K E OSBORN

***USA Today* Bestselling Author**

HESITATE
The NOLA Defiance MC Series Book 3

K E OSBORN
USA Today Bestselling Authors

This book is a work of fiction. Any references to real events, real people, and real places are used fictitiously. Other names, characters, places and incidents are products of the Author's imagination and any resemblance to persons, living or dead, actual events, organizations or places is entirely coincidental.

Disclaimer: The material in this book contains graphic language and sexual content and is intended for mature audiences, ages 18 and older.
There is content within this book that may set off triggers, please check back of book for more details of where to find help.

ISBN: 979-8353557685

Editing by Swish Design & Editing
Formatting by Swish Design & Editing
Proofreading by Swish Design & Editing
Cover model by Dylan Horsch
Photography by FuriousFotog
Cover design by Designs by Dana

First Edition

DEDICATION

To all of those who are fighting.
For love. For freedom. For sanity.
Whatever your fight may be, this one is for you.

NOTE FOR THE READER

For your convenience, below is a list of terms used in this book. Any questions, please do not hesitate to contact the author.

1% — When a 1% patch is worn, it represents the one percent of bikers who are outlaw clubs.
Cut — A vest with club colors.
Chapel - The room where the Defiance club members congregate to have their 'church' meetings.
Church - The name of important club business meetings where only patched members can attend.
Hammer Down — Accelerate quickly.
La Fin — Means The End. Also the Club's pet alligator.
Road Name — A road name is earned, given, and bestowed upon a biker. They usually have a story behind them.
Six — Watch your back.
The Heat — Police.

HESITATE

PROLOGUE

NOVAH

My heartbeat thrashes hard against my chest.

I'm sure I would hear it pulsing in my ears if the yelling wasn't so loud. My jaw clenches as my breathing quickens, my palms coating with a thin layer of sweat while I frantically usher a shaking Morgan and her two young crying children into the side office.

"You're gonna fucking pay for this. I swear to God!" Johnny screams at the top of his lungs while I push the rest of his family inside the room away from him.

"It's okay, guys, it's going to be okay," I try to reassure them. "I'll make sure you're protected." I slam the door shut behind us, closing Johnny and his yelling out.

Morgan bursts into tears, her arms wrapped around her two kids, trying to shelter them from their father's tirade. "Thank you, Novah. You're going above and beyond for us."

I place my hand on her shoulder. "Your life starts now, Morgan. Everything is going to be okay."

Suddenly, the door bursts open, and the kids scream when Johnny rushes inside. His face contorts in rage as he races straight for me. I move to stand in front of Morgan. It's my job to protect these families, and I will, no matter the cost. Tensing as he rages toward me, I brace for impact. Morgan screams at him to stop, but before he reaches me, one of my coworkers, Tim, rushes in to restrain Johnny. The only problem is, Tim's too slow, and Johnny's body slams him into the wall. I gasp when Tim's head hits the wall *hard,* and he falls to the floor unconscious.

Panting frantically, I stand in front of Morgan and the kids with my arms out in full protection mode. "No, Johnny. You will *not* come near them again."

He glares at me, his head menacingly tilting to the side. "I used to give Morgan presents, did you know that?"

Morgan lets out a sob like the memory is haunting for her. I glance back to where she and the kids are shaking with fear, and I know I have to keep Johnny talking until security arrives.

"Okay, what kind of presents?"

"We kept rats in the house as pets, and whenever Morgan was getting out of hand, I would show her what I would do to her if she didn't pull herself into line..." *Oh God, his eye twitch makes me nervous.* "Do you know what a rat's insides look like, Novah?"

Scrunching up my face, my heart races even faster, if that's possible. "No, Johnny. How about we step outside, and we can continue this conversation away from the kids?"

He steps forward. "They remind me of your face... both exquisite in beauty and perfectly flawless."

I'm not sure if I should be horrified or flattered.

Maybe both.

"That's very kind of yo—"

"The problem is... things that are perfect on the outside are often endlessly flawed on the inside. And you *are* flawed... *aren't you, Novah?"*

My skin begins to prickle.

Morgan sobs behind me. "Johnny, please, no," she begs.

"Morgan, you made your choice. Now you need to live with the consequences of your actions. *For every action, there is an equal and opposite reaction.* Newton was a smart man."

My stomach churns as I look into his eyes. I try to find something. Some depth. Some emotion. But there is nothing in those piercing baby blues, just emptiness. A vast soulless chasm, creating a void of darkness and depravity. Swallowing hard, I stand my ground. I won't let Johnny near his family even if it is the last thing I do.

He begins to chuckle, the sound so fucking haunting as he tuts his tongue on the roof of his mouth while shaking his head. "Oh, Novah, you disappoint me. I thought you'd have a little more fire. Let's see if we can ignite you."

I don't have time to think before he lunges, his hand reaching for my throat. I gasp when he pushes me back up against the wall, my feet almost coming off the ground as my fingers grip his hand. My eyes bug out of my head, and I try to let out a scream, but all I can do is gasp for air while Morgan cowers in the corner with her kids rocking back and forth. Mentally, she's no longer with us.

His eyes bore into mine, and this time I can see something there staring back at me. *Pure evil.* There is something in this man that is irrevocably broken. *He can't be saved.* My fingers dig into the flesh of his hand, trying with all my might to get him off me, then his mouth moves in against my ear. "The inside of a rat is pure perfection, Novah. I bet your insides are fucking perfect too."

He pulls back, licking his lips menacingly while I gasp for air...

Then two officers rush into the room.

Johnny rapidly drops me and takes three large steps away. He chuckles, raising his hands in the air. The police slam him up against the wall while I rub at my throat and pant for breath.

"I'll be seeing you *real* soon, Novah," he states as the police lead him out while my boss hurries inside and over to me.

"Novah. God, I am sorry it took us so long to get the police up here. I was dealing with another problem on a different floor. As soon as I saw what was happening, I called to get them in here. Are you okay?" Wanda asks, moving to my side and wrapping her arm around me.

Nodding, I sigh. “It’s not me you need to be worried about.” I glance straight at Morgan. “Are you okay? The kids?”

Morgan visibly shakes as her terrified eyes finally meet mine. “Novah, you need to protect yourself from him.”

Smiling, I rest my hand on her arm. “It’s okay, hon. After the stunt he just pulled, he’s going away for a *looong* time.”

Morgan visibly relaxes, tears filling her eyes. “I don’t know how to thank you for everything you’re doing for the kids and me.”

“It’s my job, but sometimes, with a case like this, it sticks with me, and honestly, I just want you to be safe. And if removing you from that situation where Johnny was going to continuously be coming after you and hurting you and the kids, I am only too happy to get involved and get you away from that toxic environment.”

Morgan moves in, wrapping her arms around me. “We could *never* have done this without you, Novah.”

I pull back, looking her in the eyes. “Let’s work on finding you and the kids a care facility to settle down in, shall we?” I ask.

Morgan smiles with a nod. “Sounds perfect.”

When I trained as a social worker, I knew I would have tough days. I knew I would also have rewarding days. I never thought I would have days where I would be fighting for my own life.

Johnny scared me today.

And it’s his menacing eyes that will plague my nightmares.

But right now, I have his family to protect, and I will do everything I can to keep them safe.

From him.

Even if it means putting myself in danger.

CHAPTER 1

NOVAH
Three months later

Letting out a loud yawn, I click through my emails, trying to get through an uneventful day at work. These are the days I love. Though boring, it means there are no clients in distress who I need to manage or handle.

Today is a good day.

A ping comes in, alerting me to a new email, and I open it seeing it's a report on Morgan and her kids' progress. Smiling, I read how they're doing well in their care facility. The kids are doing much better, not having their father yelling at them incessantly and constantly threatening their mother. They're coming out of their shells. Morgan is happier. She's even got herself a part-time job.

A wave of pride and emotion swarms through me. I can chalk this one up to a success. I put Johnny away for abusing his wife and kids and managed to set Morgan and the kids up in a new life where they can move on and flourish without the threats hanging over their heads. This is the part of the job that gives me purpose.

Another ping alerts, and it's red flagged as URGENT. Clicking, I read the email and my skin instantly prickles.

Johnny Myers has been released on good behavior with a reduced sentence.

It has come to our attention that Mr. Myers has been out in public for the last three weeks. Please be alert but not alarmed. We deem there is no threat to Mrs. Meyers or the Meyers children at this point in time.

Mr. Meyers appears to be sincerely remorseful for his actions and has undertaken appropriate mandatory counseling. As a result, he was approved to be released into the public and may return to full working capacity as soon as possible.

If you have any concerns or questions, please do not hesitate to contact us...

Cold sweat instantly invades my skin, followed by a chill that runs down my spine. Johnny is not the kind of man you can simply release back into the public. He's not the kind of man who can do some in-house counseling and be 'instantly' reformed.

How did they not see he's playing them?

It's plain and simple.

The only saving grace from all this is that he has no idea where Morgan and the kids are. And he has no way of finding out. I don't even know where they are. That's part of the protection process. I get my updates on their progress from a third party.

He *won't* get to them.

But he *can* get to me.

So much for an uneventful day.

Glancing up at the clock, it's almost time to head home. I figure with this news, which I wasn't expecting this soon, it's okay for me to take off early. So I pack up and shut down my computer. I need to take some time to clear my mind. In all honesty, though, they said Johnny had been out for three weeks already, so if he was going to try anything, he would have by now, right?

I say my goodbyes to my coworkers, make my way to my car, and head home. My mind wanders, thinking about whether I should talk to Bayou and Hurricane about this issue. My stepbrothers are brothers in the NOLA Defiance MC, and if I want to have someone watching my back, who better than a 1%er?

But maybe I'm overreacting.

I don't want them to blow this whole thing out of proportion.

Sure, Johnny scared me during our last interaction. I've never had anything like that before or since, but I'm sure with everything that was in the email, I won't even see him again.

The drive home doesn't take long, and as I pull in, the sun has set and only the dull hue from the streetlamp lights my drive. My eyes shoot to my front porch, where there is a feint outline of something sitting on the step. So I pull the car into the garage, then jump out without pulling the door down so I can retrieve it.

It must be a delivery from Amazon or something?

I play on my cell while I walk over to the front door, but as I approach, I gasp, spotting a dead rat, laying on its back with its insides flayed out and spread over the porch. My stomach churns as I cover my mouth, turning away for a moment to compose myself. I take a few deep breaths, then spin back, spotting a red apple with a small blade sticking straight up out of it.

Oh my God.

My stomach lurches while fear races through me so intensely bile surges up my throat. I gag as I race for my car, panting for breath once I get there. My heart's pounding so hard in my chest I feel like I will pass out as my fingers frantically dial 911.

My hands shake uncontrollably as I open the car and move to sit inside, then lock the door.

The operator answers, "911, what is your emergency?"

"Yes, hello. My name is Novah Harrington, and I'm a social worker. Three months ago, I pulled a man from his family, and he ended up spending three months in prison. However, he's been let out on good behavior, and I have arrived home from work to find a rat completely dismembered on my front porch."

"Ma'am, I'm sorry, but a dismembered rat isn't much to go on. Are you sure it wasn't a wild cat?"

Gritting my teeth, I begin to hyperventilate. "It was Johnny. The last time I saw him, he talked about how he had pet rats and how he liked gutting them. So it's not a coincidence."

The operator exhales down the line. "I'm sorry, Miss Harrington, without solid proof, we can't follow up with him."

"Well, can you at least come over and look?"

She huffs down the line. "I think the best thing you can do, ma'am, is clean up the mess and put this down to a schoolyard prank."

Anger flares inside of me so hot that I can't help myself. "You didn't see it. The rat was mutilated. A fucking school kid didn't do—" I scream.

"Ma'am, if you're going to raise your voice to me, I will have to end this call."

"So you're not going to send someone to check this out? Or at least send police to talk to Johnny?"

"There's not enough to go on, ma'am. Anyone could have done that. Do you have CCTV surveillance?"

"No, I never thought I needed it."

"Then, ma'am, there is little we can do about it. It would be a waste of police resources to send them out to check a dismembered rat with nothing else to go on."

Rubbing at my temple, I clench my eyes shut in frustration. "Thanks for nothing." I end the call, then jump back out of the car, my eyes searching around to ensure Johnny is nowhere to be seen. Thankfully, the coast seems clear. So I make my way back to the front porch, my stomach churning at the godawful sight, and I bring my cell up and take a couple of pictures of the mess. Then I spin around quickly, making my way to my car, and slide back in.

There's no way I am staying here—I'm heading for the clubhouse.

If the legitimate channels won't help me with this, I have no other option than to go to the club for help. Because right now, I don't feel safe. Johnny is sending me a message, and I have received it, loud and clear. I am not stupid, and I know this is a threat. There is no way it's not.

It doesn't take me long to get to the clubhouse. I don't know what my stepbrothers are up to, but all I do know is the thought of seeing Bayou always makes me feel better. I know Hurricane will step in and fix the problem, but Bayou is the one who will ensure I'm okay. He always has that knack for making sure I am taken care of. He has this way about him where he is always looking after me.

Over our entire lives, he's been the one stepping up to the plate. We've always had an unbreakable bond, even when we've been at each other's throats.

He. Just. Gets. Me.

Pulling up at the clubhouse, Grey opens the gates. I smile up at him, then park in my usual spot. Everything is going by in a blur, and my head is so foggy. Johnny is coming for me, and I simply don't know how I will fix that.

Walking into the clubhouse, my mind is all over the place as I meander aimlessly. I'm not even really sure what I am expecting my stepbrothers to do. I know what they will *want* to do, but am I okay with that? I am in the business of helping people. Bayou and Hurricane make bad people disappear. I'm not so naïve to think that doesn't mean they don't end up in a ditch somewhere or more than likely in pieces and fed to the club's alligator, La Fin.

Why else would the club have a pet alligator?

Bayou and City walk over. City smiling on approach. "Hey, you here for the party?"

I shake my head. "No. I'm here because I'm not really sure what to do."

Bayou's nostrils flare. "Tell me what's going on? Did someone hurt you?" *Always to the rescue.*

"No, well… not yet."

"Novah, you better start talking, so help me, God." Bayou grunts out the words.

I roll my shoulders. "There's this family at work I've been trying to help."

"You're a social worker, right?" City asks.

I nod. "Exactly. So this family I was working with, the father and partner were clearly abusive, so I reported him to the police, and we had him arrested. In the meantime, we had the mother and two children placed in a care facility where the husband doesn't have access or knowledge of where they're located."

"Okay, I'm following," Bayou states.

"The father just got let out on good behavior."

"And you're worried about the family?" City asks.

I pull out my phone and open the photo app, showing Bayou and City a picture of the dead rat and apple.

Bayou snaps his head up to look at me, a terrified expression crossing his features. "That's a direct threat to you."

"I know, and the cops won't do anything about it."

Bayou grits his teeth, his chest heaving like he's ready to murder everything in his path. "Then we will."

Hurricane steps up and places his hand on Bayou's shoulder as he stares at me. "What's goin' on?"

I go to speak, but Bayou cuts me off. "Some fucker's threatening Novah."

Hurricane snaps his head to me, his eyes turning glinty hard. "Then tell me who we have to kill?"

I let out a long breath. "Okay, I love you both, but you need to take it down a notch."

"Some asshole dismembered a fucking rat on your doorstep, and you want us to… *take it down a notch?*" Bayou says through gritted teeth.

Hurricane growls. "He *what?*"

"In fairness, I did take his entire family away from him and have him incarcerated for three month—"

"Don't care if you pissed on him and gave him herpes. He can't make threats like that."

"God, Hurricane, do you have to be so descriptive?" I smirk.

"You find this funny, Novah? Because I sure as hell don't. Dismemberin' animals only leads to more *permanent* problems," Hurricane snaps.

Raising my hands, I tilt my head. "I don't find *any* of this funny. I'm actually quite shaken. Last time I saw Johnny, we had an altercation that, quite frankly, I never wish to repeat."

"Did that fucker hurt you?" Bayou snaps, his eyes focused on me intently, my body quivering under his intense gaze.

Swallowing a lump in my throat, I let out the breath I didn't know I was holding and say, "He had me held by the throat until the police arrived and put a stop—"

"Jesus Christ, Novah!" Bayou interrupts with a groan. Turning, he starts pacing, his fingers running through his hair in frustration.

Hurricane lets out a long exhale. "Why didn't you tell us?"

"It was handled. Johnny was arrested, and he went to prison. His family is safe. That's all that mattered."

"Yeah, and now the fucker is out, targeting you. You *should* have *fucking* told us. We have people on the inside. We could have *dealt* with him no matter what prison he was in," Bayou chides.

I huff, folding my arms over my chest. "Not everyone has to be *dealt with,* Bayou. There are other ways to handle things."

He snorts. "They're not the *right* way."

I roll my eyes, and he scowls at me.

"I'll get La Fin to show him the *right* way," he mumbles, but I clearly hear him.

"I came here because I just wasn't sure of my next move. I don't think you guys should *deal* with him over a rat. Maybe it was just his way of saying, 'You took my family, I hate you,' and that's it."

"Novah, he shouldn't even know where you live. He's gone out of his way to find you. He's tauntin' you," Hurricane states.

Slumping my shoulders, I sigh because I know he's right.

"All right, so what's *our* next move? The cops know I think it was Johnny, so if he goes suddenly missing now, it's going to look suspicious. Then they will trace me to you guys, and it's not hard to figure out what happened to him. Sooo..."

Bayou inhales deeply but says nothing.

"You're one smart cookie, Novah. You know how to manipulate us..." Hurricane rubs at his beard. "Okay, fine. We won't go after Johnny, but you *will* stay at the clubhouse until further notice. No arguments," Hurricane demands.

Folding my arms over my chest, I groan. "Hurricane, c'mon. How about you station a brother outside my hou—"

"No arguments, Novah. You're our damn family. So we won't have anythin' happen to you on our watch, right, Bayou?"

My eyes shift to Bayou, and I bite my bottom lip as his eyes flick to me. So hard and yet so full of longing at the same time.

Maybe he thinks I can't see it?

Maybe he believes he is hiding it?

But I see right through him.

I know because I saw that look in his eyes once before.

Bodhi, the club's prospect, moved in next to me. A flirtatious look instantly crossed his eyes, making me curl up my lip at him. "No, Bodhi," I stated before he'd even said anything.

The girls all laughed as he slid his hand along my thigh. "Novah, I heard a rumor that you're still a virgin. If you're what? Twenty-seven. And you haven't had a good time yet, well, I can be the one to teach you how to fuck."

My eyes widened, my thoughts running rampant on how the hell he knew. I hadn't told anyone at the club I was still a virgin. Maybe I was giving off some kind of signal. All I knew was that I felt so vulnerable and exposed at that moment, and I hated how he was trying to flirt with me. His hand rose higher up my thigh, toward my pussy, and I gasped, pushing his hand from me abruptly. I went to stand, needing to get away from his physical and emotional taunting, but he instantly pulled me down into his lap. I wriggled, struggling to get out of his grasp, his hand sliding down over my breast as my eyes instantly flooded with tears.

"Get off her," Izzy snapped.

Kaia stood, shoving him.

But it was Bayou who rushed over, yanking me from Bodhi's grip and pushing me to the side. I stumbled as Bayou balled his fist tight, then socked him straight into his already swollen nose from a previous fight that evening. Blood burst out for the second time as Bayou didn't let up. Bodhi fell back onto the seat, and Bayou slammed his fist into Bodhi's jaw with such force that he fell off the chair and onto the floor. Bayou was panting so viciously, he looked like a raging bull as he turned his rage toward me. "Why were you leading him on?"

I widened my glistening eyes, blinking a few times to stop the tears. "Excuse me?"

Bayou grunted. "This is bullshit, Novah. You know how these guys can get. You're pristine to them. Perfect meat."

"The fuck are you talking about?" I threw my hands in the air.

"You can't stay out here. Not like this. Not dressed like that."

Everyone raised their brows as he grabbed my wrist and started yanking me toward the bedrooms.

"You can't go around wearing the shit you do around here, Novah. The guys are going to cling to you like leeches as you've just seen." Bayou snapped at me while leading me to my room.

I stormed inside, and he followed, slamming the door shut behind me. "I'm not dressed slutty. I never dress slutty. I don't know what the fuck you're talking about."

He stepped closer, his fingers dragging along the shoestrings of my white top. "This. It's too much. You need to cover up. I don't want them looking at you."

Throwing my hands in the air, I let out a grunt. "It's just a fucking top."

"It's not just a fucking top, *Novah. You look goddamn amazing. They'll eat you alive."*

Jerking my head back, I was confused.

Angry but flattered.

Furious but electrified.

Dumbstruck but amazed.

It was so strange to be feeling this way toward him. Panting, my eyes met his. The energy in the air swirled around us as if we were on a carnival ride, spinning so fast I couldn't contain my excitement. Both of us, staring at each other, breathing fast, feeling the electricity of the moment.

We started inching forward. A longing look in his eyes mixed with lust. It was intoxicating as he brought his hand to my cheek, both of us falling silent, fighting our attraction, knowing this was all kinds of wrong. Wanting each other so damn bad, lost in the moment as he inched closer.

I licked my lips.

Wanting him.

Needing him.

My breath caught in my throat as I leaned in, and...

Izzy shoved the bedroom door open, stepping inside.

Bayou and I both gasped, realizing the moment we were lost in—and just caught in—as we jerked away from each other dramatically.

My eyes widened as I realized the enormity of what had just happened.

"Sorry," Izzy blurted out, spinning and rushing for the hall like she couldn't get out of the room fast enough.

Bayou took off after her, leaving me in the bedroom reeling. My breath caught in my throat as I heard him threaten from the hall, "You saw nothing... that was nothing.*" It sounded more like he was trying to convince himself than intimidate Izzy. Then I heard his heavy stomping boots taking off down the hall.*

I was lost in a daze when Izzy turned back. "You okay?"

I nodded.

But honestly, I was far from okay.

"It was nothing," I repeated the same phrase Bayou said to Izzy, but my voice was minuscule, and then I rushed past her and out the door.

Bayou and I have never talked about that 'almost' kiss. In fact, we have pretty much tried to avoid each other as much as possible since then. We talk when we need to, but we both know being stepsiblings, growing up with each other, and having feelings is not the right combination.

So we keep our space.

Now that I have to live here at the club, we will constantly be around each other.

It's going to be a nightmare.

That forced proximity will be too much to bear for both of us.

"Maybe it would be better to station someone at her home? She has to go to work. It will be a disruption to her routine," Bayou states, his eyes shifting from me to Hurricane.

He's trying to avoid me being here.

A pang of hurt flows through me, but I get it.

We're dangerous around each other.

We both know it.

There's definitely something that *can't* be ignited.

No matter what.

It's just wrong.

On all levels.

Even if, in the moment, it feels so fucking right.

Hurricane scoffs. "Bullshit, Bayou. She can drive to work from here just as easily as she can from her house… it's only a few extra minutes. And I'm havin' someone come to work with you too. Actually, Bayou, you can do it. No one protects family like family, and I need to be here for the club, so you're in charge of protectin' Novah."

Bayou and I widen our eyes, staring at Hurricane like he's lost his damn mind.

"It's fine, honestly. If Johnny wanted to hurt me, he would've waited for me until I got home," I counter.

"He still could. It was a warnin' shot. A warnin' that he's comin' back for you. He wanted to scare you, Novah. He wanted you to know he's comin' back... well, not on my watch. Not my fuckin' stepsister," Hurricane declares.

Warmth radiates through me as I lean forward and take Hurricane into a tight embrace. Kaia has softened him, if only just a fraction. But it's nice to see him relax a little. "Thank you... I appreciate you looking out for me."

He wraps his arm around my shoulders, pulling me to him. "I'll protect you with my life, Novah. Any man who comes near you is gonna get a bullet right between his fuckin' eyes."

Bayou wracks his jaw from side to side but says nothing.

I exhale and nod. "I'm gonna need to go back to the house and grab some of my things."

Hurricane shakes his head. "No fuckin' way. You're stayin' right here. You're not allowed to step foot back inside that house. It's a hot zone. Bayou, go 'round and pack some shit for her."

Widening my eyes, I snap my head toward Bayou, and he scowls.

"I do have shit I need to do here, Hurricane. Plus, I have no damn clue what women need."

He grips Bayou's shoulder, turning up his lip. "I gotta send a brother in case that asshole shows up, and I'm not havin' any of these idiots rummagin' through our sister's panties. You're the only one I can trust with this shit, brother."

Widening my mouth, I suck in a deep breath as I drop my eyes from Bayou's in sheer embarrassment.

Holy shit.

"I don't particularly want anyone rummaging through my panties. Can't I go with City, or hell, what about Grey? It's his job to do the grunt work no one else wants to do, right? Let the prospect take me home, and I can grab exactly what I need. He can keep a lookout and then bring me back. Easy," I beg.

"Yeah." Bayou nods in agreement.

"*No.* Bayou gets your shit, or you stay here with the dress on your back and nothin' else, Novah. You're not goin' back to that house. Not till *we* deem it safe."

Slumping my shoulders, I nod. "Okay, fine."

"Good. Bayou, get goin'. Clean up the rat and bring back the blade. It might give us a lead on this idiot."

"Got it." His eyes meet mine for the briefest of moments. Hesitation is clear in his ice-blue orbs. Then he turns, heading for the door. My anxiety increases with every step he takes away from me, knowing that he's going to be running his hands through my things. I'm not sure why, but it unsettles me. Is it because Bayou is going to be alone in my home, and he might find my journal—the one where I have written countless entries about him? Or is it because having him in my space fills me with something I can't quite put a finger on?

Maybe I wish he would be there more often?

Hurricane pulls me to him, planting a tender kiss on my temple. "We're gonna take care of you, Brat."

Giggling at his nickname for me, I smile. "Thanks, Doofus. I knew you always would."

CHAPTER 2

BAYOU

Pulling up my ride at Novah's home, I am all kinds of tense. I haven't been here in so long because I always feel awkward. I grew up with Novah, and I shouldn't look at her the way I do. She's my stepsister. I shouldn't find her attractive. My mind shouldn't always drift to pinning her against a wall and kissing the shit out of her. Or when I'm alone in my room at night, and my cock starts to harden, I shouldn't jerk off thinking of her face in my mind.

It's just fucking wrong.

But I can't help it.

Can't stop it.

I'm all kinds of depraved.

And coming here now isn't fucking helping. I've been trying to avoid Novah since that *almost* damn-it-all-to-hell kiss when Izzy walked in on us and stopped it before it started. Because once I've kissed Novah, I doubt I will ever be able to stop.

Thank God Izzy burst in when she did.

Guilt swallows me whole as I hop off my ride and make my way to the front porch. My eyes instantly focus on the dead rat carcass on the doorstep. Fists ball at my sides while a wave of rage flushes over me so intense I want to fucking hurt something.

Instead, I let out a long, controlled breath and step up to the front door. My focal point remains on the rat, studying how it has been dissected. It's meticulous. Done with precision. This guy took his time to pull out the organs one by one and lay them out in this type of pattern. Which can only mean one thing—he's done shit like this before. And men who take their time being this meticulous with animal kills don't take long before they move on to humans.

Pulling out my cell, I take some photographs, documenting the scene properly in case we need evidence. Then I grab my keys and make my way inside Novah's house to grab some shit to clean this crap up with. I first need to find something to wrap up that apple and blade to take them back to the clubhouse with me. Then, grabbing all the cleaning gear I need, I head back out and start my task. Once I have the rat collected, I place it in a bag and throw it in the neighbor's trash can, which is out front.

Then I grab the hose and clean down the area. It's a real fucking mess. Then while I am at it, I water her front garden because I don't know how long she will be at the clubhouse—much to her disgust—and I know how much Novah loves her Louisiana Phlox. She spends hours in this fucking garden making sure it's perfectly manicured.

Finishing up, I head inside to pack her a bag. Rolling my shoulders—this is one step too far even for me, as I am invading her personal space. Everything about Novah is so goddamn pure and innocent. Even her bedroom is all white and fluffy throw pillows. Let's face it. She even has a stuffed unicorn on her bed. A *unicorn.*

So fucking innocent.

I'm a depraved asshole.

The comparison is not lost on me.

And even worse that I think of her as anything other than my stepsister. How I can even look at her and then sexualize her is despicable.

We practically grew up together. We were inseparable as teens. Always having this strong bond. Then she started growing up, and I began to look at her differently. Whenever she would talk, my insides tingled, and my skin prickled with goose bumps. Even though I knew it was wrong, and I would never act on it, I could see the reaction in her eyes too.

She was looking at me like she felt the same electrical current.

Her mother, Ingrid, has never picked up on it. Hurricane is oblivious as hell, and Nash, her blood brother, is too caught up in his business drama to be focused on his sister. The one thing I do know, the one thing that's always been drilled into Novah by all of us—any man who goes near her will have to answer to Hurricane, Nash, and myself. Now hypothetically, if that man were me, it would be insurmountably worse because the betrayal would be all that much greater.

Pushing my rambling thoughts to the side, I move to her closet and pull out a duffle bag she used to use for ballet when she was younger. My thoughts fall back to seeing her dressed in those leggings and a tiny skirt and how my young teenage cock would ache for her. Back then, it was easier to manage. Girls were clinging to me like a magnet, so it made it much easier to scratch the itch I had for Novah with the bitches from school or whores from a bar as time passed. But seeing her blossom into the perfect, flawless, beautiful human she is, has made it harder for me.

All I see is her.

All I want is… *her.*

Everything I shouldn't desire.

Everything I can't have.

The forbidden fruit.

The impossible catch.

The one woman I crave more than anything.

But if I take one single bite, I know I would ruin her completely. And I can't do that to her. I could never be the reason behind people looking at this amazing woman like she's worth anything less than pure perfection.

I'm her stepbrother—it's not a relationship I can steer toward romance.

Novah is off limits.

And I need to remember that while I'm rummaging through her things.

Stepping to her closet again, I slide open the doors. The walk-in closet mostly consists of dresses, generally white. Shaking my head, this woman is so fucking angelic it kills me. How can I—a man who has a pet alligator used specifically for the disposal of bodies—be infatuated with a woman who is the purest darling I have ever known?

It's ridiculous.

Huffing, I grab a few of her dresses, curl them up around my hand and shove them in the bag. Glancing down, I pick up her floppy sandals. I notice the few pairs I always see her alternating between, so I shove them into the bottom of the bag. Then, heading over to the chest of drawers, I slide open the bottom drawer for her pajamas and grab a couple of sets, throwing them in for good measure. Finally, with force, I pull open the top drawer where there are medications, including birth control, which raises my brow. A wave of resentment rolls over me at who she might be using that with as I shove it into the bag with a little more force than necessary. Then I turn to her other drawers running my hand through my hair to try and relieve some tension.

It's not working.

Goddammit!

So I act like a grown man, step up and open the top drawer.

My cock instantly springs to attention when her panties stare up at me. My heart races so fast as I try to control myself.

Don't be a pervert.

Don't be a pervert.

Don't be a pervert.

Shaking my head from side to side, I crane my neck as I pick up her lacy white and pink panties. They're exactly what I pictured her wearing. They ooze Novah's personality in every way.

I swallow hard, walk a bunch of them over to the bag, and quickly throw them in. Turning back to the drawer, I grab a couple of bras. Again they're so exquisitely feminine and uniquely Novah. How can they be sexy and innocent at the same time? Placing the bras in the bag, I walk back to close the drawer when something catches my attention. A hint of something red and black underneath the rest of the panties has me curious.

Hesitating for a moment, I inhale, then glance around to check if someone is looking. Then I shake my head over my stupidity and shift the panties to the side to find a black corset with black silk frills over the breasts and red ribbon inlets leading to a red bow in the middle of the breasts. At the bottom of the corset, more red ribbon decorates the lower edge in a pattern, and another two red bows line up on top of each thigh. Out of the thigh-bows are black and red suspenders where I am guessing stockings clip.

Mind control, dick.

Holding the sexy little number up, my cock goes rock hard—yeah, there was no control—as I imagine Novah wearing this devilish delight. My heart races so fucking fast I can hardly think when I glance down at the matching panties that go with it. Picking them up, they're crotchless, and when my thoughts run rampant, I let out a low growl.

"Jesus Christ, Novah," I grumble. My stomach swirls at the thought that whoever she is taking the pill for and wearing this outrageous number for, he obviously wants her to be a bad girl, not the good girl she constantly portrays.

This guy's a fucking asshole.

I'm gonna kick his fucking ass.

Scrunching the crotchless panties up in my hand, I spin, trying to calm myself down. I have a raging boner, a corset in one hand, panties in the other, and emotions flowing through me I don't know how to handle. I need to calm down before I destroy her fucking bedroom in a fit of murderous rage. Unfortunately, the only way I can think of to do that is to smother myself in Novah.

She is the one thing that calms me.

The one person who can tranquilize my mind.

Glancing down, I grit my teeth, hesitating, my breaths low and heavy, but if I don't do something soon, I'm going to lose my shit.

Completely.

Rapidly, I bring her panties to my nose and take a deep whiff. They smell of her fruity perfume. And the instant it hits me, it sends my body into contentment like her presence surrounds me, and simply smelling her makes me come alive in ways it shouldn't.

I shouldn't react to her like this.

I shouldn't be turned on so much by rummaging through her underwear.

But there's something about Novah Lee Harrington that absolutely slays me.

Makes me come undone.

And I loathe every tormented second of this so-called pleasure.

Inhaling, I curl the panties up, scrunching them into my face needing her closer, holding the corset to my chest. Letting out a long exhale, I groan as my rock-hard cock aches so fucking intensely I feel like laying on her bed and jerking the fuck off.

But I'm not *that* far gone.

Not yet.

Maybe another ten minutes in this house, and it could be another story.

Pulling her panties away from my face, I shake my head as I look at them.

So much for not *being a pervert.*

They're completely not her style.

I can't imagine her wearing them.

But she obviously has—they smell like her.

And I want *her* to know that *I* know she isn't the good girl she is portraying to everyone. I want *her* to know that *I* know about whoever this asshole is she's sleeping with and using birth control for.

I want her to know that… *I. Am. Livid.*

So I walk over to her duffle bag and place the corset and panties right on top, so it will be the first thing she sees when she opens the bag.

Petty? *Maybe.*

Am I thinking clearly? I glance down at the giant bulge in my jeans and grunt. *Maybe not.*

But right now, I don't care if I am thinking with a clear head. I need her to know that I am going to figure out who this guy is, and I might just kill him and then feed the fucker to La Fin.

My motto has always been *no one is good enough for Novah*, and my brothers concur. We have always been about protection. Therefore, I *will* find out who this asshole is and shut him the fuck down if it's the last thing I do. How dare he try to change perfection.

Zipping up the duffle—probably with a little more force than necessary as the zipper tag comes off in my hand—I move back to her panty drawer to shut it when I spot a book, and on the front is the word JOURNAL in big, bold letters. My eyes widen as I crane my neck to the side.

"Don't do it," I warn myself as I pick it up, running my thumbs over the pink satin fabric.

"Fuck!" I grunt, then flip the book open to the latest entry.

Her handwriting is scribbled all over the pages with little doodles and drawings of random things. It's exactly what I would imagine her journal to look like.

"You're going to hell, Bayou," I mumble to myself as I begin reading the last few sentences.

> *I can't help how attracted to him I find myself. I have to stop. Ever since whatever that was in my room at the clubhouse, our relationship has been strained. Bayou…*

As soon as I see my name, something inside of me clicks.

I *am* invading her privacy.

I've already done far too fucking much here today when it comes to invading what's hers. I need to take control of myself. But what I did read has given me the little buzz I need to make it through. Even though we both know this is so morally and ethically wrong, now I have confirmation she feels this too.

I can't blame Novah for fucking her frustrations out with another guy.

Lord knows, I fuck other women to get *her* out of my head.

So I close the journal and let out a heavy sigh. Walking it over to her bag, I slide it under the corset. It seems like it is something she uses as a tool to vent. She might need it at the clubhouse with what's going on.

I move to the bathroom and grab the basics. Toothbrush, some makeup—I have no idea if I am even grabbing the right shit—but I pick up what is readily available and some facial products, then shove them in an overnight bag I found in the vanity.

I slide that down the side of her duffle and…

… I am done.

I take one last look around her bedroom, spotting her fluffy unicorn, and I reach over, grab it, then shove it on top between the straps. Cracking my neck to the side, I'm glad my fucking boner is finally under control.

Quickly, I hoist her duffle up over my shoulder and walk out of her home, checking for anything else I might need as I go. I attach the bag to the rear of my bike, then head back and ensure her home is secure.

With one leg slung over my ride, my mind wanders to what her face is going to be like when she spots the corset.

Will she be mad at me?

Will she be embarrassed that I know her darkest secrets?

But most of all, I want her to know I am pissed.

Maybe I have no right to be.

She's not mine.

She doesn't belong to me.

She can fuck whoever she wants.

But I hate that she is changing who she is for some random asshole.

That devilish corset is not her, and I hate to think of the shit this guy is making her do.

Revving my bike, I take off so fast, my back tire skids out, fishtailing it as I burn rubber down her street back toward the clubhouse.

CHAPTER 3

NOVAH

My anxiety is almost crippling me at the thought of Bayou in my home. I have no idea what is taking him so long, but my knee won't stop agitating as I sit chatting with Kaia and Lani in the main clubroom. The girls are laughing about how City is so whipped by Izzy.

I smirk, turning to Kaia. "And Hurricane isn't whipped by you?"

Lani bursts out laughing. "Oh snap. Truth bomb. This is why we love you, Novah."

Kaia rolls her shoulder. "Hurricane is still alpha, though."

"You gotta give City some credit. He's been in love with Izzy his entire life. That's devotion. He finally got his woman... it's *romantic*," I tell her.

Lani nods. "Exactly, you're just a hardass, Kaia. *Let them love.*"

Kaia snorts. "Fine. But I do love, love. Hurricane, and I love *plenty—*"

"Oh, we know... we *hear* you loving *alllll* the time," Lani quips, and I burst out laughing.

Kaia rolls her eyes. "He *is* very good at *loving*."

My stomach flutters wondering what it will feel like the first time I have sex. I'm not entirely sure the reason why I haven't. I'm twenty-seven years old. I should have by now. But with having three older overbearing brothers—one blood, two step—and them being so damn protective, it's never felt right to take that chance with anyone. The other reason could be because I can't get past the fact that every time I think about going there with a guy, Bayou pops into my mind, which is equally as much of a turn-off as a turn-on.

I'm undeniably attracted to him, but the fact is, I can't go there.

There's no possible way.

Nash and Hurricane would kill Bayou for starters, and there's still that one rather large problem—he's my stepbrother.

It's not right.

It can't happen.

Suddenly, Bayou steps up to our table and lumps my ballet duffle bag onto the table between the three of us with a heavy huff. "Here's your shit," he grumbles, then storms off, not saying another word.

Widening my eyes, my mouth drops open in shock at his aggression.

"Geez, something sure crawled up his ass and stole his good humor," Lani mumbles under her breath.

"I don't understand... why the hell is he mad at me right now? I mean, I get that he had to go out of his way to grab my things for me, but *I* didn't make him do that. Hurricane did," I say more to myself than anyone else, trying to figure out what that display means.

Kaia places her hand on my shoulder. "The thing I have learned about these Ladet twins is just when you think you understand where their head's at, they go in a completely different direction. I'm only starting to now be able to read Hurricane and how his mind works, but shit, is it taking some time to wrap my head around him and his um... *logic*. Bayou is probably the same, seeing as they're twins."

"You think I should know that growing up with them for

basically my entire life. But maybe that's the problem. I know them so well that when I can't read them, it throws me," I state.

"Could be. All I know is… you and Bayou have always had this special bond…" She smiles. "I'm willing to bet whatever he's angry about, you will find answers in that duffle there," Kaia states.

Glancing down at the duffle, I nod and stand from the table. "Thanks, ladies. I better go unpack and see what I find."

"We'll be here if you need us," Kaia offers, and Lani nods her head.

I take off for my room, bag in hand, wondering what in the hell is Bayou's problem. He's never looked at me the way he just did. Anger mixed with disappointment with a side of lust and longing. So much to feel in a split second.

Making my way to my room, I ensure the door behind me is closed. Placing the bag on the bed, I reach for the tab, but it's missing. My brows pull together, so I slip my finger under the zipper and slide it open, smirking when I see my unicorn on top that Nash gave me. It might seem childish for a twenty-seven-year-old woman to still have a stuffed toy unicorn, but it has a load of sentimental meaning.

Nash gave it to me just after our father left us for the other family he had on the side. Dad had two other children and a baby on the way, our half-siblings, who we have met maybe two or three times, and our father's new wife, the lovely Sarah. Yes, that was sarcasm.

I pick up Sunshine and hold her tight to my chest while closing my eyes, remembering how much pain Nash, Mom, and I went through back when I was only ten. Nash gave me Sunshine to brighten my days. So I had something, anything, to cling to and remind me that even in the darkness, there is always something bright with a rainbow at the end. My eyes begin to glisten.

Bayou doesn't know what Sunshine means to me, but the fact he put her in shows he doesn't care that I still have her on my bed for comfort. Nash has his way of dealing with what happened with our father, and Sunshine is my way of dealing with it.

Clearing my throat, I wipe the stray tear from my eye and place Sunshine on the mattress by my pillow where she belongs, with a warm smile. Then, turning back to the bag, I pull the zipper back further, and my eyes just about burst out of my head when I see the sexy corset my best friend, Xanthe, bought for me in all its ridiculous glory. My breath catches, and my heart leaps into my throat. *Holy hell.* I reach in, pull it out and spot the crotchless panties with it.

My head shakes frantically. "No... no, no, no. Oh God, what the hell is Bayou gonna be thinking seeing all this?"

He knows I'm not going to be wearing a corset here. He wanted me to know that he saw it, and wanted me to know he's angry about it.

But this isn't me.

I wouldn't wear something like this.

Honestly, I don't know why I kept it.

I tried it on once when Xanthe bought it to appease her, and we laughed obnoxiously loud, then both said how ridiculous I looked in it. I've never worn it again.

It's been sitting in the bottom of my panty drawer ever since.

Until now.

"No wonder he's so angry..." I huff. "He probably thinks I'm off whoring it up." I throw the corset and panties to the mattress and move back to the duffle to continue pulling the rest of my stuff out. I grab the toiletries bag and see he's attempted to grab my makeup and facial products. He's missed a few crucial things, but he didn't know what to look for, so I can forgive him for that—I am sure I can borrow from the girls what I need. Grabbing my panties and bras, I gnaw down on my bottom lip while inhaling sharply, wondering what he was thinking when he was sorting through all this. *I wonder if he pocketed a pair?* I smirk at the thought. I don't think he's the perverted type.

Maybe I want him to be, though.

Shaking my head at that thought, a flash of something pink catches my eyes, and I dig deeper to find my journal.

I stop dead still.

A lump gets caught in my throat.

Shit.

Oh, fuck.

Jesus fucking Christ.

Please, no.

I pull it out and flip through the pages to see if they're all still there and intact. They are, and I get to the last page, nothing has changed, but an uneasy feeling floods over me.

Maybe he sat and read my journal?

Would he invade my privacy like that?

Surely not?

A sinking feeling assaults me, and a wave of dread pummels through me like a tidal wave. What if Bayou read it, saw how I feel about him, and he doesn't, in fact, feel the same? What if I am imagining his reciprocation, and he is completely disgusted by how I feel, and *that* is why he is angry with me?

Oh God.

What if that moment we shared in the bedroom, that *almost kiss*, was a moment of weakness brought on by me, and that is why it failed because he realized what was happening and stopped it? Because since then, shit has been weird between us, and maybe that's because he doesn't feel the same.

I'm making an idiot of myself.

But he's the jerk who read my journal.

A wave of emotions crashes through me. Fear, rejection, guilt, sadness, loss, anger, disappointment, resentment, irritation, everything bouncing back and forth as my breathing almost becomes non-existent, and I start to feel faint. The only thing I want to do right now is to take all my frustrations out on the *one man* who is causing them all.

Stiffening my posture, I storm out of my bedroom and go in

search of him. I make my way outside to where he's aggressively laying into the boxing bag. He's shirtless, covered in sweat, his chest tattoo looking so fucking delicious.

I stop still for a moment staring at his glistening abs.

The way his muscles move, pulling taut and sturdy with every thrust.

Oh, good God.

I swallow a lump in my throat as his gorgeous ice-blue eyes are so laser-focused he doesn't see me ogling him. His short dusty-blond hair is dripping in sweat. His beard covers his jaw, where his clenched teeth are hissing with each hit. The way his gorgeous face scrunches like that is making me think all kinds of inappropriate thoughts as I clench my thighs together, loving the way his ear gauges give him that edgier look.

But then I snap my head out of it and remember I am angry at him for reading my journal. So I storm up to the boxing bag, and just as he goes to take another swing, I push the bag to the side, forcing him to punch forward into thin air. He loses his footing because he thrusts too much, missing the bag but catches himself before he falls.

He turns, glaring at me. "What the fuck, Novah?" he snaps, panting to catch his breath.

"You read my journal. That's an inappropriate invasion of my privacy, and honestly, I thought you were a better man than that."

He starts pulling off his gloves and walks over to the bench to take a drink, then pours some water over his head and chest making me have to look away because it's such a damn sexy move.

"I read a sentence to see whether it was something I needed to bring for you or not. I saw it was something you clearly still use, so I brought it. It was literally one sentence, Novah. Once I saw my name, I stopped reading because I agree… it is an invasion of your privacy, and I wouldn't do that to you."

Slumping my shoulders, I weaken my stance just a little. "Then why the fuck are you so mad at me?"

He scowls. "Who's the birth control for?"

Scrunching my brows together, so I am sure they are now in one line, I jerk my head back in confusion. "For me. They're a hormone therapy, not birth control, but that's *none* of your business."

He nods his head, gritting his teeth. "Avoiding the question... *great.*"

"I just *answered* your question. What's wrong with you?"

He grabs a towel, patting himself down. "So fucking much, Novah."

I reach my hand out, placing it on his arm. The second I touch him, my fingers ignite like a sparkler. Tingles prickle all the way up my arms, wrapping around my heart and squeezing until it's hard for me to breathe. The way he is looking at me with his breathing hitched, I feel like maybe he *is* feeling this too. "Why are you angry with me?"

His nostrils flair and his hard glinty eyes lock onto mine. "Is this sweet innocent thing you have going on just an act? Or are you really a whore like how you dress in the bedroom?"

A sharp and sudden pain tightens in my chest as a blurring sensation fogs my eyes while I try to blink away my tears. My throat tightens with pain while my body flushes with heat. My fingernails dig into my palms, simply trying to keep myself together.

But my emotions overwhelm me.

I can't contain myself and let out a single loud sob, my hand rapidly slamming across his cheek. The sting reverberates through my palm as his head snaps to the side with the force. "You're an asshole," I snap and turn, heading back for my bedroom.

"Novah... *Novah*!" I hear him calling out to me, but I don't stop as I run for the sanctity of my room. Once inside, I flop onto my bed, shoving the fucking corset to the floor and grab Sunshine. Cuddling her to my chest, I pull my knees up and cry into my pillow.

I don't know how long I will be at this clubhouse, but I am starting to think maybe I should take my chances with Johnny and his rats because right now, they're looking better than Bayou and his downright hurtful insults.

BAYOU

Watching Novah walk away like that as I rest my hand on my stinging cheek, feels like she may as well have slammed a sledgehammer into my chest, not her palm against my face.

For fuck's sake, what was I thinking?

I didn't mean to call her a whore.

Novah could *never* be a whore.

I just keep picturing her wearing that sexy thing with some other man fucking her while wearing it. Some other guy who forces moans from her mouth while I want to capture them with mine.

She makes me so goddamn wild, like a man untamed, when I think about any other guy with her. Tainting her perfect body. Screwing with her innocent mind. I just can't fucking stand it. It turns me into a motherfucking asshole. All because I want to be the one to make her scream. I want to be the name leaving her lips when she comes.

But it's just not in the cards for us.

There are rules about this for a reason.

"You okay, brother?" Grey asks out of nowhere.

I snap my head to him, my eyes bulging out of my face. Then, trying to shrug it off, I nod. "Siblings, hey?"

"That didn't look like a sibling kind of argument to me—"

"Prospect, leave it."

Grey raises his hands in surrender and walks up to my side. "All I am saying is..." He scratches his head, unsure about whether to continue but does anyway. "Sure, Hurricane might be mad at first, but honestly, the only two people who have a real hang-up about it... are you and Novah."

"Prospect, I won't say it again," I warn with a growl.

Grey smirks and dips his chin. "I hear you... just think about it."

Curling up my lip, I huff. "Take some of your own advice," I snap back at Grey as he starts walking off. He turns back to me, raising his brow in question. "Lani... she's a great chick..."

Grey smiles. "She is. One of the best."

"So what the fuck are you holding out for then? If it's Christmas, that's only a few days away."

Grey shakes his head. "It's complicated."

"Said the pot to the kettle."

"You ever think about putting a call into Chains over in Houston?" Grey asks, conveniently changing the conversation back to me.

I jerk my head back in confusion. "What the fuck about?"

"You've seen how him and Chills are. They're one of the happiest couples at that club. Got a kid, madly in love—"

"What's your point, prospect?"

"They were foster siblings before they got together. Grew up almost their entire lives together... *sound familiar?"*

"Don't know what you're getting at." I try to shrug it off.

Grey dips his chin. "Well, just think about it. If anyone is going to know what you're feeling right now, it's Chains. He was pretty torn up about having feelings for Chills. Thinking it was all kinds of wrong. That it shouldn't be allowed—"

"It *shouldn't* be allowed—"

"Why? You're not related in any way? Not one ounce of DNA or blood that runs through your veins is a match. You're not siblings. Not at all. *Your* father married *her* mother. That's the extent of it. *That's it.* Plain and simple, Bayou."

"Since she was ten, I've treated her like she's my sister—"

"But she's not… *that's* the difference." He grips my shoulder and lets out a heavy exhale. "Take my advice… or don't. But from what I just saw, you have intense feelings for each other. The chemistry is there. Don't waste it on a technicality that isn't even fucking legitimate."

Sighing, I dip my chin. Being reamed out by a prospect is a new feeling for me, but for some reason, I welcome it. "Thanks, Grey. I mean that." He smiles and takes a step to walk away before I state, "Sort your shit out with Lani. She won't wait around forever, you know?"

He chuckles and keeps walking.

Seems like he can dish out advice, but when taking it, he's not so good at receiving it.

But he helped.

I have to find Novah and apologize.

Now.

Making my way inside, I'm ground to a halt by Hurricane as he steps up to me. "We gotta ride out to The Plantation. There's a problem with Felix."

Rolling my shoulders, I glance toward the bedrooms knowing Novah is probably in there, but the club *always* comes first. "Let me get dressed, and I'll meet you in the yard."

"Hurry the fuck up. This shit is urgent."

Nodding, I jog to my room, grab a fresh shirt, pull it on, and then slide my cut back where it should be. Racing out, I jog past Novah's room and hear her crying inside. My chest squeezes so fucking tight knowing I did that to her.

I'm such a fucking asshole.

But I can't talk to her.

I *will* make this right.

But right now, I have to go with Hurricane, as much as I wish I didn't have to.

It's not like I can tell Hurricane I have to sit this one out because I called Novah a whore, and I need to fix it.

Hurricane would beat the shit out of me.

Damned if I do, damned if I don't.

Taking in a deep breath, I take off, feeling the weight of my guilt eat at me as I make way for my ride. Jumping on, the other guys are already starting to take off, so I make quick work and race off after them on our way to The Plantation.

Riding should give me a sense of relief, a wave of pleasure. The vibration generally puts me at ease. But after what's going on with Novah, all I feel is tension. I need to get this shit dealt with and get back so I can straighten this out with her.

We pull into The Plantation and walk into Felix's office to see Maxxy on the floor above Felix performing CPR on him. His shirt splayed open, and the guy is as white as a damn sheet. "Well, don't just stand there, you fuckers. Help me," Maxxy calls out.

Hoodoo rushes over to the portable defibrillator on the wall and gets to work placing the pads on his chest while we all stand back. "Maxxy, stand clear," Hoodoo instructs, and she shifts back, raising her hands in the air. Then Felix jerks with the shock to his heart.

"C'mon, you fucking bastard." Maxxy grunts as she brings her hand out, slapping Felix across the face. "Wake up."

"Clear!" Hoodoo states again.

Maxxy backs up as the pads charge, and Felix's body jerks with the electricity. We all stand back staring, waiting, hoping, when suddenly Felix takes a big gasp of air, followed by the color slowly returning to his pale face.

"We got him back, but his pulse is weak. We gotta get him to the hospital, Pres," Hoodoo states as he takes Felix's vitals.

Maxxy sits back on her knees, letting out a long exhale like she's in shock, and I walk over to her. "You did great, Max."

She rubs the back of her neck and nods while Hoodoo continues to work on Felix.

"All right, let's get Felix situated. But in the meantime, what are we gonna do about the shipping distribution?" I ask.

Hurricane starts pacing, running his hand through his hair. "I don't know what the hell we're gonna do. Felix ran every fuckin' thing. Not only the trucks for this place but also the new freighters we've started for the Mississippi ship run."

Maxxy snaps out of her haze and widens her eyes. "Well, I know how Felix works. He runs all the details past me. I help him with both land and sea shipping, Pres. I mean... I might need to get myself up to date on some of the more logistical and accounting side of things, but in the interim, while Felix is out, I can step in. The poppies only take up so much of my time anyway, and the rest of the time, I'm pretty much spending on social media to keep myself occupied."

We all raise our brows.

"Oh, you do, do you?" Hurricane quips.

She shrugs. "I thought you knew?"

"We're not on social media, Maxxy. How would we know?" Hurricane groans.

She smiles. "True. I did know that. But anyway, I can totally manage everything here. It will keep me busy. I've wanted something a little more challenging."

"Growin' and maintainin' a giant field of poppies and gettin' them ready for production isn't challengin' enough for you, Maxxy?" Hurricane grunts.

She rolls her shoulders. "Hurricane, our enemies strung me up on a pike and basically flayed me alive... I'm ready for something that's going to stretch me to my limits."

We all glance at Hurricane to see what he is going to do. "Okay, Maxxy, you're takin' over. But the second you need help, you call and ask us, okay? We don't need this place fallin' in a fuckin' heap."

"Oh, ye of little faith."

"Okay... let's get Felix to the hospital before he keels over on us again," Hoodoo calls out. "Maxxy, can I borrow your car? I'll bring it back later?"

She dips her hand into her pocket, pulls out some keys, and hurls them at Hoodoo. "You break it, you buy it, my friend."

Hoodoo smiles at her as he and Omen hoist Felix, carrying him out to the parking lot. We help get Felix into Maxxy's car, and then as a club, we ride surrounding Maxxy's car to the hospital.

We take Felix in, and because we're not what the hospital classes as family, we all sit around for hours on end with no fucking news. My anxiety levels are going through the roof at leaving it so goddamn long to fix shit with Novah.

She's going to hate me so damn much.

And I'm going to deserve it.

It's been hours, and I mean hours since our fight.

I should have never left.

But there's no going back now.

I don't know how the hell I am going to fix this with her.

I can't stop pacing the halls of the hospital.

We are waiting, begging for someone to tell us something about the state of Felix so we can get the hell out of here.

Suddenly, thank God, a doctor steps into the waiting room. "Friends of Felix?"

We all turn and race toward the doctor, but Hurricane is the only one to answer, "What's happenin', Doc? Is he okay?"

"Felix suffered an almost complete blockage of his—"

"I don't care much for the medical talk. Just tell me what you did to fix it, and if he's gonna be okay?"

The doctor tilts his head. "We had to perform a quadruple bypass, but with all the damage to his heart, I can't give you a firm nod that he will recover. It's going to be a long convalescence period for him. And even when he does fully recuperate, he will have to keep his stress down and change his lifestyle."

Jesus.

Hurricane rubs the tension away in the back of his neck. "Okay… thank you, Doc."

He turns and walks off as we all circle together.

"I hope Maxxy can handle her shit. Otherwise, just when we're startin' to get our business back up and runnin' smoothly, it's all gonna fall dramatically into a pile of steaming shit again."

"There's not much more we can do here tonight. Maybe we should head back to the clubhouse?" I suggest.

Hurricane nods. "Yeah, agreed. C'mon, boys… let's ride."

It's late, and we've been gone for longer than I would have ever thought, leaving the girls back at the clubhouse to fend for themselves. As we ride back in the gates, the music blares, and we all look at each other in confusion.

We make our way for the clubhouse, wondering what in the hell we're about to walk into. And as we enter, the girls are all in the middle of the clubhouse dancing, with drinks in their hands like they didn't even notice us walk in—except for Lani, who's sitting back watching with a sad smile on her face. They've even dressed up like they're going to a club.

Fucked if I know why?

"Who started the party without us?" City calls out, and Izzy rushes over to him, jumping into his arms and planting a kiss on his lips.

I smirk as Hurricane waggles his brows at an extremely inebriated Kaia, who is having trouble even standing. Her arm is wrapped around Novah, who seems a little less drunk but definitely not herself. She must have borrowed a dress because I certainly didn't pack *that* for her. It's a shiny silver, quite low-cut, and high above her knees, and when she turns, it drops down, showing her back. She obviously isn't wearing a bra. It's sexy as all fucking hell. But she can't wear shit like that around these guys. My cock jerks in my jeans, watching the way her hips move to the music, and I grit my teeth together.

Hurricane moves in next to Kaia, sweeping her into his arms. "I thought I was the alcoholic. You provin' me wrong, Sha?"

Kaia giggles and leans in, kissing his nose, completely missing his mouth. "We're just having…" she pauses, swallowing like maybe she is thinking about puking, then starts again, "… fun. While you go off galivanting around…" hiccup, "… and breaking people's sphincters." Her finger comes up, and somehow, she bops him on the nose.

He laughs as he turns his head to Novah. "And you, little sister. I thought you were supposed to be the good influence on this bunch of rebels."

She snorts, downing the rest of her beer. "Me? A good influence? Ha! I'm nothing but a *whore."*

My eyes widen. *Jesus Christ, Novah.*

Hurricane instantly scowls, but I push past him, grabbing her bicep. "Pull yourself together. You've had enough for tonight. Go to your room and change. Right. Fucking. Now. You can't wear shit like this here for these guys to see you, Novah. You're our stepsister."

She rips her arm from my grip, her eyes glaring into mine with a hard stare. "I am *painfully* aware." She huffs, then turns, heading for her bedroom.

"You're too tough on her, Bayou. She's just trying to let loose… have a little fun. You're *not* her keeper," Kaia snaps.

Hurricane rolls his shoulder, glancing down at Kaia's short dress while tugging at the bottom hem. "This *is* fuckin' short now I think about it."

Kaia slaps at his hand, then shoves him in the chest. "No fucking way. I'm not changing. I'm the First Lady of this club. I have to have some balls to stand up to you."

"You better *not* have any fuckin' balls, Sha," Hurricane quips, his hands running up the insides of her thighs, and she swats them away.

"Later, I will prove it to you. Tonight, however, we party."

Hurricane chuckles, but his laughter stops dead when his eyes shift to the hall for the bedrooms. He gulps and quickly averts his eyes, looking at the other end of the clubroom like his eyes are burning. "Fuckin' Christ!"

I snap my head in the direction he was looking to see Novah sauntering into the middle of the clubroom wearing the fucking corset and crotchless panties with a set of black stockings and some black high heels.

"Fuck!" My cock instantly springs to attention. My breathing becomes rapid as everyone stops and turns to look at her.

"What the *hell,* Novah," I snap.

"You told me to get changed... I got fucking changed."

Hurricane grunts. "Where the fuck did you get that? Bayou brought your clothes from your house. Why the hell would you bring that for?" His head snaps to me, and instantly the color drains from mine and Novah's faces.

Yeah. Wasn't so fucking smart now, was it, Novah?

Lani stands from her seat near the back. "It's mine. It's *my* lingerie... I showed it to Novah today."

Grey chokes on thin air, coughing a little as Novah and I both snap our heads to Lani, a silent 'thank you' being said to her. Hurricane simply furrows his brow and nods. "Okay, well, I don't know what stunt you're tryna pull here, Novah, but you need to get that fuckin' shit off *right the fuck now,* and I need to wash my damn eyes out."

I race forward, hoisting the throw off the King Chair and wrapping it around her.

She glares at me, and I shake my head. "Do *not* fight me on this."

She swallows, and I push her toward her bedroom, my cock aching almost as much as my anger is seething. It's bubbling on the surface, threatening to wreak havoc over this whole clubhouse and everyone in it.

When I close her bedroom door, she throws the blanket off and stands with her hands on her hips. I glare at her, my cock so fucking hard I can barely stand it.

"What the hell do you think you're doing?"

"Just being what *you* think I am."

I groan. "I don't think you're a whore, Novah. I just can't stand the thought of you wearing this for another man while *he* fucks *you."*

She jerks her head back. "I've never worn this for another man. Not ever. No one has ever seen me in this except Xanthe. She bought it for me as a joke."

I breathe harshly out my nostrils and grit my teeth. "You're telling me that every brother out there got to see you dressed in this fucking thing the same time I did, and no one else has seen you in it... *fucked* you in it?"

She shakes her head. "No one."

"Fuck! I was going crazy. *You* drive me *fucking crazy."* I start pacing, trying to figure out my next move. I'm so turned on right now, so fucking angry I can't stand it. I want to punish her for making me feel this way. My stomach knots, and I can't fight this goddamn feeling anymore.

"Fuck it!"

I turn around and grab her, slamming her body against the wall. Her breathing hitches as she molds her body into mine. My hands grab her wrists and pin them next to her head, securing her into place as our eyes lock, staring at each other, the energy exploding around us. My heart races so fast that I feel lightheaded as I stare at her supple lips. I try to fight it, but I see she is too. The chemistry between us is so intense that I try to hold myself back, but when she licks her bottom lip, I am done for.

I can't restrain myself any longer.

CHAPTER 5

NOVAH

Bayou slams his lips to mine.

The instant his lips touch me, fireworks spark inside me so powerfully I can't contain myself. It's explosive, euphoric, intoxicating. I've wanted this moment for as long as I can remember. I just never knew it would be this intense, this primal, this hot.

His tongue slides into my mouth, his tongue ring feeling like a devilish delight as he kisses me intensely. I can't hold back. I've needed this, been fighting this. It's so wrong, but right now, it feels so damn right. His hands drop down to my thighs, and he hoists me up, my legs instantly wrapping around his waist. I moan into his mouth as his hard cock presses into my crotchless panties.

I was drunk, but the heat of this kiss has evaporated all the alcohol. So now I am here in the moment, enjoying every second of this as Bayou moves us over to the bed. My adrenaline spikes, my heart rate increasing. I always knew Bayou would be my first. But other than kissing a guy, I haven't done anything else, and this is heading into territory I know nothing about.

But I am *so* ready to go there with him.

Even if he doesn't know it.

He stands at the edge of the bed and throws me down onto the mattress. I pant at the forceful nature of his actions while his salacious eyes devour me. "I'm gonna make you feel so fucking good, beautiful."

He slides in over me, his teeth dragging along my skin as I let out a whimper, loving how he is touching me.

I have thought about this moment.

Dreamed about this moment.

And it is *everything* I thought it would be.

My fingers run through his hair as he moves in beside me on the bed, his fingers gliding toward the top of my corset, and he squeezes my breast, sliding the material down and freeing my nipple. Swallowing a lump in my throat, my stomach flutters in nervous butterflies and my palms begin to sweat when he leans down, taking my nipple into his mouth and sucking. He swirls his tongue ring around my taut bud, sending a pleasurable shudder down my spine. "Oh God," I whimper.

Why is everything so sensitive?

He groans, taking my nipple between his teeth and clamps down, sending a shockwave straight to my aching clit. My fingers clench in his hair as I bite my bottom lip. "Bayou, fuck!"

"That's it. I need to hear you scream my name." He groans, his voice husky and laced with lust. It's driving me insane.

He tiptoes his fingers down the center of my body while my breathing becomes labored as he continues to suck on my nipple—I'm already feeling so damn good. *Why the hell have I held out this long?*

My body trembles a little the closer he edges toward my pussy, not out of fear but out of impatience. I have waited so long for him to touch me. I am so ready for this. "I need to feel you, Bayou. Touch me."

He growls, his fingers sliding down through my crotchless panties into my already-wet-for-him folds. The second I feel him touching me, my back arches off the bed, and I let out a whimper.

"Yes." I moan as he begins to pant heavily.

"I've been waiting to claim this sweet pussy of yours." He grunts, then slides a finger inside me.

The feeling's like nothing I have ever felt before. Like every nerve ending has come alive while Bayou moves in and out of me, pushing all the right places. I tingle everywhere, and it's almost too good. My hands ball into the sheets forming fists as my breathing catches. My body shudders with the sensation.

"Oh, God, it feels... so... good." I can barely get the words out.

Bayou slowly chuckles under his breath, his tongue sliding out over my nipple, that freaking ring working up my nipple as I focus on the pleasure rolling through me.

"You look so fucking beautiful... skin all flushed and worked up like this. I need you to come for me, Novah." He places his thumb on my clit, and instantly the sensations are taken to a whole other level. I gasp, barely able to catch my breath as my hips begin riding his hand, needing to draw out the friction.

"Fuck, more." I beg.

He growls. "You're making me so fucking hard." He pushes his fingers inside me and draws them back in such a way that I begin to see stars. I've made myself come before, but I have never had anyone else bring me to the edge, and this right here is the most intoxicating moment of my life.

My hand reaches up, frantically gripping hold of his cut, needing to feel him. And I grip tight, my fingers digging into the leather as I drop my head back into the pillow, clenching my eyes tight. "I'm so close."

He leans down, biting my nipple at the same time as he presses hard on my clit. It sends a blast wave through me I can't even comprehend. I let out a noise I have never heard before as I throw my head from side to side while my hips ride his hand, searching for that delicious high.

"Come for me. Come now, Novah," he demands.

Goddammit! It's like he lights a fuse inside me. My body flames in an insatiable heat that it swarms every molecule of my being. My skin flushes, my body trembles, and my muscles pull tense. My breathing catches, lights dance behind my eyes, and time stops for a brief moment before the tidal wave hits and rolls over me with such an epic blast that I scream out his name, not giving two shits who can hear me. My muscles relax as my body tingles, going completely numb, and I struggle to catch my breath. Finally, I lay back, clenching my eyes, trying to stop the spasming.

"I've waited so fucking long for this. I'm gonna fuck you till you can't walk." Bayou grunts.

The sound of a belt buckle undoing makes my eyes snap open as I try to calm my racing heart.

I've just experienced my first shared orgasm.

Bayou doesn't know I'm a virgin.

I know this will hurt, and he's basically said he's going to do this quick and rough. My breathing starts to race as he yanks his jeans down, pulling out his cock. My eyes duck down between us, and they widen, taking in his size.

He's so fucking big.

Oh, fuck.

Oh, God.

Oh, shit.

This is it.

My nerves are hitting me tenfold as my stomach flutters with butterflies.

I should tell him.

Bayou moves in over me, his eyes burning with lust and desire.

I've waited twenty-seven years for this moment. I can't ruin it now. But I feel myself tensing.

His hand comes up, caressing my face as he narrows his eyes on me. "Relax, Novah, I'm gonna make you feel so good."

Letting out the breath I was holding, I lean up, pressing my lips to his. Kissing him feels so fucking right. We've been fighting this attraction for so long. We've finally given in, and it feels so good.

Why am I letting one small factor get in my head?

He lines his cock up with my pussy, his thick tip sliding up and down, and I moan into his mouth at the feeling.

This is it.

I'm not going to be a virgin after this.

Bayou was always going to take my virginity, he just never knew it.

"I'm gonna fuck you so fucking good." He grunts, then goes to push forward. But my anxiety gets the better of me, and I grip his chest and push back a little.

"I'm a virgin!" I practically yell the words in his face.

He stops.

Stills for a moment as he stares at me wide-eyed.

Then it's almost like he has been electrocuted. He pulls back, jumping off me and standing from the bed at the end of it, with his hands raised like he's just been infected by some terrible disease.

I have to admit, the horrified expression on his face as he stands at the end of the bed, his cock hanging out while his hands run through his hair, is a little daunting.

He begins to pace. His breathing sounding more like a bull. "You're a *what?"*

My anxiety skyrockets through the roof as I sit up and pat the bed next to me, trying to take his tone down a notch. "Sorry, forget I said anything. Just come back."

He puts his cock away so quickly I almost miss it, and he begins walking toward the door.

The fact he is leaving right now sends an ache right through me, and my insecurities sky high as I simply stare at him. "So what? Now you don't want me?"

He turns back. "You should have told me, Novah... it changes *everything."*

"Bayou..." I pause. "Blaise, please?"

His heavy eyes stare at me when he runs his hand through his hair. "I just can't do this..." He hesitates, then turns and walks out of my room.

Just. Like. That.

My chest feels like a herd of elephants is sitting on it as he closes the door behind him. I thought we had finally made it past our barriers, only for him to put even more up. With my bottom lip trembling, I stand and rip off the stupid fucking corset. This thing has brought me nothing but trouble. I can't help but feel dirty now, so I need to get clean. I make my way to the bathroom and jump in the shower, turning the faucet up to as hot as I can stand, trying to keep my emotions in check. I just had one of the most amazing moments of my life, followed by the most earth-shattering.

How the hell do I process that?

Bringing my fist up, I slam my palm into the tiles, letting out my frustration, and then I turn, sliding down the wall while letting out a loud sob.

I feel completely wrecked.

Ruined.

I let Bayou in.

I let him into my heart only for him to completely annihilate it.

Sinking onto the tiled floor, I let the hot water wash over me as I cry, sobbing so much I feel sick, while I scrub at my skin to try and stop me from feeling so damn dirty.

Bayou said he didn't mean that he called me a whore.

Well, he just went and made me feel like one.

CHAPTER 6

BAYOU

My heart races so fucking frantically I can hardly stand it as I bolt out of her room. I feel like an asshole for walking out on her like this, but I am so goddammed turned on right now I have to firmly control this situation. If I stay, I'm going to go about this all fucking wrong. So I hightail it out of her room as fast as fucking possible.

Novah is a virgin.

Fuck.

That thought runs through my mind over and over like a record stuck on repeat.

Novah is a virgin.

Novah is a virgin.

There were rumors around the clubhouse she was, but I never believed them for a single second. A woman as incredibly sexy as her—there's no way a man hadn't swept her up. But the fact that no one has tainted her only adds fuel to my fire—another reason I had to leave. I'm going to be the first and only man to take her body, make her scream, and give her pleasure in ways she's never known.

That's a high I will *never* be able to come back from.

Once I've had her, there's no coming back.

But Novah being a virgin changes how we need to do things for her first time—an angry, drunken fuck is not it.

I will *not* have her first memory of sex being after an argument, her memory impaired by alcohol, and her inhibitions lowered to the point where she might have given herself freely when in reality, she might not want to.

I can't be the guy to ruin her that way.

Any other woman, I wouldn't think twice.

But not my Novah.

Not the woman I care so deeply about.

The woman I have known longer than most of the people in my life, besides Hurricane, of course. There's something about Novah that is ingrained deep in my soul.

She is who I compare every other woman to.

She is who I want every other woman to be.

The one woman I shouldn't have, but I desire so fucking desperately.

We gave in to temptation tonight, and tasting her was like fucking nirvana. So fucking sweet. So fucking right. I need to take some time now to ensure that because of the alcohol in her system, she really wants this because there will be consequences if we move forward.

For her, yes.

But especially for me.

She's going to be hurt and confused that I left, but she blindsided me, and I just need a beat to get my mind focused on the right path.

Right now, I'm too fucking worked up.

I need someone to talk me off the ledge because honestly, I don't know what the fuck to do. I need someone sensible to talk to. Normally, when I need a voice of reason, I head straight for Novah, but I can't do that. So, maybe I have to go to the next best thing.

Making my way for my ride, Hurricane spots me, raising his

brow. "Everythin' good with Novah?"

Growling, I roll my shoulders. "She's upset. I said some shit to her I probably shouldn't have. She just needs to sober up."

Hurricane hums under his breath. "You push her too hard. I get you wanna look out for her… hell, I do too, but she can have a little fun while she's at the clubhouse."

My mind shifts back to the sounds she made climaxing around my fingers, my cock jerking at the thought. "She's doing fine… I gotta head out for a bit. I'll be back later."

Hurricane curls his lip. "Where the fuck you goin' this time of night?"

"To get some advice."

Hurricane narrows his eyes. "Somethin' goin' down I should know about?"

Shaking my head, I huff. "Nah, just boring mundane shit. Nothing of any interest."

He slaps my shoulder. "I might be your president, but I'm your twin first and foremost… I'm always here if you need me. You know that, right?"

Huh!

I'm not sure why, but I'm surprised to hear his words. "Thanks, brother… I'll keep that in mind." I smack him on the back and take off for my ride.

I need to feel the wind in my hair.

The open road.

The thrill of speed.

Jumping on, I rev my engine and take off. Grey opens the gates for me, and I race down the stretch of road. The engine's vibration rattles through me, giving me that thrill I need right now.

Though I can't help my mind from wandering to how shattered Novah's face was when I left.

I've never seen her look so broken.

I did that to her.

But I had no idea how to handle the situation other than

to leave.

I know it was wrong.

But it was my only thought at that time.

I hope our relationship, whatever capacity that may be, isn't irreparably broken at this point.

I pull the throttle down harder, needing to get to my destination, so I can get this shit off my chest.

Pulling into the quaint little home, I instantly feel warmth and love radiating from within the second I step off my bike. This place holds so many amazing memories, as I glance at the tire swing hanging from the old oak in the front yard.

Novah sat in the tire, giggling like anything as I pushed her. Lynx and I put the swing up on the oak tree for her because she was having trouble with her friends at school picking on her for having biker brats as stepbrothers. The girls wouldn't play with her after school, so Lynx and I said, 'screw it, we'll make our own fun,' and we built her this damn swing. The problem was, she loved it so much we always had to be out here playing on it with her. Finally, Lynx gave up and got tired of it, but I lit up every time I heard her giggling like the way she was right now.

"Higher, Blaise, higher," she chimed.

"If you go any higher, you'll fall." I chuckled.

She glanced over her shoulder. "It's okay. You'll catch me." She smiled.

And I would.

I would always catch her.

Tensing, I let out a long breath at how naïve those two kids playing on the tire swing were back then. If only they could see the mess they have gotten themselves into right now. Rubbing the back of my neck, I step up to the front door, and before I can even knock, it opens to Ingrid wrapping a robe around her. She yawns like she was sleeping, but her warm smile is the best part of coming home.

Seeing her dressed like this and half asleep makes me step back toward my bike. "You were asleep. I should have known. It's so fucking late. I'm sorry, I'll go—"

"Blaise Ladet, you get your ass inside right now, you hear me," she snaps, looking down at me through her lashes, though the warm smile on her face tells me she isn't angry.

Huffing, I step up onto the porch. "I'm sorry I woke you."

She snorts, waving her hand through the air. "Pfft... I was onto chapter twenty-seven of a really good book. I kept thinking, *just one more chapter and I'll go to sleep*. I started the book when I hopped into bed, so..."

Smirking as I step up and kick off my boots before I walk inside, she wraps her arms around me for an embrace. "Must be a good book. What's it about?"

"Nothing you'd like. It's about a cougar."

I raise my brow. "Is that one of those paranormal animal smut books they talk about?"

She chuckles. "No, darling, an older woman and a younger guy... it's giving me ideas. I'm not past my prime, you know?"

Scrunching up my face, I shake my head. "Jesus, Ingrid. You're gonna scar me for life talkin' like that."

She snickers, pulling me further into the house and closes the door behind me. "I'm joking... your father left too much of an impression on me. He took my heart with him when he passed."

I frown as she leads us into the living room. I'm actually sad to hear that. She should get out and meet someone new because if anyone deserves to be happy, it's Ingrid.

"You know my dad loved you more than anything. You gave him, Hurricane, and me a chance at a life we would never have had. But Dad wouldn't want you pining over him... he'd want you to move on and be happy."

She weakly smiles, patting my leg. "I have a feeling you didn't come all the way out here to talk about me and my problems."

Shifting to look at her, I grip her hand. "My problems can wait. You've put so much of your life into Hurricane and me. All we want is for *you* to be happy."

She looks into my eyes intently. "Bayou, listen to me. Your brother, you, Novah, and Nash are the single most important people in my life. The four of you make me the happiest I could ever be. You're the *only* people I need in my life. As long as I have the four of you, I am as content as I will ever need to be. I don't need a man to make me whole. *I don't.* I am completely fine being an independent, single woman. Honestly darling… I'm good."

She seems genuinely content with her life. Just hearing her missing Dad is something I haven't heard from her before. But I guess we all have our moments of missing him.

"Okay… but if you need us to help you get out there… to find you a younger man—" She playfully shoves me in the side as I chuckle. "But in all seriousness, as long as you're happy."

"I'm fine. But you, on the other hand, are obviously struggling with something to come here this late at night. So talk to me… tell me what's on your mind."

Groaning, I slump back on the sofa, scrubbing at my face. I don't know what I came here expecting to tell Ingrid or ask her. She's Novah's mother. She's my stepmother. It's not like I can just come out and tell her I almost stole Novah's virginity tonight.

Yeah, that would go down real well.

Her hand smooths out along my back, caressing me soothingly. "Bayou, something is obviously bothering you… is it Hurricane?"

Inhaling deeply through my nose, my terrified eyes glance up at her.

Keep it vague. Easy.

"It's a girl."

Her eyes light up, and she tries to hide her smile but fails. "You're having woman trouble?"

"Like you wouldn't believe. I fucked up… so goddamn huge."

She steadies her shoulders and faces me a little more. "Okay, so you obviously care about this woman, so whatever you did or didn't do, you make sure to find a way to make it up to her."

Craning my neck to the side, I flare my nostrils. "That's the thing, Ingrid. Being with her is complicated. I want to fix it. I want to show her why I did what I did, and I want to do it the right way. But if I do, there will be ramifications. Big ones... for her *and* me."

Ingrid narrows her eyes. "What kind of ramifications, darling? Will either of you be in danger?"

Will Hurricane and Nash kill me for being with Novah? Possibly.

One thing is for sure, they're not going to be happy.

"The hesitation in your answer tells me there is a problem, Bayou. What is it about this girl that you have to go after? Why her?"

My chest squeezes, and as I glance past Ingrid to a picture of Novah, Hurricane, Nash, and me on the mantle, I stare at a younger version of Novah and exhale. "She's everything I've always wanted."

"So something has happened between you, a reciprocal attraction?"

Nodding, I swallow a lump in my throat upon hearing Novah's moans in my mind. I push them away to keep focused as Ingrid grips my hands tighter. "I've been waiting for this day to happen."

Widening my eyes, I tilt my head. "When I would find someone?"

"When you and Novah would wake up to your feelings for each other."

I jerk my head back with a gasp. "What?"

Ingrid raises her hands in defense. "It's okay, don't panic... I'm not angry or upset. In fact, I've known since Novah was about sixteen that you two would end up together. Actually, it was your father who noticed the connection first."

Shaking my head, I scrunch my brows. "H-how did you know?"

She sighs. "Darling, chemistry like that, you can't fake. Honestly, I'm surprised it's taken you so long to get together.

You've fought it for a long time."

"She's my stepsister."

Ingrid shrugs. "And? You're not related, Bayou. You might have grown up together, but the only ones putting a stigma on yourselves is you two."

"I think Hurricane and Nash might have words to say about it."

Ingrid smirks. "They're protective. They don't want anyone to hurt her. They want a man who will look after and cherish her... do you plan on doing that?"

"With every fiber in my being."

"Then tell them, and they will be glad it's you and not some asshole who is gonna treat her like shit."

My mind flashes back to her face when I walked out of her room. "But, I did treat her like shit."

Ingrid sits taller. "Okay, tell me about it."

Grimacing, I groan. "Let's just say we were about to..." I dip my head while widening my eyes, so she gets the idea without me having to say it out loud.

Her eyes bulge out of her face as she gasps. "Oh. Okay, I'm following... yes, go on."

"Then, just before I... went for it, she told me something I didn't know, and I freaked out, backed away, and left."

"She told you she's a virgin?"

I gawk at her. "How did you know that?"

She chuckles. "I have three boys and only *one* girl. Trust me... me and Novah talk about *everything."*

"Right..."

"How did she take you leaving?"

"She looked devastated. It fucking killed me, but we'd just had a fight, and she was a little drunk. There was *no way* I was about to angry fuck her for her first time. No matter how much she felt like she wanted it. She was inebriated, and her inhibitions were down. She wasn't thinking clearly. And as soon as she told me about her virginity, all I could think of was that if I went through with it, in the morning when she sobered up… if she remembered any of it… Novah's first time wouldn't be a special memory like she deserves."

Ingrid's eyes glisten as she reaches out, pulling me to her in a tight embrace. "Novah may be mad at you right now, but if you can explain to her what you've just told me, she will thank you." She pulls back, looking into my eyes. "You're a good man, Bayou. You're looking out for her needs before your own, and that is all I could want for her."

"That's if she ever talks to me again."

Ingrid pats my hand. "She will. She's hurting. She might feel rejected right now, so prove to her that you want her, that *nothing* else matters."

"I'm still so conflicted. Every part of me wants to be with her, to claim her as my Old Lady and make a life with her. But then there's this voice inside my head that makes me feel so fucking guilty. Like I'm breaking some goddamn sin or something by wanting her this much."

Ingrid frowns, but she nods. "I figured that was why the two of you had never acted on your attractions until now. But darling, don't worry about how people will judge you. Bayou, you're NOLA Defiance, an outlaw, you have a pet alligator you feed enemies of the club to, and you treat him more like a part of your damn family than Nash sometimes. You're a 1%er. You don't take shit from anybody, so why the *hell* are you letting *this* worry you?"

Exhaling, I run my hand through my hair. "I worry for Novah. She has an important career. I don't want her clients looking at her differently because of me."

"Don't you think that's *her* choice to make? You *can't* decide that for her."

Slumping back on the sofa, I nod, rubbing at my beard. "I need to talk to her, don't I?"

"Yes, darling, you do…" Ingrid smiles. "I love you equally, and no matter what happens, I will be here for the both of you. You never have to worry about that, okay?"

"She's your daughter, and I want you to understand that if this all falls to shit, you should support her."

"Bayou, I may not have given birth to you, but I love you as if I did. That does not make a difference to the fact that you and Novah are destined to be together. Do you hear me?" Her hands grip either side of my face and force me to look into her eyes. The crow's feet at the edges of her eyes are even more pronounced as she glares at me intensely.

"I hear you. Thank you."

She pulls my head forward and plants a kiss on my forehead. The way she always used to do it when we were young and heading off for school. I smirk while she pulls back, this time with a smile on her face. "I love you. I'm so glad you came to talk to me about this."

"Please don't tell Novah I was here."

Ingrid pats my leg again. "Your secret is safe with me. I'm just glad you two are finally giving in to your feelings. It's long overdue."

"Well, we will see how it goes when I get back to the clubhouse. She might not talk to me."

"She'll come around, and if she doesn't... *make her."*

"Anyone ever tell you how good you are at advice and talking people down off the ledge?"

Ingrid exhales. "I was married to your father. He was the president of the club, remember? I constantly had to talk him down from the ledge."

Smiling, I tilt my head. "And now you have to keep doing it with Hurricane and me. Not what you signed up for."

"I didn't sign up for anything, Bayou. I do it because I love you all. No other reason. Now, how about I make you a cup of your favorite hot cocoa before you head back and deal with this mess?"

Fuck.

I loved her cocoa as a kid and haven't had it in years. "Fuck it! Why the hell not."

CHAPTER 7

NOVAH

I can't stop thinking about the way Bayou made me feel.

Sure, I've made myself climax thousands of times, but he is the first man to ever get me to that high, and it was everything I could have ever imagined.

I wanted more.

I've wanted more from him for so damn long. We've been fighting it for so long, at least I was, but now I wonder if he even has feelings for me at all. Maybe he just wanted a quick fuck, but as soon as I pulled out the V-card talk, he repelled from me so fast it was like I repulsed him or something.

I've never felt more unattractive in all my life.

The way he flew out of here like I was infected, like any second longer in this room with me he was going to catch the dreaded virginal disease. I've never been more humiliated, devastated, and disappointed. My entire life, I have waited for Bayou to be the man to take my virginity. I think that's partly the reason I never dated. I blamed it on my brothers, said it was their fault, but deep down it was because I didn't want to run the risk of letting anyone else in.

I was saving myself for *him.*

But the fact is, he doesn't want me.

I'm not stupid. I know Bayou's been with countless other women—I simply don't measure up to them.

Wiping the tears from my cheeks, I walk to the closet and yank out my duffle bag.

I have to pack.

I can't stay here.

I can't stand to see him every day, knowing I finally put myself out there and he rejected me.

Trying to pretend like everything is okay in front of Hurricane when it is anything but.

I simply don't have the strength.

So, I begin shoving all my shit into my bag, packing everything except that stupid fucking corset. My eyes fall to it on the floor, and I walk over and pick it up, then walk it to the trash can in the bathroom and shove it with a little extra force. I slam the lid down tight and then lean over the basin looking at myself in the mirror. My face is red and blotchy from crying—I look a fucking mess. But right now, I don't care. I just need to leave. I'll take my chances with Johnny and his rats at this point, I'd prefer his company over Bayou's.

Grabbing my bag, I head for the door and walk into the clubroom. It has quieted down for the night, seeing as it is so late. Most of the brothers have taken off for their rooms for the night, and only a few stragglers remain. Kaia walks to the kitchen but spots me getting ready to leave, her eyes widening.

Then as I almost reach the door, Bayou walks through it. His eyes fall directly on the duffle. His nostrils flare, the vein in his neck pulsating as he shakes his head. "Going somewhere?" he asks.

"Like *you* care."

A low growl reverbs from deep within his chest, and he reaches forward for my bag, but I yank it from his grip. "No. You don't get to tell me what I can and can't do."

He glances around the clubhouse, wondering how to play this with our onlookers. "Novah, you can't leave the clubhouse. It's not safe, and we have shit we need to discuss."

I laugh in his face. "I think your actions told me plenty. I heard everything you were saying loud and obnoxiously clear. I don't need to know anymore. Now…. Let. Me. Pass." I grunt in his face.

He folds his arms over his chest. "Don't be stubborn, Novah. It doesn't suit you."

My bottom lip trembles when my eyes meet his. "Just another thing you don't like about me, huh?" Sniffling, I go to shove past him, but he grabs my shoulders and steadies me, breathing rapidly.

"I don't want to make a scene out here."

Rolling my eyes, I scowl. "Then… *let me go."*

"You can't leave, Novah."

"Why? Because it's not safe? *I don't fucking care, Bayou.* It hurts more to stay here than to get hurt physically out there right now," I scream at him.

He jerks back, his face contorting like I've killed his puppy. "Novah… I—"

Kaia suddenly steps up beside me and reaches for my arm. "Novah, how about we go and have a talk, woman to woman, let whatever is happening here cool down… if you still want to leave after we've talked, we can figure that out then, okay?" Kaia asks.

My adrenaline surges, and I want nothing more than to walk out of here, but Kaia and I have always gotten along so well.

Maybe I do need to talk to someone about what happened.

Get this off my chest.

I shove my duffle toward Bayou, and he takes it with a heavy exhale as I turn with Kaia, and we head for the bedrooms. She wraps her arm with mine, and I try to control my erratic heartbeat while she walks us to my room because obviously, Hurricane is in hers.

Entering, I move over to my bed, and she sits in the desk chair.

As she rolls it up in front of me, I flop back on the bed, staring at the ceiling, wondering where on earth to start.

"Novah, you're like family to me. It's obvious there's some tension between you and Bayou. We saw it when we were dancing. Are you guys just having one of your typical fights, and it's making you want to leave?"

Letting out a small laugh, I place my arm over my eyes to stop myself from crying. Again. "If only it were that simple."

She exhales, her hand resting on my knee comfortingly. "You don't have to tell me anything you don't want to, but sometimes talking things out can help."

Letting out a long breath, I groan. "Everything is so fucked up, Kaia."

"I'm sure it's not as bad as you think. Sometimes our minds make shit worse than it really is."

I sit up dramatically, my terrified eyes meeting hers. "No, this *is* bad. For sooo many reasons."

She rolls her shoulders. "Okay, you know whatever gets said here is between us, Novah. I'm not going to say anything to Hurricane unless you want me to or unless the club is in real danger."

That makes me feel better, knowing I can talk to her, and it won't go anywhere. "You won't tell Lani?"

"It's just you and me. No one else will hear a word of this. I'm the First Lady of this club, and I have a duty to take care of the members. You may not directly be a member, but you're club family. So I'm gonna take care of you, Novah... let me help you."

I feel like I can trust her, like she will have something insightful to tell me. Of course, Bayou will probably hate me for telling her, but fuck it. He lost any rights to what we have the second he showed me how he truly felt about me. "Bayou and me... we've always been much closer than me and Hurricane. I mean, don't get me wrong. I adore Hurricane, but Bayou and I automatically clicked when we were younger."

Kaia nods in understanding. "I get it. I see that when you're together, I also see that you get on each other's nerves more too."

Slumping, I sigh. "I thought it was because we were fighting our attraction for each other."

Kaia widens her eyes, a slow smile crossing her face. "Oh… I see. So there *are* feelings between you both?"

Groaning, I shake my head. "No. I thought there were… seems it's one-sided. How fucking stupid could I be?"

Kaia chuckles. "You're not stupid… all us girls notice the way he looks at you. The way his body reacts when he is around you. Iz, Lani, and I have talked about it… Bayou is most definitely into you. We just never wanted to bring it up to you because it is a delicate subject."

"Right. He's my stepbrother, for crying out loud. It's wrong on so many levels."

Kaia rolls her eyes. "Stop that. It is not. You two are perfect for each other. What I meant is that when Hurricane finds out, he is going to freak. He's so intent on making sure the guy you're with is perfect for you, knowing it's going to be his twin is going to knock him around."

"Well, you don't have to worry because Bayou and I are over before we begun."

Kaia furrows her brows. "Why?"

"I haven't had sex before…" I pause, trying to gauge her reaction. There is none, so I continue, "Anyway, things were getting heated between us after our argument in the clubhouse. I was ready to let him take me, so willing to let that moment be it, but the guilt of not telling him I was a virgin was eating at me. So as he was about to… *you know*… go for it, I blurted it out."

Kaia stiffens her posture. "Blurted what out?"

"That I'm a virgin."

Her eyes widen, and she gasps. "Let me get this right… just as Bayou was about to enter you, you told him?"

"He was right there, and I just spat it out."

"He had his cock out coming toward you?"

"It was actually going in a little bit."

Kaia throws her hands in the air and lets out a groan. "Oh my God, Novah."

Tensing all over, I stare at her. "What?"

She turns back to me. "Bayou freaked out, didn't he?"

Wrapping my arms around myself for comfort, I nod. "Mm-hmm... ran out of the room quicker than I could say fucker."

"You threw dynamite at him and lit the fuse, Novah. That's no small thing you told him. The woman he deeply cares about told him something that is a big deal in a woman's life. I can't say for sure what's going through his mind, but I bet whatever it is, it's not whatever you *think* it is."

"His face was scrunched. He looked like I repulsed him, like my virginity was some disease he would catch. He didn't want to be near me. Like at that moment, I couldn't have been uglier if I had tried. I've never felt more unattractive in my life."

"Oh, Novah. I'm sure he doesn't think that way."

"That's sure how it feels. Like the very thought of me is disgusting to him."

"From the look in his eyes just now, he doesn't think you're disgusting. If anything, he wants to talk to you, probably about this very issue. Clear the air. I'm sure he wants to make it up to you."

"I just don't think I can look at him right now. It's the way he took off... I just can't stand being near him..." My breath catches in my throat. "It hurts too much."

Kaia nods and reaches out for my hand. "I understand. He hurt you, really bad. But Novah, there's a direct threat to your life outside these walls. You know if you leave, Hurricane is just going to drag you back and demand to know *why* you left."

Fuck.

She's right.

"Why do you have to make so much sense?"

She smirks. "You don't have to talk to Bayou tonight. Hell, you don't have to talk to him for a week if you don't want to, but just know that if you two are avoiding each other, Hurricane *will* notice and want to know why. Eventually, you're going to have to tell him there's something between the two of you."

Snorting, I shake my head. "He'll kill Bayou, probably feed him to his own damn alligator."

Kaia giggles. "I won't let him. Bayou is too important to us all. Will Hurricane be angry? Probably, but he might also be relieved. Like I said, he wants a man that is worthy of you."

"Right now, Bayou is *not* that guy."

"Give him time to make it right."

Nodding my head, I bite my lip. "I hate that I let him have the power to make me feel like this."

Kaia sighs. "I know the feeling well. When Hurricane kidnapped me, I was devastated that he could do that to me. I felt so fucking betrayed. I thought we had made such progress for him to just shoot it all to the ground like that. I didn't think we could come back from it... but we did. And look at us now. If I can forgive Hurricane for kidnapping me, I'm sure you and Bayou can work through this too."

Well, she put that into perspective.

"Thanks, Kaia, for helping me."

"I think the thing you need to remember is... the news you gave Bayou at the eleventh hour was a huge shock. I don't think he reacted because he didn't want to be near you. I think he reacted because he wanted to take care of you in that moment."

"Maybe... it sure didn't feel like that at the time."

"And that's why you need to talk to him, find out what he was really thinking, but only when you're ready... it's okay to let him wait a bit. Get some of that power back." She grins at me and winks.

"You're good at this advice stuff, you know that?" I tell her.

She snorts. "Hardly, I just say what I'd like to hear." She laughs as she stands from the chair. "Want me to go grab your bag and tell him you'll talk to him tomorrow *if* you're up for it?"

Nodding, I exhale. "That would be great. Thank you... for talking me into staying. I didn't want to go back out there with Johnny gunning for me."

"You're welcome to stay here as long as you want, Novah. You just have to be willing to. Our house is your house, and these guys will protect you with their lives because that's what we do for family."

"The word of the hour."

"Family?" Kaia asks.

"Mmm..."

"Don't get caught up on a six-letter word, Novah. Yeah, Bayou is family, but I'm also your family. Lani is your family. All those brothers, who are a part of this club, are your family... it's just a word, Novah. It's what you make it."

She has a point.

I need to let go of this hang-up I have. That's if Bayou and I are even going to be something. Which, at this point, I can't see happening. "I'll try."

She pats me on the shoulder and then turns for the door. "Novah, if you ever need to talk, I'm here... always. Please don't feel like your only option is to leave."

"I understand that now."

"I'll go get your things." She pulls the door open, then turns back to face me. "For what it's worth, I think you and Bayou together will make an amazing couple." She winks at me, then closes the door behind her.

Exhaling, I slump back down on the mattress, staring at the ceiling. Maybe Bayou did stop for my benefit? But I just can't stop the way it makes me feel when I think he doesn't want me, like I'm not good enough for him. I've never felt anything but support and kindness, even adoration from him.

When he fled from my bed, it was like an icy dagger slammed

straight into my heart. I can't just erase that feeling. It's etched deep inside me, spreading like a noxious weed.

He might have been trying to do the right thing—*maybe*.

But in doing so, he's hurt me so inconceivably, and I don't know if we will ever be the same.

BAYOU
Christmas Eve

The last few days have been tense.

Novah is doing everything she can to avoid me at the clubhouse, even though I have tried to corner her alone multiple times. She simply finds some excuse to get away from me. I guess she's not ready to talk to me.

I royally fucked up, and I have no clue how to fix it.

We have a giant Christmas Eve feast tonight, and Ingrid and Nash are here to celebrate with us as usual. The last thing I want is for Nash to have *any idea* that Novah and I are on shaky ground. As it is, trying to hide it from Hurricane is bad enough, and I'm worried about what he would do if he found out. But Nash, he's a whole other ball game being Novah's blood brother. If anyone is going to put a bullet in me, it's him, and we're the assholes who taught him how to use a damn gun.

Ingrid steps up to my side with a warm smile while I sit at the bar, drink in hand when the party starts around me. She rubs my back soothingly. "You don't tend to drink that often, Bayou. But I see you're changing that tonight?" She looks directly at the three empty shot glasses and one beer bottle in front of me. Plus, the half-empty bottle in my hand.

"I'm a little tense, Ingrid," I reply, knowing I am being sarcastic but honestly not having a clue as to what else to say.

She glances over her shoulder to where Novah, Nash, and Hurricane are all sitting together talking and laughing. "The only way they're going to find out, darling, is by you being a sad sack of shit all night..." She dips her chin. "It's Christmas Eve. Enjoy the festive spirit."

Finally cracking a smile, I take one last sip of my beer and place it on the bar. "Thanks, Frankie." The club girl wipes down the bar and takes all my empties away.

Standing, I walk with Ingrid over to the table where the rest of my family is sitting and being rowdy.

"I can't believe you're actually doin' it, you sonofabitch. I'm gonna just say it... I'm damn proud of you, man," Hurricane tells Nash.

He beams with pride as he dips his chin. "Ensure Asset Management will be trading as of the third of January. I stole Lucas from my father's company. He will be my COO, and Zoey, my PA, is coming across with me too. I may be starting the business from the ground up, but as long as we can get a couple of big clients when we hit the ground running, it will be icing on the cake. Most of my clients are moving with me, which helps."

My eyes shift to Novah, who is beaming with pride. "I always knew you would step out from under our father's shadow, Nash. I am *so* proud of you."

Nash smiles at Novah and rests his hand on her knee. "Thanks. Lucas can sometimes get out of control, so I need to keep him in line."

Novah snorts. "Good luck with that, the guy's an animal when he's not at work."

The hairs on the back of my neck stand to attention. *How the fuck would she know that?* Jealousy flairs inside me, and even though I know she is a virgin and hasn't been with any other man, the idea that this asshole might have tried to make moves on her is making me borderline deranged.

"You all right, Bayou? You look like you're ready to kill someone?" Nash asks.

Novah turns to look at me. Her eyes widen like she didn't even know I was here.

Clearing my throat, my nostrils flare in frustration and downright rage. "How do you know this Lucas, Novah?"

She rolls her eyes. "Through Nash's work. He's harmless, just a flirt."

"Why are you letting guys flirt with you?"

Ingrid clears her throat, obviously to gain my attention. I glance at her, and she widens her eyes with a tiny shake of the head. I quickly get her meaning—I'm becoming obvious and obnoxious—that I need to cool my shit. "All I am saying is… don't attract unwanted attention."

Ingrid slumps her body, sagging her shoulders like she is disappointed, and there is a whisper of a sigh.

"Because all I can get is *unwanted* attention. Because no one could *possibly* want me, right?" Novah snaps back.

My fists clench together to stop me from standing up, racing over to her, and swooping her into my arms right here and now. I don't care who sees. "That's not what I said."

"But it's *clearly* what you think."

"Okay, you two, back to your corners. Why the fuck are you always bickering?" Nash grunts, seeming disinterested, whereas Hurricane's eyes are solely focused on me and how angry I am.

"Because Bayou is an arrogant asshole," Novah states in a hard, stony voice.

Ouch.

"Won't argue that." Nash chuckles, not seeming to be able to read the room right now.

"I think we should give out the gifts. What do you say, Hurricane?" Ingrid calls out.

Hurricane dips his chin. "Yeah, I think that's a good idea." He sends a whistle around the clubhouse, the twinkling lights from the decorations flickering in their Christmas cheer. The tinsel hanging from the rafters sends twinkles around the room, and a giant tree stands tall at the end of the clubhouse with a massive pile of presents around it. "Yo, I think it's about time we opened some gifts. What do you fuckers think?"

Kaia gets up and walks to the tree along with Lani, who is bouncing on her toes in her excitement. And the two of them start handing out the gifts.

I hang back, watching as they are handed out, knowing I wrapped Novah a gift marking it from anonymous. I'm hoping she will know it's from me. My eyes follow her as Kaia hands the box to her, and I light up when she smiles, looking at the tag like she is curious as to who it's from. I can't hear anything she is saying from back here, but she opens it to find a little unicorn holding a love heart. I know that the unicorn Nash gave her brings her comfort, so my hope is this one will be a sign that I want to bring her nothing but comfort too.

I want her to think of me as a safe place—not her enemy.

She glances over her shoulder, her eyes meeting mine, and her lips slowly turn up. "Thank you," she mouths, and I dip my chin as she places it back in the box so no one else can look at it.

Progress.

Ingrid steps up to me and hands me a card. "What's this?"

She shrugs. "Open it and find out."

Flipping it over, I open the envelope, and as I do, a photograph falls into my hands. It's of a young Novah and me, embracing, and it's clear the chemistry between us in this picture is there for all to see just from how we're looking at each other.

My eyes shift to Ingrid, and she smiles. "This was when I knew. So, darling, I know Novah is fighting you, but you two have only had eyes for each other since you were young..." she points to the picture, ".... and right here is the proof. You make her see it too."

I pull Ingrid in for a giant hug and plant a kiss on her head while everyone continues unwrapping presents around us.

"Hey, there's another anonymous one here for Novah," Grey states handing her the large box.

Furrowing my brows, I spin because that's definitely *not* from me.

She smiles. "You guys are spoiling me," she chimes, ripping off the wrapping and giving the box a little shake. She opens the packaging, and we all jump when a small blast of confetti erupts sending glittered candy canes through the clubhouse.

Everyone laughs.

Novah shakes her head. "Jesus! Way to scare a girl."

She reaches inside the box and pulls out an ornament, one you hang on a Christmas tree, but it's a bit bigger than normal. It's an apple, and as she spins it, she gasps because there's a miniature blade sticking out of it.

My skin prickles as I race forward at the same time as Hurricane and Grey, but Grey reaches her first. Then, grabbing the apple, he takes off running.

"What's going on?" Novah yells, the panic in her voice becoming more apparent.

We all turn to watch Grey as he hightails it for the front of the clubhouse. My heart's racing when he reaches for the door and throws the apple. But as it flies through the opening, he ducks, then an almighty blast follows. I rush forward, jumping for Novah at the same time the shockwave hits, and I shove her to the floor. Falling on top of her, my body covers hers from the debris. Shrapnel flies through the clubhouse at the same time as the heatwave hits. Nails and razors zoom through the air, hitting people before they can dive to the floor. A razor slides up my arm, a nail lodging in my leg while I shelter Novah from the chaos. I groan in pain as the front door of the building collapses, and part of the roof crumbles over the top of Grey. Screaming and cries of panic and pain sound through the clubhouse as it shakes and rattles from the explosion's aftermath.

I'm panting, trying to calm my racing heart. I glance down, seeing I am completely over Novah, so I lift a little to see I have sheltered her from any of the shrapnel.

Her eyes are watering as her fingers instantly rush to the gash on my arm. "Bayou, shit!"

I glance down but ignore the mess and instead slide my hand over her cheek. "You okay? Did *anything* get you?"

She shakes her head as I shift back, my leg hurting like a bitch. I glance over my head, hearing the moans of Grey under the rubble. Quickly, I help Novah up, my eyes checking her over, my hands running over her body.

Novah pushes on my chest. "I'm okay. Go. Go help Grey."

I hesitate, but she shoves me, and I take off following the rest of my brothers. We start shifting the paneling off Grey piece by piece.

"Grey, you okay, brother?" I call out as we hoist the shit off him as fast as we can.

"Got a… f-few holes… in m-me," he grumbles.

We start to work quicker as a team to pull the debris off him, and when we pull the final panel away, Grey is covered in blood—head to toe in blood.

Shit.

My eyes shift to Hurricane. Unfortunately, it looks like Grey copped the full brunt of the razor blades.

"It's gonna be okay, kid. We got ya," Hurricane offers. "Frankie, I'mma need some towels and a whole lotta gauze."

Frankie nods, a line of blood streaming down her face, but she merely swipes at it, running off with Davina and Storm to collect the supplies for Grey.

"Is he going to be okay?" Lani calls out as Kaia holds her back.

We all look up to Hoodoo, the most experienced medic here. "He's lost a lot of blood. We need to get him to the hospital."

"Oh shit, Lani," Kaia calls out.

We all spin, and in what seems like slow motion, we watch Lani fall to the floor, her body contorting and jerking in one of her seizures.

"Kaia, you got her?" Hurricane calls out as Kaia starts crying.

Izzy and Novah rush to her side to help.

Everything is happening at the same damn time.

"Fuck. *Nash? Ingrid,"* I call out, the thought suddenly slamming into my brain that I haven't seen them. Hurricane snaps his head around as they step out into the chaos.

"We're okay. Just standing back letting everyone focus. Let us know if we can help in any way?" Ingrid states.

"Either of you hurt?" I yell.

"Not a scratch. We were too far away from the blast," Nash replies.

Hurricane and I both slump our shoulders. "Thank God."

Turning back, we swarm around Grey, the prospect zoning in and out of consciousness with his blood loss. I glance over my shoulder to watch the girls focusing on Lani as she shakes with her violent seizure.

Hurricane stands, pacing like he is torn, while a couple of brothers race out the front to see if an attack is imminent or if the explosion *was* the attack.

I glance up at my twin, my president. "Hurricane, go be with Kaia and Lani. We got Grey. It's okay."

He runs his fingers through his hair and kneels, placing his hand on Grey's bloody shoulder. "You hang in there. We got the EMTs on the way. We are Defiance. You got it?"

Grey nods his head in reply.

Hurricane dips his head at me and then takes off to be with his Old Lady and her sick sister.

City and I press our hands onto the more severe cuts as Hoodoo kneels next to him, checking his vitals. "Just hold on a little longer, Grey?"

Grey coughs, his body shaking as he lies on the floor. "I g-got this. W-walk in the p-park."

We weakly smile, making sure to press harder on his wounds.

He looks up at me. "L-Lani?" he asks.

She has finally stopped seizing, and Kaia has her in her arms, stroking her hair. But this seizure lasted a long time, much longer than I have seen her have before. I don't know what that means, and she certainly isn't awake. "Just worry about yourself right now, brother. You did so fucking good getting that bomb away from everyone. You're a goddamn hero."

"C-can you g-guys give me my p-patch before I b-bleed out," he teases with a big smile.

I shake my head. "You're making a fucking mess on the clubhouse floor. You clean it up, then we can talk about a patch, all right?"

He chuckles, then starts coughing, instantly grimacing in pain.

Finally, the sound of an ambulance siren wails outside the clubhouse.

"They're here, brother," City tells Grey. "We got you."

Grudge and Raid race in with the EMTs, and they both glance around at the chaos of the clubhouse, hesitating at the carnage right in front of them. One of them stops in their tracks. "Maybe we need to get the police here? Is this safe?"

"It was a gas leak," Hurricane states upon walking over and ushering her toward Lani.

The second, less intimidated male EMT smirks. "With razor blades and nails?"

Hurricane grunts and his eyes remain apathetic. "We're not makin' any official report. I just need you to help Lani and Grey. Can you do that?"

The male EMT nods. "Show me to the patients." He walks over to us while the woman tends to Lani. Kneeling, he takes Grey's vitals. "We need to get him to the hospital, he's lost a lot of blood. *We have one for transport,"* he calls out to the female.

She shakes her head. "Make that two. Non-responsive female

suffering epileptic seizure. We need to get her assessed."

The guy nods. "Two for transport. We can't take anyone with us as the ambulance will be full, but you can ride to the hospital behind us if you'd like."

Kaia steps forward with a pained expression on her face. "I'm going, Hurricane. I have to go."

"I know, baby..." He pulls her to him and kisses her head. "City, Grudge... I need you to go with Kaia, protection for her and Lani. The rest of us will stay here and clean this shit up."

Everyone nods. Brothers are scattered everywhere, but some are already picking up the debris.

They load Grey onto a gurney and lift him into the ambulance, followed by Lani, and then watch as it drives out of the compound along with City, Grudge, and Kaia in her car.

Turning back to Hurricane, he rubs the back of his neck. "This was a clear attack. We just need to figure out who the fuck it was from. Though it's gonna be hard now, seeing as the fuckin' evidence is blown to smithereens. But this is where Raid comes in, I guess. First things first... fixin' up the wounded." Hurricane sends out a whistle to grab everyone's attention. "Listen up... this was a huge hit. One we didn't see comin' but one we will surely find payback for. In the meantime... Goul, you're in charge of construction, fixin' and securin' the front of the buildin' is our top priority. Hoodoo, I need you to tend to as many of the wounded as you can, clean up what you can clean up. We need to band together. We're always a family, but right now, we need to show that strength and resilience we are known for... let's get to work."

Everyone takes off in all different directions. I even see Nash walk over to the front door that's demolished and start lending a hand with the cleanup. He's never been a part of anything like this. Perhaps it's given him a newfound respect for us and how we come together to help each other in these times.

My leg is killing me as I hobble over to Hoodoo, who has already set up a medical station, and he eyes me up and down. "Sit!" he instructs, and I do begrudgingly.

He kneels beside me and hikes up my jeans—a nail lodged in my calf. He chuckles, shaking his head. "I don't have any Lidocaine to numb the area, so when I pull this out, it's gonna hurt."

Exhaling, I dip my head. My eyes search the room, finding Novah helping with the cleanup. Instantly my tight chest relaxes a little. "Just do it, brother."

Hoodoo grabs a betadine swab, swipes down the area, and then grabs some plier-looking things. I try not to look, keeping my eyes focused on Novah.

I need her to distract me.

Even if she doesn't know she's doing it.

"On the countdown of three," Hoodoo tells me. "Three..." I tense, gritting my teeth, then he yanks the nail out of my calf, forcing a groan. I snap my head down to him.

"What the fuck, man?" I glare as he presses a piece of gauze to the bleeding wound, then proceeds to patch me up.

"Sorry, brother, had to do it. If you tensed up anymore, it could have done more damage."

Snorting, I grumble under my breath. "I'll be fine."

"I'll need to give you a tetanus booster and keep an eye on it for infection because it's so deep we don't want it getting into your bones."

"Yeah, yeah, whatever. Can I go help now?"

Hoodoo smirks. "Let me finish patching you up, give you some antibiotics, then you can go."

"Do I really need antibiotics?"

Hoodoo places the rusty nail in my hand. "See this. That shit will go into your bloodstream, and if I don't treat it with a heavy dose of antibiotics, you *will* get sepsis, which will lead to massive inflammation throughout the body, multiple organ system failures, and ultimately... your death. So you choose... do you *want* the antibiotics?"

My eyes shift over to Novah again. The idea of leaving this

world without sorting this shit out with her kills me. I need to fix this with her, but first, I need to fix my injuries. Turning back to Hoodoo, I smirk. "Fine, I'll take the damn drugs."

Hoodoo smirks, dipping his chin. "Good. I'll be grabbing a whole bunch of them for pretty much everyone who was hit by the nails, and I'll bring them to you when they're ready."

I grip his shoulder. "Thanks, Hoodoo. I appreciate it."

He snorts. "Just doing my job."

My skin prickles at how close it came to the bomb blowing up in Novah's hands. "They came so close to hurting Novah."

Hoodoo nods. "I know. We'll figure it out. Let's just get everything cleared away. Then we can go full revenge mode."

"Sounds fucking perfect. Some asshole needs to pay for this."

Hoodoo taps my shoulder, then gestures for me to head off. "Now, get lost, I have other patients to see."

Chuckling, I stand. "Thanks for the fix."

Making my way to the kitchen, Ingrid and the club girls are already preparing food and drinks to keep everyone hydrated and fed throughout the cleanup. I continue on to Ingrid and spin her to face me. She smiles, then spots the line of blood on my face, her hand coming up to caress my cheek. My hands run up and down her arms. "Are you hurt?"

She shakes her head. "No, I'm fine. Not a scratch. Just want to make sure you're all taken care of through this cleanup."

"Well, I want to make sure you and Novah are okay."

"I'm fine, darling. Novah is keeping busy lending her hands where she can... you saved her, Bayou. She didn't get a scratch on her because of *you.*"

Dropping my eyes to the floor, I nod in thankfulness. "Good... good."

"You could talk to her, you know?" Ingrid chimes full of hope.

"Now's not the time, but I will."

"Okay, darling... in the meantime, keep up your strength."

I lean in, plant a kiss on her cheek, and turn for the door.

I need to keep focused.

We spend the next couple of hours cleaning and ensuring everything is in some kind of working order. Once everything is functioning, Hurricane calls Raid and me into his den to figure this shit out.

Standing back with my arms crossed over my chest, I need to know who the fuck this was.

Raid glances over the fragments of what's left of the bomb, he huffs. "It's obviously a pipe bomb. I think the intent was to cause carnage, not the explosion so much. Whoever this was wanted dismemberment and disfigurement as their main priority. They wanted wounds and lots of them."

"It was addressed to Novah. The reason she is staying here is because that Johnny guy left a rat and an apple with a blade through it on her doorstep. It can't be a coincidence that the ornament of the bomb was an apple with a blade through it, can it?" I ask.

"How the fuck did Johnny know she was here?" Raid asks.

"How did he know where she lived in the first place? The guy is crafty. Which can only mean one thing."

"We have to deal with him. She won't be safe until he's taken care of," Hurricane states.

"Exactly," I reiterate.

Raid types frantically into his computer. "I'm going to have a look at our cameras and see if we can figure out how that gift came into the fucking clubhouse."

He searches, pulling up footage. Then zooms in showing a parcel being dropped off at the front gates by none other than Johnny. Davina spots the package hours later and brings it in. She's our newest club girl and probably doesn't know the protocol like the other girls.

"Fuck, we have to tell her," Raid states.

"She's gonna need a punishment," I grunt out the words, anger seething inside me.

"It's going to need to be severe to compensate for all this damage, Pres," Raid states.

"Privileges taken away. No special treatment. She's on cleanin' duty until we tell her she isn't. She can't attend functions or parties. The only thing she can do is come when she is called. She wants the club girl experience… we'll give her the bottom of the rung version. Fair?"

Nodding, I fold my arms over my chest. "She might walk?"

Hurricane shrugs. "Then she fuckin' walks. She needs to know her place and how we run things. If she can't follow simple instructions, like not bringin' in fuckin' unmarked parcels that are outside the gates without one of us checkin' it first, then she doesn't belong here."

It's harsh but true.

"So what do we do now? Do we wait until the club is settled before we take off to find Johnny, or do we mount the fuck up?" I ask.

Hurricane rolls his shoulders. "I don't know about you, we might be battered and bruised, but I am itchin' to cause some carnage of my own tonight."

"Merry fucking Christmas, Johnny." Finally, I feel like I might be able to let off some of this pent-up frustration.

Hurricane smirks as we turn, heading out of the den to tell the guys to mount up.

We're going to catch ourselves a damn grinch.

CHAPTER 9

BAYOU

My mind is on one thing—payback.

Johnny is in my line of sight, and I am going to make him pay for trying to hurt Novah. But first things first. I need to see her before I ride out, to make sure she is okay.

She's been with Ingrid and Izzy while Nash has been helping with the cleanup. I walk up to her, gently reaching out for her arm and pulling her aside. Her gorgeous blue eyes meet mine, and she looks at me like she's confused.

"I... I just need to know that you're okay... that you're not injured in any way."

She sighs. "Bayou, I'm fine." Her hand reaches out for the cut on my arm. Not a priority compared to the nail in my leg, and she gently grazes it with one finger. "I'm more worried about *your* injuries."

Well, damn! My chest squeezes that she still cares. "I'm fine. Hoodoo took out the nail in my leg and patched me up." I smile, but it drops away when I say, "This was *clearly* a move made by Johnny."

Novah jerks her head back, a gasp leaving her lips. "What? This was my fault?"

I reach out, pulling her to me. I don't care about all our fucking weird shit. Right now, she needs me to comfort her, and I need to make her feel better. This isn't her fault. Not at all.

My hands smooth up her back as I embrace her tightly, her arms clinging to me for her comfort. "We're going to fix this... right now."

Novah pulls back from me, her eyes wide as Ingrid steps up beside us. "What the fuck does that mean?" Novah rasps.

"I think you know what that means."

Ingrid pulls Novah to her for comfort.

"He attacked the club. If he goes missing, they're going to come here looking for him," Novah begs.

"They're not going to find him, Novah." She looks terrified, but I try to reassure her. "He's not going to stop coming for you. He's a danger to you and our family. He won't stop hurting people. This *is* the right thing to do. But... the less you know, the better your plausible deniability will be."

"Bayou, we're leavin'. Hurry the fuck up," Hurricane calls out, waving me on.

I lean in planting a kiss on Ingrid's cheek, and my eyes meet a glistening Novah's. "I'm gonna take care of you."

Novah nods her head, then I turn and walk for my ride.

Hurricane slaps me on the shoulder as I pass and falls in step with me. "You tell them what we're doin'?"

"Just enough so they got the hint but enough for plausible deniability."

Hurricane smirks. "Good, as it should be. Raid's got a location on where he thinks this fucker might have gone. We're gonna head over there now."

"Let's get this asshole."

We walk out toward our rides. I have a fire in my belly and vengeance in my soul. I need to end this fucker for trying to hurt Novah, for threatening her. No one comes near the people I care about.

Jumping on my ride, I rev the engine. Raid takes off in the lead. We pull out behind him, the tires burning rubber with the anger fueling our bones.

The ride doesn't take long, as we make our way inside a trashy trailer park. People gather around burning trash can fires. It's a real shithole of a place. Junkies are doing drug deals behind the back of their tents, and God only knows what else.

We pull up our rides close to where the ping is located. The trailer is practically falling apart as we all gather, sliding on knuckle dusters and yanking out baseball bats from our saddlebags.

We turn to Hurricane as he drops his eyes to Raid. "You sure this is the place?" he confirms with Raid.

"Yep, his cell is pinging inside."

Craning my neck to the side, a slow smile lights my face. "Then let's get this fucker." I state as we approach his door.

Hurricane steps up, slamming his boot into the flimsy door. It smashes off its hinges and circles a few times before falling inside the trailer, and we all rush inside. Johnny is sitting at the table about to snort a line of coke. He jumps so high from the intrusion that the coke flies through the air. "What the fu—"

But we don't hesitate.

Hoodoo and Omen rush forward, grabbing him, while Quarter, and Hurricane slam their bats into every fucking thing in his trailer, demolishing the joint. Plates and glass fly as Johnny is held back. I step up, look him in his terrified, high-as-fuck eyes and slam my fist right into his crooked, weasel nose.

He yelps out in pain, struggling in Omen and Hoodoo's grip. "W-who are y-you?" he snaps.

I slam my fist into his jaw, making him spit out a line of blood and a tooth for good measure. "Don't be a smart ass with me, Johnny. Why the fuck did you bomb the clubhouse? Was Novah your target?"

Johnny's scared demeanor shifts in an instant, and he slowly turns his swollen and bloody head to face me, looking through his narrowed eyes. "Novah? Oh... I see... I have no idea what you're talking about. Maybe you need to do some fact-checking before you come in here smashing up my joint."

"Do you hold a grudge against Novah for taking your family away from you?" I snap.

Johnny chuckles. "Of course, I hate the bitch. She took *everything* from me. I'd love to get a moment alone with her and tell her what I'd *reeeally* love to do to her."

My insides burn, but Hurricane steps forward while I try to control myself, and he slams his knuckle-duster fingers into his nose. A snap resounds through the trailer, his head slams back into the headboard behind him, and it knocks Johnny out cold.

Letting out a long breath, we all gather, my muscles tense as fuck as I stare at the asshole out for the count. "He's lying, right?" I ask.

Hurricane tilts his head. "Gotta be..." He runs his hand through his hair. "Hoodoo, Raid... wrap him up and chuck him in the van. Once he's secure, we'll all ride back to the clubhouse."

The guys move about getting Johnny wrapped for transport.

Hurricane steps up to me. "This feel right to you?"

Rolling my shoulders, I crane my neck to the side. "It's gotta be him. Who else has got a grudge against Novah? She's pristine, innocent. No one else is going to have a bad thing to say about her, Hurricane."

He exhales. "Yeah, I've heard about enough of this guy's bullshit. We need to teach him a lesson."

"Then let's stop yammerin' and get back to the clubhouse so we can finish this," I snap.

Hurricane smirks, gripping my shoulder. "You're gonna have too much fun doin' this, aren't ya?"

Smirking, I simply dip my head, then turn for my ride. Making it back to the clubhouse doesn't take long at all, after all, we have something to look forward to, so we ride in record time. Omen and Raid take Johnny into the Chamber as Hurricane and I stroll in behind them. Omen holds onto Johnny. His mouth has been gagged because there is nothing worse than a hostage babbling and carrying on while you're trying to set them up for torture.

Raid pulls on Johnny's clothes and strips him down.

This is part of the Chamber process.

Every man who sits in that silver chair is there for a reason.

Because they have wronged the club.

Because they are our enemy.

We want them to feel low.

Embarrassed.

Like they are shit on our shoes while in here.

That is why we strip them. We want them to feel completely bare. It makes them vulnerable. More susceptible to talking. It is the way we do things. Some might think of it as a violent and degrading way to treat people in their final hours on this earth, but if they're here, they deserve everything we throw at them.

Raid pulls Johnny's stained, white briefs away from his body and then forces him and his limp dick to sit in the silver chair. Omen straps Johnny in while Johnny's eyes are wide with fear the entire time. Like he is unsure if he is being pranked and we're about to yell 'just kidding' or if this is really happening.

I step up to him. He pants furiously through his nose while I stare into his soulless eyes. "You threatened Novah. You hit the club in a way that cannot go unpunished."

His eyes bug out of his head, and he shakes it adamantly. But all I want to see is the pain in his face as he screams for me to stop. Hurricane steps up, carrying a special saw that Raid made. It's shaped like a hacksaw, only ten times sharper. "You sent the box to our stepsister… you were tryin' to hurt her. Now we're gonna hurt you."

Grinning from ear to ear, I fold my arms over my chest.

Hurricane steps forward first. Johnny wriggles in his restraints, his eyes wide as saucers. Hurricane moves to Johnny's right arm, placing the saw just above his elbow. "This is for making a fuckin' mess of my clubhouse and the people in it." He starts hacking back and forth on his skin. Johnny screams as blood gushes from the site, pooling on the plastic underneath the chair. A thrill runs through me as Hurricane saws fast and deep. Johnny's screaming so frantically that he is hyperventilating. Snot bubbles out of his nose while his entire body shakes with the sheer pain rolling through him.

As Hurricane hacks through the last part of his arm, the saw taps the silver chair scraping the metal and tinging with the sound. I smirk as Hurricane chuckles, pushing his severed arm to the side. The lower half of Johnny's limb is hanging on the chair by his wrist restraints. "Such a beautiful sight," Hurricane states, proud of his accomplishment while the rest of us laugh.

Johnny sinks into the chair, panting like he is having trouble even keeping awake as Hurricane hands the saw to me.

Now it's time to really enjoy this.

Stepping up, I squat in front of Johnny and tilt my head. "You hurt so many people in your life, Johnny. You're a fucking waste of space, but your biggest mistake was trying to hurt Novah. You stepped into shoes that were too big to fill. Maybe I should wipe those sorry feet from existence?" I bring the saw to just below his left knee and start hacking. He screams out again into his gag as blood pools all around me on the floor, but I don't stop. The push and pull of the sinew feel like heaven—like justice—like vengeance. I saw through the muscle, cartilage, and bone until only a fragment is left hanging there. I pull the bottom of the leg, and it collides with the floor, making a loud thud.

As I stand, Johnny zones in and out of consciousness from the pain, from the blood loss—maybe from both—but I don't give a fuck. We don't want him to miss a second of this. So I gesture to Raid, and he steps forward with a giant injection, stabbing it right into his chest. He injects the shot of adrenaline, which surges his heart awake, and Johnny jerks his entire body with the hit as he pants like he simply wants this to be over. But he should know better.

I lean in, his frantic and panicked eyes finding mine. "This is what happens when you hurt women. You lost your path, Johnny. You couldn't see clearly… so I guess there's no need for you to be able to see anything, right?"

Hurricane chuckles as I drop the saw and rush forward, jamming my thumbs right into Johnny's eye sockets. Johnny screams the loudest he has since this started, the warm gel teamed with blood oozes around my thumbs, his body shaking violently with the pain wracking through his mangled body.

He's so close to death I can smell it in the air.

Hurricane leans in next to Johnny's ear. "You're a waste of space, and we need to save all the space we can get."

Smirking, I draw my thumbs from his eyes, gunk and shit pulling out with them, and I shake my hands to get it off.

Hurricane grabs a giant blade, swings and slices, aiming for Johnny's head. With a precision hit, Johnny's head slams to the floor, rolling a few times, his entire body flopping over on the seat.

I let out a relieved sigh, feeling relaxed now that I know we have stopped the man trying to kill Novah.

Hurricane looks at me, and I dip my head at him. "I'll prep for La Fin," I tell him, and Hurricane chuckles.

"You're gonna enjoy feedin' time."

"Oh, fuck yeah." I beam with excitement.

Raid and Omen detach what's left of Johnny and bring his body over to the meat saw. I move with them and reach up for my apron, sliding it on, then switch on the rotary blade, the high-pitched groan of the saw swirling through the room as the others start the cleanup.

There's something so calming, so soothing in cutting up the body of the man you just killed out of vengeance. I don't know why, but it almost feels like a chorus of classical music plays harmoniously in the background. There's something so raw and unbridled in it. Seeing that the handiwork I created of the final moments of his life is being made into the food for my pet alligator. It's a symphony, an orchestral genius. It's magical. Something so uplifting and freeing about being about to provide for La Fin by taking an evil asshole out of this world.

It might make me a monster by taking out the monsters, but I am one hundred percent okay with that. If they can't hurt my family or the people I love, I will gladly be the villain.

After spending some time slicing Johnny up into the portions I need for La Fin, I leave Omen to package the rest up for the freezer. Hurricane and I walk out to the bayou with a bucket full of Johnny to finish off the last of this task.

Cracking open the gate, I walk down first.

Hurricane follows me. "Do you ever get tired of this?".

Glancing down at the hand, foot, and part of a forearm, I shake my head. "Never. I don't know what that makes me, but I live for this shit."

Hurricane chuckles as we step out onto the rickety dock. I stomp my foot twice, my general code for La Fin to let him know his dinner is ready. The vibration will hum through the water, and if he is close enough, he will raise to the top and let us know he's here.

La Fin was only a baby when I found him trying to cross the road. I was out on a ride and there he was, far from any stretch of water. Someone obviously had him in captivity then released him in the middle of suburbia because the thought of what he would grow up to be was probably too much for them. But the second I saw him, I felt a bond. I know it sounds strange, but it's true.

I've always had a connection with Novah, a connection I could talk to no one about except for La Fin. He obviously can't talk, so I tell him *everything.*

He is the shoulder I lean on whenever I have a bad day. We have a bond—not one anyone can understand—and I'm sure given half the chance, he would eat me if he were hungry enough. But, he has been here for me, and I am grateful for that.

A crazy kind of therapy I always needed.

Suddenly, breaking me from my thoughts, his scales break the murky water's surface. A smile lights my lips as I reach in, grabbing one of Johnny's hands and roll my shoulders. "Make sure to enjoy this one a little extra, my boy." I hurtle it into the water, and his massive jaws open, snapping the hand without warning.

A majestically beautiful sight.

The loud snap filters through the bayou, and I turn to Hurricane, who shakes his head with a chuckle. "Never get tired of seein' that."

Warmth floods me at the thought that Johnny tried to outsmart us, but in the end, he got what he deserved.

He beat his wife.

In front of his children.

Then he went after Novah.

He almost demolished the club.

Yeah, this is a fitting end for him.

Asshole.

I throw his foot, and La Fin jumps out of the water, snapping it forcefully, and when he lands, he does a belly roll. I chuckle, loving the show he is putting on for us. It's almost like he knows how important this moment is to us.

Again La Fin is helping ease this intense moment.

Some people need therapy dogs.

I say, *Why not have a therapy alligator?*

Throwing in the last of Johnny's parts, I smile widely.

Hurricane chuckles. "Feel better?"

Smirking, I crane my neck to the side. "Asshole had it coming." I wipe my blood-stained hands on my jeans.

I'm covered in blood. *It's not a good look.* "I need a shower, I have to get every ounce of this cunt off me."

Hurricane bursts out laughing as he slaps my shoulder, and we turn, heading back for the clubhouse. "Tomorrow is Christmas, brother. Now, we *really* have somethin' to celebrate."

CHAPTER 10

NOVAH
Christmas Day

My body aches all over as my eyes slowly flutter open.

It's Christmas morning, a time to be merry and bright, but last night the club was literally rocked to its foundations because of me. Johnny intended to take me out and ended up hurting Grey and Lani in the process.

Grey is still in hospital, Lani is recovering from her seizure, and the clubhouse has to be partially rebuilt. Add to the fact the guys went out to find Johnny, and I have no idea how that went. So I am crazy anxious this morning.

Yeah, today is not looking so festive after all.

Stretching, I amble out of bed, my muscles aching from having Bayou tackle me to the floor when the explosion hit. But I don't begrudge the ache, it's better than being hit by the razor blades and nails. He saved me, and I need to be thankful for that.

Getting dressed, I slowly make my way out to the main room, expecting to see a war zone, but my eyes widen in surprise when all the Christmas decorations are back up in place, and the front of the damaged clubhouse has been propped and the structure stabilized. It just looks like the clubhouse is undergoing renovations rather than damage repair.

Goul has done a great job.

Spotting City and Izzy sitting together at a table, I walk over and let out a long exhale. They're sitting with a planner out, looking over wedding details.

I can't help but smile as I sit. "Planning on Christmas morning?" I ask.

Izzy smiles. "There's so much to do, and if last night showed us anything, it's that you never know what can happen. So we need to be prepared for all possible outcomes."

Sinking in on myself, I exhale. "I'm so sorry. I never meant to bring all this shit to the club."

Izzy widens her eyes. "Oh crap! No, I didn't mean it like that, Novah. I'm sorry. What I mean is, at the club, even when you plan something perfectly, something will inevitably change, so you need a contingency plan because there's always something happening. This isn't your fault, Novah, so please don't think that way."

City nods. "The club is going to be under attack no matter where it is coming from or who is the cause. It's because of who we are as a club. We expect this shit frequently. It's no one's fault. It comes with the territory."

Gnawing on my bottom lip, I dip my head. "I feel like I led Johnny here."

"You honestly think Hurricane and Bayou wouldn't do everything in their power to protect you? They adore you, Novah. They would burn this place to the ground if it meant you were safe," City states.

The problem is, I think he's right.

They would throw it all away to protect Mom and me.

I have to cut myself some slack.

"You're right. I should be grateful. It's Christmas, my problems are taken care of, and I'm here with the people I love. There's nothing for me to be mopey about."

Izzy smiles wide. "That's the Christmas spirit."

Slowly, everyone starts making their way out of the hall and into the clubroom, my eyes subtly watching for Bayou. We were on shaky ground before the explosion last night, but the way he lunged for me, the way he put his body on the line for me, helps me to soften toward him.

Maybe he's not so terrible after all.

He strides into the room with a bright smile like he is exceedingly happy this morning. I can't help but wonder what that's about when he spots me. His eyes brighten, and he grins at me but keeps walking.

God, he is so fucking attractive.

Maybe I should be the one to make the first move today.

It's Christmas, and I'm in the mood for giving.

Walking over to Bayou as he stands with Mom, I step into their chat. They both turn to me and smile. "Morning, darling, how did you sleep?"

"It was a rough night if I'm honest. But in the light of day, and with some kind words from Izzy and City, I'm feeling better this morning."

Mom wraps her arm around me. "Good, I'm glad. It's nice to see you smiling again, isn't it, Bayou?"

He dips his chin. "Definitely."

"So, umm… did everything go to plan when you went out last night?" I ask.

Bayou chuckles. "Plausible deniability, Novah."

"Okay, but just tell me this… do I have to worry anymore?"

Bayou glances from me to Mom then back to me. "He won't bother you again."

A wave of relief flows through me, and I race forward, wrapping my arms around Bayou. He's tense for a brief moment, but then his nose falls into my hair, and he embraces me back. The feeling of him holding me is so fucking comforting as we stand for probably a moment too long, simply holding each other. My eyes close as I inhale his aftershave—all leather and sandalwood. He smells so fucking delicious it's making my clit throb, and the second I clench my thighs together, it's like a switch goes off in my mind. We're in the middle of the clubhouse, standing right next to my mother, being *far* too obvious.

I pull back from Bayou, probably a little too dramatically. I clear my throat and straighten out my dress. "Thank you," I say, but it comes out as a breathy whisper. I risk a glance at Mom. The smile on her lips is bright, but she says nothing.

"You know I'm always going to take care of you, Novah," Bayou states.

My mind flashes back to when he couldn't get out of the bedroom fast enough. *He didn't take care of me then.* Rolling my shoulders from the tension gathering in them, I clear my throat. "Maybe you need to work on that a little more?"

Mom raises her brow, and I think for a second I have said too much when she glances past me. "Oh, there's Hurricane and Kaia. I'm going to go see how Lani is doing," she says, not seeming to care about our conversation, and takes off, leaving me with Bayou.

He exhales, reaching out for my hand, and I let him take it. My skin prickles in goose bumps, my heart fluttering so fast I feel faint. "I wish you would let me explain what happened," he says.

Pulling my hand from his, mainly because it is incredibly distracting, and I need to focus on the conversation right now. "I already know what happened, Bayou. You freaked out because I suddenly became repulsive to you."

His nostrils flare, the vein in his neck pulsates. He reaches out, grabs my hand again, and starts dragging me into the hall. My feet can hardly keep up with him as he pulls me down and into the kitchen. "Bayou! What are you doing?" I snap as we enter the kitchen to Frankie and Davina cooking breakfast. Their eyes shoot up, and he glares at them.

"Out!" he orders, and without hesitation, they both turn, scurrying out of the room.

"Bayou, what in the world are you—"

Without wasting a second, he spins and hoists me up onto the island in the middle of the kitchen. I gasp as he steps in between my legs, one hand rushing into my hair gripping tight, the other running straight down between my legs, pressing on the thin fabric over my pussy.

I let out a gasp as he pulls my head back, lining his lips up with my ear while his fingers rub against my folds. I pant frantically while his breath against my ear makes me hotter for him. "Don't you ever, and I mean *ever,* think that you repulse me, Novah."

I breathe excitedly through my nose as I clench my eyes tight, feeling the heat wash over me. I can't help but wriggle against him needing to feel more pressure against his fingers. His lips slide along my neck, his tongue darting out and licking my tender skin, causing a small moan to whimper from my lips.

"You don't know what you do to me. You're making me so fucking hard—"

"Then fuck me," I beg.

His eyes move in, staring into mine. Nothing but undeniable lust peering back at me. "No, Novah. Not here, not now. But our time will come. Just be patient." His hand grips tighter on my hair, and he slams his lips to mine. Our tongues dance together as he slips his finger under my panties, pressing on my clit. I whimper, my hands clenching on his cut's leather to drag him closer while he circles, pulling nothing but pure pleasure from me.

My hips rock against his hand, just needing that high I am so desperately chasing when the sound of footsteps creeps into my ears. "Bayou, you fucker, where are you?" Hurricane calls out from the hall.

We quickly pull apart.

Bayou removes his fingers from underneath my panties while I try to control my breathing. He takes a couple of steps to the left away from me but stays behind the island to hide his erection while I pull my dress down and tussle my hair, trying to calm my erratic heart rate. Hurricane enters the room, my back to him as Bayou shoves his finger into his mouth. I widen my eyes as he sucks my juices off his finger.

"Frankie said you were in here… you in the festive spirit this mornin', Novah?" he asks, stepping up to the Island.

I glance over my shoulder and smile. "Just waiting on some breakfast. Came to see if the girls needed any help."

Bayou continues to suck on his finger, and, with his other hand, he slides a jar of whiskey cream toward Hurricane. "They outdid themselves with the cream, it's delicious." He grins at me, and I can't help but smirk, knowing he's not talking about the damn whiskey cream.

Hurricane chuckles. "Stop shovin' your filthy fingers in the food, brother, and get your ass out here. Grey should be comin' back soon. I wanna run somethin' by you."

My eyes widen. "Is Grey getting his patch? After him getting that bomb away from me, he deserves it."

Hurricane narrows his eyes on me. "That's what I was gonna talk to Bayou about. Thanks for havin' the meetin' for me, little sister."

Smirking, I shrug. "You're welcome. So it's decided, Grey will get his patch. We just need to think of a road name."

Bayou and Hurricane both laugh. "You thinkin' about patchin' in? Or you want to let us *actual* brothers organize club business?"

Smiling, I wave Hurricane off. "Fine. Spoilsport."

He narrows his eyes on me. "You comin' down with somethin'? It's not particularly warm, and you're all flushed?"

I widen my eyes. *Think, Novah, think.* Glancing to the other side of the kitchen, I see jalapeno poppers ready for Christmas lunch. *Perfect.* "Before you walked in here, Bayou made me eat one of those Jalapeno poppers. You know what I'm like with spicy food…" I fake a cough. "I can't handle even a little bit."

Hurricane glares at Bayou. "Why the fuck did you do that, Bayou? And on the same token, why the hell did you eat it, Novah?"

Bayou chuckles. "'Cause I said if she did it, she could make me do any one thing she wants. It will probably be something like clean her fucking car, but still, I said if she didn't, then she would have to sing karaoke tonight in front of everyone."

Hurricane smirks, shaking his head. "So you ate it because you don't want to sing in front of everyone?"

Smiling, I shrug. "Have you heard my voice? I may look like an angel, but I certainly do not sound like one. So I ate that fucker, and now Bayou owes me one do-anything-I-want token."

Bayou side-eyes me like he knows I'm going to hold him to it.

Hurricane groans. "You two still act like kids. I swear. Placin' bets on each other. All right, Bayou, when you're done makin' out with your cream, come see me. We need to figure out Grey's road name."

"Got ya, be there in a sec. I'll just clean up in here."

Hurricane nods then spins to walk out of the kitchen.

Bayou waits for a few extra moments, then turns back, stepping in between my legs. I wrap my arms around his neck, my fingers threading in the hair at the base of his neck. "Jalapeno poppers?" He smirks.

"Would you rather I tell him the truth?"

Bayou curls up his lip. "Nope... as it is, he's gonna kill me for this." He leans in, pressing his lips to my neck. "And this..." he runs his tongue up under my ear, "... and this," he murmurs as his teeth clamp down on my earlobe and tug, sending a shockwave straight to my clit.

"Fuck," I whisper, my fingers thread through his hair holding him to me. "You know I could use my token and demand you fuck me right now?"

His teeth glide out along my neck, grazing my skin as he grinds his erection into my pussy. "Mm-hmm, but Hurricane is expecting me, so I couldn't give you the attention you deserve in the time you need. It would be a waste."

Dammit.

"Guess I'll hold onto it then... for a rainy day."

His head pops up, his eyes meeting mine, his hand sliding out and caressing the side of my face. "When I fuck you, Novah, you're not going to need a token for me to take you. I'm gonna make you feel so fucking good you won't be able to sit for a week."

My eyes bulge and meet his, my clit throbbing as I stare at him. "Promise?" I ask.

The corner of his lips turns up, and he leans in pressing them to me briefly before pulling back. "Fucking promise."

"*Bayou,*" Hurricane yells from somewhere in the clubhouse. We both chuckle, and he pulls back, glancing down at his erection.

"You're gonna get me in so much fucking trouble."

Smirking, I slide off the counter and straighten out his cut. "Hope I'm worth it." I turn to walk away, but he grabs my wrist, pulling me back against his chest, causing me to let out a small squeal. But my arms slide up around his neck holding him to me as he presses his lips to mine once more, our tongues colliding in a deep passion. My heart beats faster as he slowly pulls back, looking into my eyes.

"You're worth everything." He presses a featherlight kiss to my nose, then lets me go and takes off quicker than I have time to gather myself.

I put my hand out steadying myself on the island, needing a moment to contain my emotions from what just happened.

We almost got caught.

By Hurricane.

That would have been a disaster.

But at the same time, it sent a rush of excitement through me I never knew could be so addictive. We've spent so many years hesitating, holding back on our feelings when we could have been acting on them in secret.

It's so much better.

As I glance at the jalapeno poppers, I giggle to myself. *Thank you, Frankie.* You just gave me something to hold over Bayou, and I will use that token when he least expects it.

CHAPTER 11

BAYOU

The festivities of the day have been great.

Food, there's so much of it as the club has come together to celebrate. Unfortunately, we've been missing that one person who we really wanted to celebrate with today, but he is due back any minute now.

We all sit around the giant table in a food coma, when the front doors open and Grey walks in— though he is a little sluggish—with Hoodoo helping him for support.

A loud cheer erupts through the clubhouse, and we all jump up, crowding the prospect, though the poor kid looks like shit. Bruises and cuts are all over him. His left arm is up in a sling. He took one hell of a battering for the club, and we're going to repay him for his duty.

Hurricane steps up to him, shaking his head. "Jesus, looks like you did ten rounds with Mike Tyson, then stepped in a cage with a fuckin' lion."

Grey snorts out a laugh. "Feels like it too, Pres."

"You did good. You understood the threat, and you took care of business, puttin' yourself in danger to save my family… I won't forget that."

"I'd do anything for this club, Hurricane. You're all more of a family than my real one, so laying down my life for yours is a given."

"Let's hope it doesn't come to that too often," I state, and Grey smirks.

"That'd be good."

"So what's the damage?" Hurricane asks.

Grey glances down to his arm in the sling. "Broken left collarbone… gotta wear this fucking thing for two to six weeks during the day to try and help heal the injury. The doctor sutured up the wounds from the razor blades and nails. Got a tetanus injection. Was pumped full of antibiotics and fluids. They said one of the nails that lodged in my neck only just missed an artery. Seems luck was on my side."

I side-eye Hurricane and smirk. "I think you showed true grit. You really showed the rest of us what you're made of."

He shakes his head. "Any one of you fuckers would have done the same."

I tilt my head. "Yeah, maybe, but you're the one who stepped up."

City steps forward with a wooden box in his hand, and Hurricane grips Grey's shoulder gently. "Normally, we'd do this differently. But it's Christmas, and we're not in the mood for hazin' today. Plus, you're fuckin' banged up, and it would be cruel to play a prank on you. You've done your duty, you've worked your way up showin' time and time again why you belong here…" Hurricane pauses. "Grey, you'll now be known as Grit." City hands him the box. He struggles to open it with his other hand in the sling. He grimaces through the pain, and I reach out to help him, but he flicks the box open with a smile.

Yeah, Grit is certainly the right name for him.

His eyes widen when he takes in his club patches and his road name sitting proudly on top. "Grit… I fucking love it."

The club cheers as everyone moves in closer, his eyes shifting to Lani who is standing back, watching him with the biggest smile on her face. She's still recovering from her seizure last night, definitely tired and slower than normal, but you can't miss the way these two are looking at each other. Pure chemistry. There's been a connection between them for months. I don't know if they have acted on it or not. All I know is Hurricane is all kinds of protective over Lani, just like he is with Novah. So the poor guy will have some *letting go* issues for him when it comes to the women in his life.

"Congratulations, brother, and welcome to the club, Grit," City says, moving in and embracing him. He grimaces in pain but uses his one good arm to pat City's back.

"You guys don't know how much this means to me." He looks down at the patches in awe.

"Yeah, brother… we do," I tell him. "Now grab someone to help you sew on those patches while we figure out how we're gonna find us a couple of new prospects."

We continue with the Christmas festivities, having indulged probably too much in the huge lunch feast. Everyone is chatting, having a good time full of laughter and fun. We're all enjoying ourselves now that the threat of Johnny has been taken care of. Novah and I sit with Hurricane and Kaia enjoying some downtime.

Kaia turns to Novah. "It's been so great having you here, Novah, I have to admit… I like having an extra female to help with the overload of testosterone around here."

Novah smirks as Hurricane and I roll our eyes. "You do have a gender equality issue, Hurricane. You need to look into that," Novah quips.

Hurricane chuckles. "Well, the guys need to hurry up and find themselves old ladies then, don't they? Bayou, what you waitin' for?"

I tense up, rubbing the back of my neck. "Waiting for the right woman."

Hurricane snorts. "You'll take anything with a tight pussy and a mouth like a hoover."

My eyes widen as I see Novah try to keep a neutral face, but I see the shock in her expression as Kaia punches Hurricane in the arm. "Shut up, show some respect for your brother."

Hurricane smirks. "What? It's true. Bayou loves to fu—"

"Shut the fuck up," I snap, making the three of them stare at me. "We don't need to talk like that in front of Novah."

"Pfft, she's grown up with us. Like she doesn't know you're a sex-crazed lunatic."

Kaia sits forward, grabbing Novah's hand. "So, Novah, it's really exciting that you're safe now, huh?" She changes the subject, almost like she can sense the awkwardness of the topic, unlike our idiot brother.

Novah lets out a long exhale. "I have to admit, I don't know what has happened to Johnny, but knowing he won't come for me or his family again… there's something so calming in that."

My muscles begin to immediately tense, as I see it register on Hurricane's face the same time it does mine. I know exactly what he's going to say next. "I guess tomorrow, once we all wake from our food comas, you can go home, Novah. And also back to work. There's no need to keep you here with the threat taken care of."

My skin prickles in unease. I want her here with me, but I have no legitimate excuse as to why I should demand to keep her here—not without blowing this *relationship* out into the open.

So as much as it's killing me right now, I say nothing.

Novah glances at me, then simply nods her head. 'Yeah… I mean, I guess that makes sense. I *should* get back to my life."

"Then it's settled. Bayou will take you home in the mornin' and make sure the house is all good, that there's nothin' waitin' for you, and then we can all move on and forget about Johnny."

"Sounds like a plan," Novah states, her eyes shifting to mine again.

"We'll come round and do sweeps every couple of days just to make sure," I tell her, to let her know I'm not giving up on us even though this puts a proverbial wrench in the works.

She nods. "That would make me feel more at ease."

"I'll do the checks myself," I tell her.

She weakly smiles and nods.

Hurricane claps his hands together. "Excellent. Now that's settled, I'm gonna go fuck my woman. Sha, if you're not in our room in thirty seconds, I'm fuckin' you on top of the leftover turkey."

Kaia giggles, shaking her head and stands, reaching out to grab the chocolate sauce from the pudding. She dips her finger in and shoves it in her mouth. "Still warm," she chimes as she saunters off toward the hall for the bedrooms, chocolate sauce in her hand.

Hurricane growls under his breath and takes off after her.

Those two are fucking animals, I swear.

Turning back to Novah, she's biting her bottom lip, her legs are clenched together, and I smirk knowing she is thinking about sex. But there are people everywhere, so I have to be careful what I say. Leaning into her side, I whisper in her ear, "When the time comes, I can arrange for chocolate sauce to be available… if you think you'd be into that kind of thing?"

Her eyes widen, and she snaps her head around to me, trying to fight the massive grin on her face. "Bayou, people might hear," she whispers so quietly that the only reason I know what she says is from lip reading.

Chuckling, I sit back in my seat, licking my bottom lip. "Mmm… I love chocolate," I tease, and she reaches out, slapping my arm with a giggle.

"Stop it!" She snickers, shifting in her seat like she is affected.

My lips turn up in the biggest smile. I love teasing her, and seeing the way her cheeks flush in that beautiful shade of red is only turning me on even more. "That sweetness, and if you team it with a little bit of salt, damn!"

She lets out a heavy exhale. "Jesus, Bayou."

I grin, glancing around. No one at the table is paying any

attention to us. "You're adorable when you're flustered."

Her eyes widen, snapping around to check and see if anyone is listening, and when she realizes no one is, her muscles relax a little, and she sighs. "You're playing with fire, you know that?"

Sitting back in my chair, I thread my fingers together at the back of my head and lean into them. "I always did like to live on the edge."

"If Hurricane finds out… hell, if Nash finds out what we're doing—"

"We'll deal with it, but they won't. Not until we're ready to tell them." I keep my tone calm and assertive to let her know we're going to be okay.

She glances over her shoulder at Ingrid and Nash at the other end of the table chatting to Grit and Lani. "How do you think Mom is going to take this?"

Smirking because I've already told her, and I know she is fine with it, I shrug. "I think she'll be cool. Ingrid is laid back. She's switched on. She can read the both of us better than we can."

"You think she knows?" Novah asks.

I should tell her, but I also don't want her freaking out that I talked about us behind her back.

Play it safe, Bayou.

"I think she has an idea, but I think more importantly, she will be fine with it. Out of everyone, Ingrid is the most accepting of everyone. The guys, however, don't want you with anyone. The second they hear it's me, they're probably going to kill me… let's be honest."

"Maybe we just shouldn't tell them?"

"Keep us a secret for our entire lives? We can't live like that, Novah. We're going to have to just wait for the right time."

"The right time for what?" Lani asks, sliding in next to Novah.

Both our eyes widen as we pull further apart from each other. We'd somehow forgotten we were sitting in a room full of everyone, and we were carrying on a vital conversation that could have cost us hugely if Lani had come by just a few seconds earlier.

"For Novah to head home tomorrow, just making sure it's the right timing," I add, trying to cover our tracks.

Lani nods her head. "Totally understand... but with Johnny out of the picture, it should be all good now, right?"

Novah rolls her shoulders. "You would think so. It all just depends on whether he's been to my house and made any adjustments to it before he..." She leaves it open-ended.

Lani hums under her breath. "You'll be going with her, right, Bayou? To check it all out?"

"No doubt. I'll be checking everything before Novah steps a single foot in that house."

"See, nothing to worry about... though I am going to miss having you around. Izzy suggested that the girls have a night out on the town, remember? I think we should do that. We all need something to relax us after the events of the last few days."

I tense up, but Novah nods, "Yes. So much, yes. New Year's Eve is in a few nights. We should all head down to Bourbon Street."

"Yes," Lani almost screeches.

I shake my head adamantly. "Do you know what Bourbon Street is like on New Year's Eve? It's going to be chaos. There's no way in hell City and Hurricane are going to let you all go down there without us."

Lani shrugs. "Then you come with, just hang the fuck back because as they say, *girls just wanna have fun*."

Novah laughs and nods. "This is going to be epic."

Groaning, I huff. "No... it's not."

They both smile, and I know with those innocent eyes and cheeky demeanors they're trying to charm me, and they're definitely going to get their way.

Fuck!

CHAPTER 12

BAYOU
The Next Day

While I pull back on the throttle, the wind whips at my face. Novah's arms are wrapped around my waist. She clings to me tightly, and I can't wipe the smile from my face. Feeling her at my back like this as I ride is a high I didn't know I needed. It's the best feeling in the world. And the thought that we're going to be all alone in her home is doing all kinds of things to my libido, but right now, I can't think about that. I have a plan, one I don't want to deviate from, and I can't let my cock steer me off the path.

Pulling into her driveway, I park my ride, and she climbs off. I smirk at her as I follow and then turn to face her. "Wait by the bike, do not come inside no matter what you hear."

She widens her eyes but nods her head.

I pull my gun out from the back of my jeans and turn for the house. Slowly making my way up to the front porch, I check for anything, trip wires, cameras, booby traps, bombs, anything and everything I can think of, but I find absolutely nothing.

So I pull out my keys and make my way inside her home, checking over every surface, every nook and cranny. Under her mattress, in the cupboards, under the sofas, and in every ornament. Everywhere Johnny could have hidden or planted something.

I find nothing.

Letting out a long exhale, I lower my gun and turn, making my way back to Novah, who's pacing the driveway like she is freaking out. Her eyes are wide, her face pale and clammy. She's definitely panicking. Racing to her, I spin her to face me, my hand sliding into her hair as I hold tight, and I don't waste another fucking second, slamming my lips to hers. She hesitates for a moment like she is stunned by my actions as I kiss her passionately, showing her how much I need her.

She slowly gives in to the kiss, relaxing at my touch and kissing me back. Her tongue collides with mine in the most irresistible way. Novah's arms loop around my neck, her body curving with mine and the panic attack gone without a trace, a heat scorching in its wake. Slowly, I pull back, utterly breathless, her body slumping a little as I let go.

"Fuck, I have wanted to do that all damn day."

She giggles, resting her hands on my chest, and playing with the leather of my cut. "I've wanted you to do it all damn day."

Grinning wide, I lean in, pressing a featherlight kiss to her lips once more, then tilt past her to grab her bag from my bike. "C'mon, let's head inside."

She nods, and I follow her as she walks straight to the kitchen.

I close the front door behind me, place her bag on the sofa and then lean against the kitchen counter as she moves about grabbing the supplies to make us a coffee. "Can I ask you a serious question?"

She continues with the coffee but shrugs. "Of course, go for it."

I fold my arms over my chest and decide to let this play out. "Did you feel weird about us, with the whole stepsibling thing?"

She hesitates, her arm hanging out of the cupboard, and then she turns to face me with a serious expression crossing her features. "Yeah... it feels weird. I think that's why I fought it for so long."

Exhaling, I scrub at my face with my relief. "Thank fuck. I was feeling so guilty over it. It's what took me so long to give in, but it was Grey who convinced me to take the leap."

She raises her brow. "Grey, as in the prospect who just got fully patched and saved me from a random explosion, Grey?"

Chuckling, I nod. "One in the same. Reminded me about Chills and Chains from Houston. Foster siblings who are in a committed relationship and have a kid."

She moves in, her arms sliding up around my neck. "Is that where you see us heading? A committed relationship?"

My arms pull her closer, sitting just above her ass, my eyes locking on hers. They sparkle so fucking intensely I could get lost in them for days with how stunning she is. "All I know, Novah, is I don't want any other man touching you. I don't want any other man near you. Just thinking of it makes my blood boil. I want to be your first and your last, your everything in between… if that makes it a committed relationship, then fuck yeah, I'm in."

Her eyes glisten as she stares at me. "Who knew you could be so sweet?"

Grinning, I turn up my lip. "Don't fucking tell anyone."

Novah laughs and leans in, gently pressing her lips to mine. Kissing her is everything I've always wanted. She tastes like sweet berries, and I can't get enough. My hands slide down to her ass, pulling her tight against me so she can feel *everything* she does to me. She giggles against my lips. When she pulls back, she rests her forehead against mine. "You know… we're all alone. No Hurricane. No Nash. No one to stop us from being together," she suggests, waggling her brows.

Groaning, I let out a sigh. "I wanna do this right with you, Novah, not just when it's convenient."

Her eyes droop. "You sure you're not just trying to avoid it? I mean, you *are* a sex maniac, apparently."

My hands grab hold of her ass, and I hoist her up. She lets out a small squeal when I walk her backward to the opposite counter and sit her on top, pressing my erection into her pussy. "Feel that? *That's* what you do to me. Don't doubt I want you, Novah. I want you *so fucking bad* it's killing me, but because it's your first time, I *need* to do it right."

Her lips turn in a slight pout. I see the disappointment in her face, but she slowly nods her head like she understands. "Okay... I've waited this long for you. A little more time won't hurt."

"That's a good girl," I tell her and press a hard kiss to her lips. She's breathless when I pull back, her eyes wide in awe, obviously affected by my words.

So she has a praise kink.

Good to know.

I rock my hips into her, causing a whimper from her mouth. I know she is desperate for some attention. *Maybe I can give her something to tide her over.* Dropping to my knees, her eyes widen as my hands grip her knees, and she tries to force her legs closed. "Bayou, what are—"

"You want to feel good, Novah?" I growl against her thigh, kissing and nipping down her leg. My fingers trail up under her skirt toward her panties.

She nods. "Mm-hmm," she whimpers.

"I'm gonna lick your pussy until you're screaming my name. Taste you until I've had my fill of you and then work you to the brink until you can't fucking breathe."

She pants breathlessly as I continue to kiss up her thigh. My fingers slide in to grab the hem of her panties. She swallows a nervous lump down her throat, and I continue speaking, "You're making me so hard, Novah, the anticipation is killing me. I'm so hungry for you. I need you to be a good fucking girl and ride my face." My fingers clench either side of her panties as she gasps at my words, and I tear them to shreds. Her breaths are hard and fast as I toss the piece of white fabric to the floor.

So pure, so innocent.

All mine.

Her fingers slide out, threading into my hair while I trail kisses along her delicate thigh. Her skin quivers at my touch. Knowing I am the first and only man who's been with her makes my cock so fucking hard I can hardly stand it.

"Bayou, I-I don't know what to do. W-what if—"

Looking up from my kneeling position between her legs, I smirk. *So pure, so innocent. I fucking love it.* "Beautiful, you don't have to worry about a thing, you're fucking delicious," I tell her.

She bites down on her bottom lip like she's unsure, so I dip my finger into her pussy. She inhales quickly at my touch while I gather her juices, then pull my finger out just as quickly and slide it into my mouth to taste her. Her eyes widen when I let out a guttural groan. "Mmm, so fucking good."

Her breathing quickens as I continue to reassure her. "Hold onto my hair, and the harder you tug, the faster I'll go. But all you have to do is hold on."

Novah swallows hard, the nerves evident in her eyes, and teamed with anticipation, it almost makes me anxious, but I want to make her feel good. I *need* to make her feel good. She nods, threading her fingers through my hair, and she gives it a sharp tug. A deep moan reverbs through my chest—she has no fucking idea how much that turns me on. How hard it is for me to control my urges around her. Instantly, a flash of her pulling on my hair as I thrust my cock deep inside her while she screams out my name in ecstasy washes through my mind. My cock hardens even more with the thought.

I have dreamed of a moment like this with Novah, wanting to taste her for so fucking long. Now it's here, I'm going to savor every second. Hell, I'm going to savor every last fucking drop of her.

I am so worked up right now that I release a groan and rub my hand over my cock, which is straining against the zipper of my jeans. But right now, I need to focus on Novah, so I trail my lips up her thigh, teasing her, my tongue darting out and licking her delicious skin. She trembles beneath my touch, and I know it's not out of fear but nerves teamed with lust. Gliding my tongue ring along her pebbled skin, her breathing hitches as I take my time with her. Her ass is wriggling on the counter, now anxious to skip ahead.

My greedy girl.

I press my lips on the apex of her folds above her clit, and she lets out a small whimper. Rocking against me, I can't help the low growl that escapes my throat when I flick my tongue out, desperate to taste her. The instant my tongue hits her clit, her body jerks, her hands tightens in my hair, and I can't help but smile, loving how receptive she is to everything.

She lets out a heavy breath. "Bayou, shit, it's so intense."

If you think that was intense, just wait, beautiful.

Grinning as I continue to flick my tongue on her in a way I can tell she likes, I slide my finger inside her. She lets out a deep moan when I push right in, hitting her G-spot. Her breathing stutters and her fingers clench in my hair so tight it makes my cock harder than I have ever felt. I rotate my finger, hitting all her nerve endings to bring her closer to the edge.

My tongue circles her clit, working her faster and higher as she rocks against my face. "Fuck, Bayou! Ahh…" She pants breathlessly.

My cock throbs so fucking much I need to feel some relief. So I slide my free hand down and pull my cock out of my jeans. Fisting my hard length in my hand, I begin to tug as I insert another finger, scissoring my action, the same time I work my magic on her clit. Her fingers grip my hair so tight it feels like she might rip some strands out, but I fucking love the pain. It only encourages me to work faster, bringing her to the edge of her climax.

She moans so loud, the pleasure rolls through me. Her head throws back, almost hitting the cabinet on the wall behind her. One hand leaves my hair as she reaches above her trying to find something to grip onto. Eventually, she finds the handle for the cupboard and grips it so tight, the handle breaks and the door flies open. "Fuck!" she mumbles as she throws the handle to the floor beside me.

I can't help but chuckle against her delicious pussy, which sends a vibration through her. Instantly, she shudders, her hand slamming back down on the counter, continuing to search for something to cling to, but she accidentally sideswipes a coffee mug, and it crashes to the floor smashing apart on impact.

Seeing her come undone like this, while I jerk myself off, only heightens the sensations running through me. I let out another guttural moan then flick my tongue. The sounds she's making are so fucking intoxicating, I want nothing more than to ram my cock into her, but I can't do that.

I have to take my time with Novah. Ease her into this.

First things first—making her scream my name while she comes all over my face.

I ramp up the speed, circling, using my tongue ring to cause friction on her clit. Simultaneously, I pump harder on my cock which causes my balls to pull tight with pleasure. My fingers work on the inside of her pussy. Novah's body quivers, shaking and shuddering with the desire rolling through her. Her body coats in a fine mist of sweat while I work her right to the brink. She's panting, tightening her muscles all over her body. She is close. So close precum forms on my cock in anticipation of bringing her over the edge. I just need her to let go. So I move my fingers in a come-here motion inside her, and she gasps as I hit the spot she needs.

"Oh God! *Oh God*," she screams, her thighs clenching tight around my face, almost suffocating me. The problem is, I'm a twisted fuck, and I love that she is so lost in her pleasure, she doesn't know what she is doing.

Her losing herself in her climax is only bringing mine closer as I try to find my breath, but her hands tear at my hair, forcing my face into her pussy, my mouth completely trapped by her cunt. I take full advantage of devouring every inch of her perfect pussy while she orgasms, squirting just a little, enough to wet my face. Smiling against her, I lick up her juices as she screams out my name.

"Bayou!" She pants.

This is the single hottest fucking thing I have ever done, and I have done a lot. But being smothered in Novah, experiencing her first oral orgasm is by far the best experience in my life. My heart races as the tingle shoots so intensely from my spine all the way to my balls. I let out a groan when she relaxes a little, her thighs softening their deathlike grip on my head, letting me finally take a breath as the rush hits me, and I explode all over my hand and the counter between us.

I inhale deeply, trying to catch my breath.

Novah's fingers turn from rough to caressing my hair, and she lets out an angelic chuckle. My eyes shift up to look at her. Her face is calm and full of bliss as she relaxes back against the cupboard. Wiping my face with the back of my arm, I let out a contented sigh and stand, my eyes meeting hers, my cock still raging hard—it's taking everything in me not to take this further. All I want to do is spread her across the floor and fuck her senseless, but she is worth so much more.

Novah's is worth everything.

She glances down between us at the mess I made, and she raises her brow like she is intrigued. I watch her fingers dip between us, and she swipes up some of my cum and then slides it into her mouth.

My eyes widen as she sucks on her finger. "Novah!" I rasp.

"Mmm, so fucking good," she repeats the words I said to her only moments ago.

I slide a stray piece of hair behind her ear and caress her cheek. "You're so fucking beautiful when you let go like that."

She smiles, releasing a long, languid sigh. "That thing you did with your tongue..."

Chuckling, I plant a quick kiss on her lips. "It's reserved only for you."

She blushes. *Fuck, she's so fucking attractive when she's all innocent.*

"You're definitely going to have to do that again."

Laughing, I move in, picking her up from the counter. Her legs wrap around my waist as she clings to me. "We have time. Now, be a good girl and behave so we can cuddle on the sofa and watch some TV." She smiles while I carry her to the living room and place her on the sofa. I slide in next to her, and she cuddles me.

She glances up, her beautiful eyes stare at me. "I'm glad I waited for you, that was..."

My chest floods with pride.

Knowing she waited for me should put pressure on my back, but all it does is make me want to show her how fucking good this can be. How good I can make her feel. She gave me the honor of being her first for almost everything, and now I have to treat that with the respect it deserves.

It's taken us so long to get to this point. But, honestly, I want to enjoy what we have before shit hits the fan. Because when Hurricane and Nash find out we are together, shit will not only hit that fan, it will annihilate it. But I'll take the knocks if it means I get to spend even a moment with Novah because she is all I have ever wanted.

And right now, I have her.

And I don't plan on letting her go.

Not for anything.

Or more importantly anyone.

CHAPTER 13

NOVAH
New Year's Eve

Don't ask me how, but somehow Lani convinced Hurricane to let us girls come out tonight. It's New Year's Eve, and we're getting dressed at the clubhouse. I brought over a little white dress to wear, but the girls are having none of it.

"Here, wear this. You looked so good in it last time you wore it," Izzy says, handing me the little glitzy silver backless number from our drunken dance party at the clubhouse.

I tilt my head, knowing Bayou had a fit last time I wore it. But I also saw the look in his eyes—there was nothing but lust. "Okay, hand it over."

The girls all cheer for my apparent lack of self-control, so I strip and pull on the silver dress that leaves little to the imagination. I glance in the mirror and shake my head. *He's going to kill me.* I smirk as Lani grabs my hand, and we all walk out into the clubroom.

We walk out, and the guys turn, gawking.

Hurricane and City instantly start shaking their heads at Kaia and Izzy.

"No," they both say in unison.

Bayou sits back, his eyes focused on me like he's desperate to come over and tell me off for being a bad girl, but he knows he can't.

"Sha, you think I'm letting you out dressed like that? Every fuckin' asshole in New Awlin's is gonna want a piece of you," Hurricane tells Kaia.

She shrugs. "Good thing my Old Man will be hiding in the shadows to tell them all to fuck off then, right? We're not changing, Hurricane."

"Then you're not goin' down Bourbon Street."

Kaia folds her arms across her chest, and I step forward, placing my hand on Hurricane's arm. "It's New Year's Eve. It's a time to celebrate, let us go out and have a good time. You're going to be there. You can watch us. We feel good, Hurricane. Don't you want us to feel pretty?" I ask.

"Fuck!" He slumps his shoulders looking at Bayou. "How am I supposed to argue with that? Dammit, Novah! Fine, we go, but we go somewhere *I* trust."

Bayou raises his brow. "Revel Rose?" he asks.

Hurricane dips his chin.

"Marcel will keep an eye out on the girls. Any shit he'll warn us."

"Okay, Revel Rose is a good place. It has amazing cocktails. We can make it work," Kaia states and starts leading us toward the door. "You guys coming or what?" she throws back over her shoulder.

Hurricane groans.

Bayou shakes his head. "We're going to regret this… I see it a mile away."

Hurricane looks at Bayou, nodding in agreement. "Damn straight."

Our heels click-clack as we walk to the van while giggling and chatting. Grudge helps us inside while the guys mount up ready to ride alongside us the entire way. But, of course, they want to ensure their precious cargo is taken care of. Who can argue—it's sweet.

The girls are all hyped up, excited for a night out, plus we'll be bringing in a new year. It's the start of exciting opportunities. Growth. Change. Tonight, anything can happen.

The four of us chat and laugh all the way into the city, the roar of the Harleys beside us the entire way letting us know our men are right there with us.

Support.

Comfort.

Protection.

Not long later, we pull into the parking lot of Revel Rose. The van's rear opens, and Grudge helps us out one by one. Excitement bubbles up inside me when I side-eye Bayou, but he's trying to keep a neutral face. We approach the lineup, but the guys walk us straight to the front. Hurricane whispers something to the bouncer, and he pulls the rope aside, letting our group walk right on through. The patrons waiting in line all heckle, but I'm not concentrating on them because I can feel Bayou's eyes on me the entire time. It makes me feel powerful, like I know I am working him up into a frenzy without even trying. And I love that feeling.

The bar is alive and buzzing. Revelers are having a great time dancing and drinking, bringing in the new year with their friends and loved ones. The guys grab a table, all moving to sit around it, while the girls head for the bar.

Lani slides in beside me.

"I'm so glad you came out with us tonight," I tell her over the loud music.

She smiles. "I mean, I can't drink, but I can still party like there's no tomorrow. You watch me."

Wrapping my arm around her, I embrace her as Kaia bumps into my side. "Shots!"

I let out a laugh. "Oh man, it's gonna get messy. Lani, you might have to carry me."

Lani chuckles. "I'm just glad you're letting me join in the fun."

Kaia slumps her shoulders, her lips turning downward. "I know I sheltered you for a lot of your life, and for that I am sorry, but I want you to live as much as you can within your limits."

"I'd love to have a job. That's my main ambition in life. To be self-sufficient, but I don't know any place that would hire me. I'm a liability."

My heart sinks for Lani because she's such an amazing person. She deserves the world.

Kaia suddenly widens her eyes and places her hand on her sister's shoulder. "Lani, I need a receptionist at Ohana street. The parlor needs someone to keep track of everything. I don't know why I didn't think of it before. You'd be perfect for the job."

Lani's eyes glisten, and she shakes her head slightly. "Are you sure? I mean, I'm your sister. Wouldn't that be cramping your style?"

Kaia pulls her in for an embrace. "Lani, there is no one I trust more to look after my business than you."

"Thank you. You're the best, Kaia," Lani says. "Shots are on me."

We all chuckle.

Marcel, the bar owner, slides three shots across the bar. Kaia, Izzy, and I pick them up and throw them back. The burn instantly igniting my insides.

"Okay, now we celebrate Lani's new job by dancing, right?" I ask.

The girls all cheer, and we walk out onto the dance floor, making sure to stand together. We know the rules. The four of us have to keep together so the guys can watch us. Small price to pay for having a night of delightful fun.

We let our hair down and dance into the late night hours, having an incredibly good time. My eyes occasionally shift over to the guys, who are chatting and drinking. They're not far from us, but far enough away not to encroach on our space.

There is one thing I have noticed—Bayou's eyes haven't left me all night. It sends a thrill of excitement through me. I wish he would come over and dance with me, but I know he can't. The fact he's watching me is making my clit throb.

Suddenly, Izzy grabs my hands and starts dancing with me, and I smile moving with her to the beat. But as the song changes to Rihanna's "Skin"—the song clearly about sex—all I want to do right now is show Bayou what he's missing. So I decide to do exactly that. Grabbing Izzy, I move with her to the music. She doesn't seem to care as she joins with me, both of us grinding against each other to the beat. My mind is thinking it's Bayou's hands on my hips as I sway. Turning in her grip, I press my back to her front, my hands moving up into my hair, and I thread my fingers through it slowly and sexily as I grind my ass against her, my eyes moving straight to Bayou. His hands fist against his thighs like he is having trouble holding himself together, his nostrils flaring while he stares at me intensely, watching my every sensual move. The song talks about skin and ripping clothes off, and that is all I want to do with him right now. My clit throbs so much I can hardly stand it.

Suddenly, City appears beside me, reaching out for Izzy, a hard glint in his eyes. "No offense, Novah, but no one is allowed to grind up against my Old Lady but me. Not even a woman."

Izzy rolls her eyes as he pulls her to him tightly and starts dancing with her. "It was just a bit of fun," Izzy defends.

"It's fine, Iz. I get these guys and their *you're mine* shit. Sorry, City, she's all yours."

He grins, leaning in and pressing his lips to hers forcefully, claiming her completely. I smirk, deciding I will go to the bar and grab a drink to cool me down. Because after working Bayou up like that, I need something to take the edge off.

Standing at the bar, I wait for Marcel to come to me, but the bar is packed full of people. When a hand on my back draws my attention, I go to tell whoever it is to get lost as it starts to move lower, and he leans into my ear. "Were you trying to make me mad?" His deliciously warm breath tickles my skin.

Giggling, I bite down on my bottom lip. "Did I make you mad or… hungry?"

He growls into my ear. "You're gonna be the fucking death of me."

I turn to Bayou. Our faces are so close as I look him in the eyes. "Did you like what you saw?"

He inhales sharply through his nostrils, his eyes darting around to see if anyone is nearby. "I've never wanted to spank and fuck someone so damn hard in all my life. If you're trying to be a bad girl, Novah, you're going about it the right fucking way."

I lean in a little closer. "Maybe I'm sick of being the innocent, pure, little good girl?"

He grits his teeth like he's trying to control himself. "Don't try so hard to be something you're not, Novah. You *are* a good girl, and I happen to *really* like that about you. You don't need to change because you think a bad girl is more suited to who *I* am. I want you as you are. A *good fucking girl."* He growls the last part.

Hearing him call me a good girl does something to me. I don't know why, but it makes my insides quiver with the tone he uses. *It's so fucking sexy.* I could hear him call me a *good girl* all day long and never get tired of it.

"I don't know how much longer I can wait, Bayou."

He chuckles, his hand slides a sweaty piece of my blonde hair behind my ear. "Delayed gratification, beautiful. Our time will come. In the meantime, don't fucking sexy dance with anyone else. I don't want any fucker touching you."

I smirk because he's doing exactly what City did to Izzy only moments ago. Except I'm not Bayou's Old Lady, and he can't take possession of me in this bar for everyone to see.

Damn limitations.

"And stay with the group," he demands, narrowing his eyes on me, then turns, walking back over to the guys.

Smirking, I swing around to grab my drink, then make my way

back to the girls, and we continue to dance.

It's getting close to midnight, and the countdown is on. The guys make their way over to ring in the new year.

Bayou steps in behind me as we gather together, and my skin prickles in goose bumps knowing he is behind me but can't do anything to touch me. The crowd huddles together, and I step back closer to Bayou, my back against his front, just needing to feel him. His hard cock presses into my back, and I bite down on my bottom lip while the countdown to midnight begins.

I am so turned on right now, I wish I could spin around at midnight and kiss him, but I know I can't.

Five...

He grinds his cock into me, making my breathing hitch.

Four...

His hand slides out, running down the side of my hip so slowly that I can't think straight.

Three...

My eyes dart around to see if anyone is watching as his hand slides up the back of my skirt.

Two...

I move my leg out a little when he shoves a knee between my knees, and he pushes my panties aside and eases his finger inside me.

One...

I gasp when a wave of desire rolls through me, the same time a heightened anxiety of being caught rises to the surface. I lean further back into Bayou as he plunges deeper inside me. I let out a whimper when everyone calls out, "Happy New Year!"

Confetti explodes from the ceiling.

Pleasure wracks through my body.

Everyone cheers, yelling and rejoicing as they bring in the new year.

Fireworks erupt behind my eyes and out in the New Orleans' streets.

A loud blast goes off simultaneously as I let out a small moan.

Suddenly, the power in the bar shuts off.

Everyone stops dead still.

Bayou pulls his finger from me abruptly, then wraps his arm around my waist, pulling me to him protectively.

"What the fuck?" Hurricane grunts out.

Everyone in the bar mumbles, turning on their cell flashlights to see what is going on.

The fireworks and revelers outside are still going off like crazy as New Orleans rings in the new year.

I turn, facing Bayou. "What's going on?"

He shakes his head. "I don't know. Stay with the girls while we go with Marcel to check it out," he instructs. Then, he takes off with Hurricane and the others leaving Grit and Grudge with us. I wrap my arms around myself, feeling uncomfortable.

Something doesn't feel right.

I turn to Grit and Grudge and shake my head. "I don't like this."

Grit nods. "Me either."

A small commotion gathers my attention. I glance toward the entry where a bunch of people are coming into the bar, while others are trying to get out. I find it weird that people are trying to come in while the power is out.

Then it hits me.

They are not partygoers.

They're the reason the power is off.

I turn to tell Grit, but he's already off and heading in their direction with Grudge. I grab Kaia and point. "I think shit is going down."

She pushes up on her toes and grunts. "Fuck! We need to find somewhere to—" She lets out a small yelp when the four of us are suddenly grabbed from behind. I go to call out to Grit that the men they're chasing are a distraction, but the guy wearing a black balaclava places his hand over my mouth and drags us away. I kick and fight as much as possible, losing a heel on the way, but they're too strong. The other girls are doing the same, but they haul us through the back of the bar to a waiting van. My heart races so fucking fast I can't breathe properly, so I do the only thing I can think of, I clamp down on the asshole's hand, getting my mouth free.

"Bayou," I scream as loud as I can.

"Shut. Up!" The guy grunts, slapping my face. My head snaps to the side with the sheer force he uses. My face immediately stings, and it brings tears to my eyes.

The running footsteps of the guys are there, but it's too late. Whoever this is, has us all in the van, and when the back door shuts, we drive off before I even see if our men have seen us. I let out a sob as the guys in the back start cable tying our hands. They place gags over our mouths so we can't scream out or talk to them or each other. The fireworks and partying continue in the streets around us, and the revelers are none the wiser about what is happening in the van driving down their street.

The four of us sit back, staring at each other with wide eyes, wondering what in hell we do now, as one of the guys looks around. Then, finally, he turns to Kaia, pulling down her gag. "You... are *you* the leader?"

Kaia nods. "Yes."

He doesn't hold back, balling up his fist and landing a solid blow right to the middle of her face. Kaia yelps as the rest of us burst into tears while blood pours down Kaia's face. My body trembles, glancing at Lani, her eyes glazing over as Kaia flops to her side on the seat. I mumble under my gag and try to signal to the asshole to pull it down. He groans and yanks the gag down with such force it splits my lip.

I wince, but fight through it. "You need to let Lani breathe properly. She has epilepsy, and she's on the verge of a seizure. Look at her eyes."

The guy snaps his head to Lani as her eyes focus in and out. He pauses, groans, then pulls her mouth gag down, leaving only Izzy with hers still on.

I may as well try to figure out what the fuck is going on, so I am not above begging. "Who are you?"

"Not your concern," he replies with a slight accent that I can't place.

"What are you going to do with us?"

"It's a new year. We celebrate."

My eyes widen. "What does that mean?"

"You figure it out, sweetheart." His accent comes through a little thicker now.

My eyes meet Izzy's, and she shakes her head.

The accent.

The threat to us.

I know who these guys are.

"Did Anton Novikov send you?" I ask, and he backhands me across my face. My split lip begins to really bleed now, as I am forced to the floor of the van.

"Shut your mouth, you whore. Or I celebrate New Year's with you, in front of your friends," he snaps.

Goddammit! I roll on my side, anxiety crashing through me at the thought.

I've been saving myself for Bayou, and if the club doesn't find us, all that waiting might be wasted on the fucking Novikov Bratva—the club's nemesis.

So much for being a good girl.

BAYOU

Grit runs to us at the side of the bar where we are trying to get the power back on.

He's panting and out of breath, clutching his broken collarbone like he's in pain. "Some assholes just took the girls in a black van. I was alone, so I couldn't take them all on. There was at least six of them."

My eyes burst out of my face, and my heart feels like it stops beating for a moment, then thumps back into a rhythm so hard it knocks the breath from me. "They took Novah?" I snap.

"They took *all* the girls," Grit reiterates.

Hurricane grunts, his face turning redder by the second. "Motherfucker! Marcel, we gotta leave you to deal with this. We gotta ride." He doesn't wait for a response as we rush to our rides. Raid pulls out his tracker and starts pinging each girl's cell. Three of them are back at the bar, obviously in their clutches on the table, but one is on the move.

Lani.

"She's so fuckin' smart. Raid, follow that ping. Get us to it as quickly as you fuckin' can."

Raid dips his chin. "On it."

We take off at breakneck speed, not wasting a second nor caring about rules or the fact that there are people everywhere on the streets tonight. They just have to get out of the fucking way. Fireworks are going off everywhere, people partying as we weave in and out of the traffic, the revelers crowding the streets while we surge through them, honestly not giving one shit.

We need our women back.

Raid signals to a black van, pulling down a side street. The girls are obviously inside, and we need to do everything to get them out. So Hurricane and I zoom up, speeding in front of it, pulling out our guns, making sure not to aim for the side of the van. The girls will be in the back, so we aim for the tires, but as we go to shoot, the windows roll down, and two men pop out, aiming directly at us.

We raise our guns as I dart out behind a car while his gun starts shooting at me. I duck down into my ride, trying to dodge the spray of bullets when they punch into the car I am hiding behind. Goddammit! I watch as innocent civilians inside are hit, then it darts toward me. “Fuck!”

I slam on the brakes. The car diverts in front of me and crashes into the fire hydrant on the opposite side of the road. Water sprays up in the air. The van speeds up ahead of me, the other guys taking off in pursuit.

Grunting, I spin my back tire, I’m really fucking pissed off now.

Gunfire blasts between the fireworks and celebrations while Hurricane and Grit ride up alongside. And as they’re dodging the gunfire, they shoot one of the guys hanging out the window, Grit aiming for the front tire. The van starts to wobble as it turns, heading for the ornate buildings.

Hurricane shoots through the windscreen, his bullet lodging in the driver. The van picks up speed like the driver’s collapsed onto the accelerator, and the van runs straight into a lamp post, it collides to the ground, while the van tips, then slams onto its side and slides down the street for a few feet. Glass shatters, the scrunching of metal grates on my ears while I ride as fast as possible to get to the girls. Pulling to a stop, I barely kick out the stand before I jump off my ride and run to the back of the van with everything in me. My heart is racing so fast I can't think straight.

As we approach, Hurricane, Grit, and City are right by my side. The back door of the van opens, and men burst out sending off rounds. But we don't falter, each of us raising our guns and unloading our bullets in quick succession. But I see City's arm jerk like he took a hit. But we fire back. Their bodies jerk and stumble with the spray as they drop to their knees, blood pooling at their feet, and they all fall to the ground. Dead.

We continue, fear almost crippling me when we yank the door open to see the girls inside, all tied up. Kaia is closest, her nose all bloodied, and she is zoning in and out. Hurricane moves straight for her as I push past in search of Novah. Her lip is split badly, with blood pooling on her chin. I move in, caressing her face, not even caring about Hurricane and what he thinks of my affection toward Novah right now. "Are you okay?" I ask.

She pants like she's trying to catch her breath. "I'm okay... Lani isn't."

Grit slides inside the confined space and pulls her into his arms, even though it's killing him right as Lani starts to seize. "Shit. Lani. I got you."

City steps in and Izzy jumps into his arms, he winces a little with the pain. She has scratches all over her from the crash, and her wrists are still tied as she wraps them around his head. But he manages to pulls her mouth gag down, and he kisses her.

I want to kiss Novah.

Wrap her in my arms.

I would fucking worship her.

Take care of her.

Give her my everything.

But I can't.

Not without everyone knowing how I feel.

"Grit, how's Lani?" I call out.

He's stroking her face, smiling down at her, his eyes looking at her lovingly. It's obvious he is into her. "She's coming around."

Hurricane holds Kaia, whispering something in her ear as I continue to sit with Novah, wishing I could say and do more for her. My eyes meet hers, and I stare. She weakly smiles, like she can understand my pain without me having to say anything.

She reaches out, gripping my hand, and squeezes. "It's okay. I'm okay."

I grab my knife and slice off her cable ties, releasing her restraints, and I hand my knife to City who repeats the process with Izzy. Then he hands it to Grit, who hands it to Hurricane.

Placing the knife back in its sheath, I focus on Novah.

We can't stay here much longer.

Luckily, there's only been the one car of witnesses.

In any case, we need to get out of here.

"Did they tell you who they were?" I ask.

"I can't be sure, but I think they were sent by the Novikovs," Novah replies.

Hurricane grits his teeth holding onto Kaia tightly. "Fuck! Hoodoo, Raid… check this van for anythin' leadin' us to where they might be. We need to find out where Anton's located and pay that asshole a damn visit."

Holding Novah, fear cripples me at the thoughts running through my mind right now. I need to know something, even if the answer will kill me. "Did they do anything else to you?"

Her eyes meet mine. "They didn't come right out and say it, but I think that was their plan."

I crane my neck to the side, a couple of audible cracks popping through the air. "I'm gonna fucking kill them."

"Can Lani ride back to the parking lot?" Hurricane asks, distracting me.

Kaia shakes her head. "She can't, not after a seizure. It's too dangerous, Hurricane."

Grit picks her up into his arms, not even caring about his injuries. Lani's awake, just seems incredibly sleepy. "I'll put her on my ride. She can sit in front of me and hold on as best she can. I won't let anything happen. I'll ride slow till we can get her in the van."

Hurricane turns to Kaia, a pleading look in his eyes. That look says *We need to get out of here*. "Okay, but if she falls off that bike, I swear to God, Grit, I will chop your balls off myself."

"Understood."

We need to leave before the heat shows up.

The Novikovs will clean this shit up before the cops even have a chance to attend this mess. They don't want to be found the same as we don't. So no need to be concerned about repercussions from the heat.

Raid wipes the scene down, and I watch as the others jump on their rides. Lani sluggishly climbs on the front of Grit's bike and clings to him bearhug style. The pain is obvious on his face, but it's clear to see, Lani's not going anywhere. He's so fucking good for her.

I gesture for Novah to move in behind me after I slide on my ride. Her arms wrap around my waist, and I swear I will never get sick of this feeling. Novah at my back is precisely where she belongs. But I can't concentrate on how good this feels or how much I love that she is here with me. I need to get her home. I need to make sure she is safe and taken care of. Right now, I must, above everything, protect her, and I can't do that if I am too busy thinking about how good this feels.

We start our rides and I hammer down, driving in formation with the guys. We make our way back to Revel Rose, and as we approach, we see Marcel has the power back on.

Hurricane sends Grudge in to fetch the girls' bags and cells. But Kaia and Izzy are really hurting, and I have to admit I am worried about Novah. Not to mention Lani has had a fucking epileptic seizure.

Hurricane's bike is next to mine, City on the other side, a line of blood oozing down his arm.

"I'm takin' Kaia to the hospital to get her nose checked out. You guys should follow. Just make sure everyone is good from the crash."

City and I both nod as the three women all groan in unison.

"We don't need the hospital, Hurricane, we just want our beds," Kaia murmurs.

"I think your broken nose says differently. And by the way you're gaggin' behind me while ridin', it says differently, Sha. We're goin'. End of discussion."

"Yeah, Izzy's got some real deep cuts I want looked at," City states.

And I nod. "Everyone needs to be checked. We should go."

"Let's head there now," Hurricane states. "Think you can keep ridin', Sha?" he asks Kaia. She nods, then winces at the pain in her face. "Right, let's go."

We start our engines and take off for the hospital. Marcel calls ahead to let his connections know we're coming in hot. Knowing the city's big players helps us hide things and get where we need to be more easily.

We make it to the hospital and walk the girls in, the triage nurses taking them straight through while another checks over City's arm.

Novah's lip is glued back together, Izzy's scrapes and cuts are tended, and Lani is checked over for her seizure but seems okay. Kaia, however, is feeling off. So they take her in for further testing. They think it might be because she swallowed so much blood from her nose. I stand back with Hurricane while she is getting some testing done, and he is pacing the floor between Kaia and Novah's room. "What the fuck is taking them so damn long?"

Novah and I look at each other, and then to Hurricane.

I step up to him. "She's in the best possible hands. Whatever it is, they're gonna help her."

He groans like he isn't convinced. "No, it's takin' too fuckin' long. What if someone has taken her? I need to go find out where she i—"

Suddenly, they wheel Kaia back in her bed, and Hurricane lets out a long breath running his hands through his hair like he's about to lose his shit. "Where the hell have you been?" he snaps.

Kaia shifts a little on the bed like she's shocked by his outburst, the nurse trying to ignore him. "Calm down, you big idiot. They were running tests. This is a working hospital... things take time."

He throws his hands in the air. "Well, you're a VIP. Shit should be expedited."

Kaia chuckles. "It doesn't work like that, baby, but it's cute you think so highly of me."

He glares at the nurse, who is fiddling with Kaia's IV. "Don't you know how important Kaia is? You need to work faster. Treat her with the utmost respect. She is the queen of our club."

The nurse rolls her eyes as Kaia laughs, shaking her head. "Okay, calm down. I might be royalty in the club, but this is a public hospital, Hurricane, and out here I'm just like any other person in need of medical attention. I'm no more important than anyone else."

"You are to me."

Kaia smiles. "And I love you for that. But please, calm your stubborn ass down. You're making a scene."

Hurricane folds his arms over his chest, and I grip his shoulder. "She's right, brother. Let them do their job."

Hurricane huffs, craning his neck to the side. "Fine. What did they say? They figure out what's goin' on? Why you feel the way you do?"

"They said the doctor will come and talk to us, give us the results soon."

Hurricane growls. "Can someone call Marcel? Get him to call his contact at the hospital again and tell them to move their asses along. We don't have all fuckin' night. I wanna get my woman home so I can take care of her."

The screen pulls back, and a woman steps into the bay. She is gorgeous with a bright smirk on her face. "No need, I'm right here."

We all turn to face her, and Hurricane looks her up and down. "You're Marcel's contact?"

She slides the curtain across and steps in further like she might be annoyed now. "I know Marcel, and I have an arrangement. But if you are going to come in here screaming it at the top of your arrogant lungs, then I can always get security to escort you outside until I'm done treating Miss Māhoe. But, if you can keep yourself respectable and calm in my ER, I can get on with my job, and we *won't* have any issues."

I smirk as I see the vein in Hurricane's neck pulse, but Kaia reaches out for his hand. "Hurricane, it's okay. Take a breath."

He curls up his lip, gritting his teeth. "Who the fuck are you anyway?"

She smiles, walking over to Kaia, checking her monitor, and typing something into her hospital tablet. "Dr. Aubree Adams."

"And how do you know Marcel?" He keeps pushing.

She exhales, turning to face him. "That... is none of your business. Now, Miss Māhoe, I have the results of your tests. Are you okay having all these people in here?"

Kaia chuckles. "Please, call me Kaia, and yes. They're family. Anything you have to say, they're gonna hear it anyway, so they can be here."

"Okay... you've suffered a fracture to your nose in the accident, it's why there was so much bleeding. Generally, this treatment would include realigning the fracture and placing on a splint. This is usually done through surgery, but that option is not on the cards for you right now, so we will have to realign by hand and see how it adjusts. We will give you some antibiotics, but again, we must be careful about what we give you. Our treatment options are limited, but not impossible."

Kaia and Hurricane both shake their heads.

"Why are the treatments so difficult, doc?" Kaia asks.

Dr. Aubree glances from Hurricane to Kaia and smiles. "Kaia... you're pregnant."

My eyes widen in shock.

Hurricane stumbles a little on the spot. I place my hand on his back as his eyes shoot down to Kaia, who looks equally as stunned. "A baby?" Kaia whispers.

Hurricane smiles so wide, then he presses his lips to hers gently, so he doesn't hurt her nose. "A fuckin' baby."

I let out a small laugh as I turn to Novah, and she's beaming in excitement.

Hurricane lets out a cheer. "I'm gonna be a fuckin' dad."

I smirk, shaking my head. "God help us all."

Now we have to figure out just what the hell we're going to do about the Novikovs.

What a way to start a fucking new year.

CHAPTER 15

BAYOU

After the events at the hospital, it was all a lot to take in. I am sure the clubhouse is in full celebration mode, but I wanted to make sure Novah is cared for. So I came home with her to ensure she is comfortable after the accident. I tried to have her to stay at the clubhouse, but she wanted her own bed.

I get that, but it would have been safer at the club.

Especially considering the Novikovs just attacked.

But she wouldn't hear of it.

So I have no choice but to stay with her—not that it's a problem.

As we undress in her bedroom, I pull the duvet back, and she slides under.

"Are you sure you want to be here and not at the clubhouse? They might come for you?"

Novah gingerly pulls the covers up and sleepily says, "I am fine right here in your arms."

So I follow her, pulling her to me. My fingers run through her hair, and I exhale out a sigh. This is a really stupid move, but I can't force her to stay at the club. And I'm not leaving her here on her own. So this is my only option.

After tonight—after nearly losing her—feeling her around me is fucking comforting. There is nothing sexual, I simply need her to know how much I care. So I stroke her hair and plant featherlight kisses on her head until she falls asleep in my arms.

The fact I nearly lost her tonight sits in the pit of my gut like a noxious weed burying itself deeper and deeper, its roots thrusting further into my soul, making it impossible to breathe.

As she sleeps, I try to calm my rage, my insatiable appetite for revenge. The Novikovs are behind this, and as a club, we must do something to pay them back before it seeps so far inside my veins I become a monster on a path of imminent destruction.

But that's for tomorrow, right now, I need to enjoy the fact she is here.

She is alive.

And I am never letting her go again.

The Next Morning

The blasting of a cell phone jerks me awake with such a shock that I reach for my gun under the pillow, and as I search for it, I realize I am at Novah's. Groaning, I scrub my face while she lays in the bed grumbling about the constant noise.

I reach over and see Hurricane flashing on the screen.

Fuck.

Swiping the call, I bring it to my ear. "Hey," I reply sleepily.

"Where the fuck are you? When I realized you didn't come back to the clubhouse last night, I thought the fuckin' Bratva got you. Goddammit! You're an idiot."

I should be honest, just not *too* honest. "Stayed at Novah's. Didn't feel comfortable leaving her after what happened. I wanted to make sure she was safe, given they came after her. Those assholes would need to come through me first."

Hurricane is quiet for a second and then hums down the line.

"Smart move. There was no movement, nothin' to see?"

"Nothing. I was on the sofa… radio silence all night."

"Good, okay, come back to the club. We gotta discuss what we're gonna do to fix this."

"Got it. Be there soon." I end the call and flop back on the bed.

Novah giggles. Leaning over, she places a kiss on my lips. "I'm sorry you have to lie to him. It can't be easy lying to your twin, let alone your president."

"It's not. But Hurricane loves you, and he doesn't want *any* guy near you. So God help me when he finds out it's me…"

She places her hand on my chest comfortingly. "I know… I know. We'll hide it for as long as we can."

Leaning up, I place my lips to hers, needing one last fix before I face the music. "Mmm… why do you taste so fucking good first thing in the morning?"

Novah giggles as I pull back and move to get dressed. She sits back in the bed, watching me. "Are you guys going to go and deal with the Bratva today?" She delicately wraps her arms around her knees like she is suddenly feeling insecure.

My eyes meet hers. "I'll be safe… I promise."

"Just come back to me, okay?"

Kneeling on the edge of the bed, I bring my hand up to her face and caress her cheek. "Always," I whisper, then gently kiss her injured lip.

She kisses me back, and I rest my forehead against hers to just breathe her in. "If you need me, at any time today, you call. I don't care if it's because you broke a fingernail. *You. Fucking. Call!"*

She giggles, biting her bottom lip. "I'll call."

I press my lips to hers once more, then turn, heading for the door. Leaving Novah right now feels all kinds of wrong, especially when there's a threat who could come for her the second I leave. But I know she won't come with me. She's too stubborn. So I walk out her front door, hop on my bike, and ride like hell to the clubhouse.

The quicker we deal with the Bratva, the quicker I can get back to Novah.

As I walk inside the clubhouse, Hurricane has Kaia sitting on his lap, and he is casually stroking her stomach. A slow smile creeps up my face as I watch my twin. The man I thought would never settle down, would never let a woman tame him, and would certainly never be whipped enough to become a father, but he is taking this all in his stride.

I step over, and they both glance up at me.

Hurricane stops talking to Kaia's stomach, and his eyes shift to me, with curiosity etched in his features. "Novah okay?" I nod. "Thanks for takin' care of her. I kinda had other things to worry about." His eyes fall to Kaia's stomach again, and she rolls her eyes.

"Is this what this entire pregnancy is going to be like, you fawning all over me?"

Hurricane chuckles. "Yes, woman. You have my kid inside you. I'm fuckin' takin' care of the both of you whether you want it or not."

"Hurricane, it's so new I didn't even have time to realize I was pregnant. Let's give the baby time to breathe."

"The baby has eight months to breathe, Sha. I'm protecting him *now*."

She raises her brow. "*Him*?" She snorts.

"Oh, yeah... it's a boy."

I shake my head as Kaia scowls.

"No, she's a girl. A mother knows these things."

"Oh okay. God, you two are gonna be fighting over this until you find out, aren't you?"

"No. Because it's a boy," Hurricane snaps.

"Fine, we'll call it a boy as long as you're not disappointed when it comes out a girl."

"You're gonna be an uncle, Bayou. How's that feel?" Hurricane asks, changing the subject abruptly.

"Surreal. Never saw you as the type to have a kid, brother. But then again, never saw you settling down either. Kaia, you've been good for him."

She smiles, cuddling into Hurricane's side. "He's been good for me too."

I scoff. "Find that hard to believe—"

"Shut up, fucker." He taps Kaia's leg, and she stands. "Anyway, let's get to the business at hand, shall we?"

"I think it's time."

Hurricane stands and sends a whistle through the room. "Yo, fuckers… everyone… church. *Now.*" He turns back to Kaia and tilts his head at her. "You…" he points, "… you're puttin' your feet up and restin'."

"Jesus Christ, no way. I'm going to work. I have a tattoo parlor to run."

Hurricane growls. "While there's a threat to you and my son. No. And I repeat for good measure… *no.*"

Kaia inhales long and deep like she's trying to control her emotions right now. "I *am* going to work. You can have someone tail me if they need to. Hell, send ten brothers… I don't give a shit. But I am *not* spending the next eight months couped up here like some damn invalid."

Hurricane narrows his eyes on her, rubbing his beard like he's unsure how to play this one. "You try my patience, *woman.*"

"Good. Wait till your daughter is bossing you around when she's in her teens."

Hurricane widens his eyes, his face turning pale as a white sheet while I let out a laugh, slapping his back. "Send Grudge and Quarter. If anyone is going to go crazy on someone, you know Quarter's going to fuck an asshole up for going near her."

Hurricane grunts, glaring at me like he wants to kill me, but I smirk. "Fine… fuck!" His hand goes straight to his head, a telltale sign he's stressed as he rubs his fingers through his hair. "Grudge, Quarter… take Kaia into work. Watch her with your life. She gets hurt, so do you."

They both react quickly and walk with Kaia to get ready to leave. I wrap my arm around Hurricane's shoulders, leading him toward the Chapel. "Good call, brother. Any other decision would have had a hormonal Old Lady on your back, and heaven knows..." I look upward, "... no one wants that."

Hurricane grins, shaking his head. "She's so fuckin' strong-willed. For once, I'd fuckin' love it if she didn't do the exact opposite of what I tell her to do."

I burst out laughing. "This is why you love her, brother. Because she calls you on your shit."

"Fuck... you're right. Dammit!"

Chuckling as we walk into the Chapel, we take our respective seats.

Hurricane bangs the gavel. "So... the Bratva. We all know they were the assholes who tried to take our women. Before this, they've been quiet. They have been for a while, but we all knew they were gonna come back. I just don't know what their end game was here."

I sit forward, my hands balling into a fist on the table to contain my raging anger. "Novah seems to think they were going to abuse the women. That's the vibe she was getting from them."

"Who knows what their plans were? To send a message? I have no idea. We just got lucky we got to them in time," Hurricane states.

Craning my neck to the side, I need to bring this up. It's killing me. "Is Novah safe being at her house alone?"

Hurricane furrows his brows. "Would they have taken Novah if she wasn't with the other girls? Is she a target? We don't know. If we work on the fact that she *is* a target, then Ingrid might be too, and we don't want to start bringin' in all the women tied to the club and cause a fuckin' mass panic... maybe keep a guard on her door for the time bein'?"

Who better to guard her door than me?

"She'll feel safer with a brother she knows well and trusts. I'll volunteer," I suggest, even though there is no way I'm letting any other fucker spend time with her.

Hurricane dips his head. "Good. She *will* feel safer with you there. Solid plan, Bayou. You can start tonight…" His head shifts to Raid. "We need to figure where the Bratva is hiding out."

Raid types away on his laptop, but he continuously shakes his head. "I have been trying for weeks, Pres, but nothing is coming up for the Bratva or Anton Novikov anywhere in New Orleans. Those assholes have gone dark, which is what I would do if I were rebuilding my forces. We decimated their ranks, and every time they come at us, we take their soldiers out, sending them another hit. Maybe they're clutching at straws? Or maybe we're not looking hard enough."

Hurricane rubs at the back of his neck, making a small groan. "Or maybe we need to broaden our horizons?"

City cocks his head to the side. "What does that mean?"

"We need to look out of the city, think bigger…" Hurricane picks up his cell and starts dialing.

We all sit back, wondering who in the hell he's calling.

It rings on speakerphone so we can all hear, and when the call connects, it's a female voice. "What do you want?"

"I hear you do deals with Defiance? We're looking for a little quid pro quo."

She chuckles down the line. "I have enough trouble to deal with, with Six and Zero from Defiance over here in Houston. What the *hell* do you want with me?"

"Well, Baroness, we're having issues with the Novikov Bratva. We've been at war with them for what seems like forever. They came for our women. We got them back, but we're having trouble locating their base location. We can't find any hits on them or their leader, so retaliation is damn difficult. But if you've worked with Houston Defiance, you know that if they came after our women, we must retaliate."

The Baroness hums down the line. "Oh, yes, I know all too well… leave it with me. I will reach out to my sources and see if I can find any information. But, nothing comes for free, Hurricane."

We all raise our brows as Hurricane tilts his head. "Never told you my name."

She laughs. "You think I don't have someone tracking your call the second the call came through? There's a reason I am the most powerful woman in the south, Hurricane. You'd do well to remember that fact." She ends the call without another word.

We all look at each other with a sense of foreboding running through our veins.

"Oh, well, here we fuckin' go." Hurricane grunts, placing his cell on the table.

We've heard about the deals Houston has had to make with the Baroness over the years.

Now we're in bed with her too.

Not sure *this* is such a good idea.

CHAPTER 16

NOVAH
Two Weeks Later

The past two weeks have been interesting.

Bayou is still holding out on me.

I'm not entirely sure why.

He says when he's at my house that he's on guard and keeping an eye out, so he has to maintain his focus.

It doesn't stop him from making out with me, though.

But it does make a girl feel a little unwanted.

I know the whole virgin thing threw him when I blurted it out in his face like that, but I thought we could come back from it. *Maybe we can't?*

Trying to work with him standing at my office door is almost impossible. Trying to explain to my boss why my biker stepbrother is constantly standing there looking like a bodyguard is even more impossible to deal with. But somehow, my boss is letting it slide.

I think Wanda likes looking at him if I am honest.

Who doesn't like looking at him?

Spinning on my chair to grab something from the printer, I spot, out the corner of my eye, a jar of applesauce on my desk.

Furrowing my brows, I pick it up and smirk. "Where in the world did you come from?"

Shrugging, I figure it must be from a client or someone I work with. It looks homemade, and I smile, loving how generous people can be. Placing it down by my handbag, I move to the printer to get my client's information and then return to the computer station when my cell rings.

Nash's name flashes on the screen and I smirk. It's not often he calls me, especially during the day. So I quickly answer the call. "You're calling me? During work hours? You butt dial me or something?"

Nash groans. "No, I did *not* butt dial you. I need your help."

"Ooh, this sounds exciting, you never ask for help. Hurricane and Bayou, I get why you asked them for help that time, but me? What on earth can *I* help *you* with?"

"Well, if you'd stop blabbering for long enough I'll tell you."

Snorting out my amusement, I love it when he gets cranky. It's so funny. "You're always so... *moody.* Okay, dear brother of mine, how can *I* help you?"

"I need you to come over and talk with my event coordinator about shit to do with a gala fundraiser I am hosting."

"Oh wow! Is this for the new company?"

"No, Novah, I'm doing it out of the goodness of my heart."

Scowling, I roll my eyes. "Okay, wiseass. You're in a mood today."

"Can you just get over here?"

Glancing around my office, I notice Bayou pretending not to listen in, but he definitely is. "I have a job too, you know? One where I help people, where they need and depend on me. I can't just drop everything at your whim."

He hesitates like he is thinking.

"Fine, tonight, my apartment... you'll come for dinner to talk over ideas with Brianna?"

My eyes widen in excitement. If Nash is bringing this woman to his apartment, he must like her. "She has a name?"

Nash huffs like he is annoyed. "Novah!"

"Yes, I'll be there. Need me to bring anything?" Bayou turns, his eyes narrowing as he starts walking toward me. His face turning redder with every step—he's going to blow a gasket.

"Your best fucking behavior would be nice."

Scoffing, I raise my hand to stop a ballistic Bayou. "I'm always on my best behavior. See you tonight, loverboy."

A low growl erupts from Nash's chest as I abruptly end the call before Nash hears whatever Bayou is about to say. "Just where in the hell did you expect to go out to tonight?"

Folding my arms over my chest, I smirk. "Wow, you really are worked up right now, aren't you?"

"Novah! You're not going out. It's too dangerous."

"It's only to Nash's house for dinner… I'm meeting a *lady friend*. Nash never wants me to meet a lady friend, Bayou. This is a *big deal*. Nash has security, I'll be fine."

Bayou raises his brow. "I can't imagine Nash settling down with anyone."

"Well, technically, she's hosting some event for him, but still… *I* can see the writing on the wall."

"Novah, I know you mean well, but maybe keep your nose out of Nash's love life? The guy's been through enough lately. He doesn't need you interfering."

"It's gonna be great." I ignore him.

Bayou groans. "I'm coming with you."

I widen my eyes. "No, you're not. You weren't invited."

He steps up to me, spinning my desk chair, and bends down, his face in line with mine. "You're not going out on your own. End. Of. Discussion."

The way he looks at me makes me want to reach forward and press my lips to his, but people in the office would see, which is inappropriate. So I bat my eyelashes at him and smile. "You can take me to his apartment and wait in the parking lot for me. Final. Offer."

He groans, turns, and starts pacing. "Fine."

"In the meantime, stop being so damn obvious. This is my place of work. I'm supposed to be a social worker, a good influence. Not showing people it's okay to flirt with your stepbrother at work who also happens to be a biker… *not* the best example, Bayou."

"People just need to get their sticks out of their asses. Fuck what they think."

I raise my brow. "Oh, fuck what people think, huh? Is that what you believe when it comes to Nash and Hurricane?" I tease, and his face falls in horror. "No… didn't think so."

He groans. "You're a menace, woman."

Grinning, I wink at him. "Now go back to guarding the door. You're distracting me from my work."

He leans in, right next to my ear. "I like this bossy side of you. It makes me want to let you take charge." As he pulls back, my thighs clench together, he spins, walking for the door with a strut in his step.

The asshole knows just what he's doing.

At least the view from my desk is really fucking nice.

Bayou is driving my car to Nash's for my dinner with him and Brianna, and he is in fine form as I sink into my seat, getting a lecture.

"I mean it, Novah. No drinking alcohol. No talking about us. For fuck's sake, don't stay too long. Don't tell Nash I will be in the car waiting for you… he will ask too many questions. I want to be the one to tell Nash about us. So—"

"Bayou, I'm not a child. I *can* handle this. Do you know how controlling you sound right now?"

He exhales, running his fingers through his hair. "This makes me nervous, Novah. We've barely started whatever this is, and already we're sneaking around. If Nash figures this out—"

"He won't. I'm not going to say anything. Anyway, I'm going to be focusing on him and his *lady friend* tonight."

Bayou pulls the car into the parking space, and he seems to relax a little once he turns off the engine. He spins and leans over, pressing his lips to mine. It's gentle but still letting me know he wants me.

As I regretfully pull back, my eyes meet his concerned gaze. "It's going to be okay. You're parked right by the elevator. You will see anyone coming or going from the building."

He nods but still doesn't seem at ease. "Just be cautious, all right?"

Smiling, I open my car door with a nod. "I won't stay long." Quickly, I press my lips to his once more, then hop out of the car, feeling his eyes on me the entire way to the elevator. I swipe the keycard and step in. Turning back, I give Bayou a quick wave before the elevator doors close, and I am on my way up to Nash's penthouse apartment.

Glancing at the reflective texture of the elevator, my white and silver lurex thread swing dress, black heels, and cross-body bag with its cute chain make my outfit look quite dressy. I wanted to look nice for Nash's new girl.

The elevator takes me up, and as it pops open, the smell of my favorite gnocchi with burned-butter sauce lingers through the air, and I inhale the aroma while walking toward the kitchen.

"Hey. Are you cooking my fave again?"

I round the corner, my eyes falling on Nash. A woman who I am assuming is Brianna dramatically takes three large steps away from Nash, then she straightens out her clothes. My brows draw together with a tiny smirk, sensing the clear sexual chemistry between them. Nash turns to the stove, pretending I didn't just interrupt something.

Yeah, you can't fool me, brother.

Nash breaks the tension as he steps over to me, pulling me to him and kissing my cheek. "Grandma's recipe."

I lean into his kiss. "You spoil me..." I practically shove him aside and walk toward Brianna. I'm just so freaking excited to see that Nash has taken an *actual* interest in someone other than himself. "Hi, I'm Novah," I introduce myself, then pull her to me in a tight embrace.

"Novah, control yourself," Nash states with a chuckle, walking back to the stove.

Smiling at me warmly, she replies, "Hey, I'm Brianna... Bri."

Pulling back, I look her up and down. "You seem like a woman who can handle herself."

Nash snorts under his breath as he continues with dinner.

Brianna nods. "I like to think so."

Linking my arm with Brianna's, I start dragging her over to the sofa. "Good. Because you need to stay strong to handle Nash at his worst."

"Novah!" Nash grunts.

"Oh, shush. You know it's true." I giggle, waving him off. "So, tell me... you're working for him?"

We sit on the sofa, and she grabs a folder and slides it across to me. "I've taken Nash on as a client, so I'm organizing an event for his company."

"This is where you come in, Novah. I need your help with all the finer details," Nash calls out.

I smile. "The pretty shit?"

Brianna grins while Nash chuckles. "Yeah... the pretty shit."

I clap my hands together while the excitement bubbles up inside me. "Okay, this I can do. I mean... I'm not qualified for any of this. I'm a social worker, but I *love* this kind of stuff. I'm happy to help wherever you need me."

"Okay, well, while Nash is working on dinner, shall we talk linens and décor?" Brianna asks.

This woman is so pretty, and she seems incredibly nice.

However, I can't help but wonder *why in the world she would be interested in Nash and all his broody bullshit.*

"God, yes. I am so in for all this. I *am* getting an invite to the event, aren't I, Nash?"

Nash smiles. "Of course."

"Can I bring a plus one?"

Oh shit, I didn't think that through. But maybe this is the way Bayou and I tell him.

Nash glares at me, but I stare him down, and he slumps his shoulders. "Fine."

"Thanks. Now, back to the important business at hand, the gala. I need all the details, and we'll plan this to perfection. Can't have my brother and his business looking like idiots, now can we?"

Nash grunts. "Thanks, Novah," he says sarcastically.

"You're so welcome," I reply. "Okay, Bri, let's get cracking while Nash cooks."

Brianna smiles at me. "Anyone ever tell you you're extremely likable?"

Smiling, I shrug. "You hear that, Nash? I'm likable."

Nash grumbles under his breath. "Debatable."

Smirking, I reach out, grabbing a pen. "Keep that up, smartass, and I won't help with your gala."

Nash rolls his eyes. "You're fucking amazing, Novah. There... that what you wanted to hear?"

Brianna chuckles as I shrug. "It's a start. Now, back into the kitchen, the gnocchi won't cook itself."

"Jesus Christ!"

Brianna giggles, and I turn to her and reach out for her hand. "You have to learn with Nash. You have to pick your battles. Sometimes you can win. Other times you can't."

Brianna dips her head. "Good to know."

"But enough about that asshole, let's talk about this gala because... fun." I state, and Brianna beams.

"Okay, so we have a theme..."

We discuss in depth all things gala, including the finer details, picking and choosing accessories, accents, and generally moving ahead in all aspects. All Brianna has to do now is clear the details with Nash and have him sign off before she starts prepping. But the thing is, spending this time with Brianna, I realize she is a take-no-shit kind of woman, and I can instantly see why Nash is attracted to her. She is definitely his type of woman and is perfect for him. And honestly, right now, I couldn't be happier if I tried to set him up with someone myself.

"Ladies, dinner is served," Nash calls out.

Brianna and I both look over at the table, set beautifully, as Nash starts pouring us each a glass of wine. *Bayou said not to drink—surely one glass won't hurt?*

Brianna raises her brow when we stand and walk over to the dining table. "I thought you were all about hard liquor? You're surprising me at all the stops tonight," she says.

Nash takes a seat. "I can drink wine when the celebration calls for it."

Sitting next to Brianna, she sits opposite Nash, and I inhale. "Big brother... this smells and looks *sooo good* as always," I say, picking up my fork.

"I still can't believe you hand-made the gnocchi." Brianna shakes her head with a chuckle.

"I'm very good with my hands, Little Bee."

My fork stops midair, my mouth wide open, staring at Nash. The sexual connotation of that comment and the fact he called her a nickname is not lost on me. Brianna clears her throat as Nash grins, knowing what he's just done.

Brianna shifts a little in her seat. "So Novah... tell me what it was like growing up with this guy?" She tactfully changes the subject.

Nash groans. "No one needs to hear about that."

I chuckle. "Oh yes, we do. I should tell her about how you used to dress up in Dad's suits when you were younger, pretending to be him. You were what... ten? The suits were *waaay* too big, and Dad would get so mad that you creased his expensive suits. But Mom, she knew you were simply trying to emulate him, so she bought a suit to fit you—"

"Novah, c'mon!" Nash grunts.

"You were always destined to be a businessman, to be high above us all in those steel towers overlooking the city." *I'm so proud of him and how far he has come.*

Brianna smiles. "I think it's sweet how you always knew your path, Nash. Not everyone is that fortunate. They go through life never really knowing what they want to do."

Taking a bite of my gnocchi, I nod. "Absolutely. I see it so much at work. But our Nash, he was always destined for great things. I could tell from the way he stood up when we were young."

"Novah," Nash warns.

Brianna furrows her brows. "What do you mean by the way he stood up?"

Nash sits taller, placing his napkin on the table like he's becoming frustrated. "We don't need to talk about thi—"

I ignore him.

"Our father is a real piece of work," I state, and Nash slumps back in his seat, folding his arms across his chest and letting out a loud, frustrated groan. "When I was ten and Nash was twelve, the asshole told our mother and us that he was leaving our family for another one he had on the side. He had other children with this woman, and she was pregnant with another one on the way. He chose them over us and left us to fend for ourselves." My stomach knots as I talk about it. The painful memory still hurts, but somehow I deal with it differently than Nash.

Brianna's eyes widen as they snap to Nash, but his are distant, and his face is scrunched like he's living the memory all over again. The pain is clear in his features. I can tell because the pain is real for me too. And if Brianna is going to be in his life, then she deserves to know the truth.

"Nash had to step up and be the man of the house... to look after Mom and me. He was so protective over us both—"

"Novah, that's enough. You don't need to say anymore." Nash sighs heavily, clearly uncomfortable now.

But I keep pushing because I want Brianna to know everything, to see Nash at his worst. After all, I like Brianna, and if she can handle him at his worst, then she is a keeper.

"Nash decided it was a good idea when he was old enough to work for our father at his company... I still can't figure out why the hell Nash would want anything to do with that asshole. The old man would never promote Nash because of the club affiliations."

Brianna widens her eyes at this information. "Club affiliations?"

Nash slams his fist on the table, making the wine glasses rattle and a fork fall to the tiled floor with a clang. Brianna jumps with shock as his face turns bright red in obvious anger. "Novah, enough! We don't need to air our damn dirty laundry."

Shit! Quietness falls over the room as Brianna subtly picks up her wine and takes a drink to stem the awkwardness flooding the room. Nash is seething, and even though I was pushing his buttons to make sure Brianna saw his demons, I never thought he would react like that. Maybe I pushed too far. I know Father is a sensitive subject for both of us, but I always thought Nash and me going through it together meant we were a team.

Maybe he is sick of me and my nonstop mouth.

Just like Bayou is trying to avoid me but in a different way.

Maybe I'm the problem here?

Maybe I'm too much for everyone to handle?

These thoughts hit me as the silence around the room is deafening.

I move to stand, breaking the tension. "I think I should go."

Brianna reaches out, grabbing my hand. "No, don't leave." Her head snaps around to Nash, gesturing for him to say something to stop me.

But he says nothing, just takes a long sip of his drink.

Yeah... I'm the common denominator here.

Dipping my chin in understanding, I gather my things while Brianna lets out a heavy exhale.

She stands, then pulls me into an embrace. "Thank you for your help tonight. It was so nice meeting you."

"Get Nash to give you my number. We can keep discussing the gala or anything else..." I turn to look at Nash. "Thanks for dinner. Love you," I say, then spin and walk for the elevator.

CHAPTER 17

NOVAH

Getting inside, I press the button.

The elevator descends, tears welling in my eyes as I finally feel like I've realized that the problem is me. I'm just not sure what it is about me that people find so annoying or uninviting.

The elevator opens, and I see my car. Bayou's lying back, his eyes shut as he chills behind the steering wheel, but I don't want to deal with that right now. So I walk straight past the car and keep walking.

It's not too far.

I'm sure I can make it without a fuss.

I need time to think.

I don't want to cry in front of Bayou.

Tears flood my eyes as soon as I think it, and I wrap my arms around myself for comfort. Then the sounds of running footsteps coming from behind me, and I turn to see Bayou jogging.

The guy doesn't miss a damn thing.

He grabs my arm. "What is going on? Where the hell do you think you're going?"

"I just need a second, Bayou. I know I'm not perfect. I know I'm this happy-go-lucky persona who always tries to be upbeat and positive, but I have feelings and emotions too, you know?"

He furrows his brows. "Okay, talk to me. You aren't feeling happy and upbeat right now?"

"*No*. I rarely ever do, Bayou. It's a fucking front. I feel miserable *all the damn time,* and I put on this act to try and make everyone else happy when inside, I feel like my entire life has been a fucking lie."

He jerks his head back. "Whoa, Novah… what are you talking about?"

I burst into tears, feeling the emotion now overwhelm me. "He left. He fucking left us for another family. We weren't good enough for him. I'm not fucking good enough for anyone. For Nash… for you. *You don't fucking want me either."* I'm screaming as my knees give out, and I fall to the ground, suddenly feeling so incredibly weak.

Bayou is by my side in an instant, and he scoops me into his arms. "Novah, I never knew you felt this way. I know your dad left, but it never seemed like it affected you. Nash, sure, but you never acted like it was an issue. And as for me not wanting you…" his hand comes up, caressing my cheek, "… I want you so fucking much it kills me. I want to do it right, Novah."

"It shouldn't hurt this much, Bayou."

His somber eyes look pained when he rests his forehead against mine. "Let me do it right. I don't want to fuck you on a whim. You mean far too much to me to treat you like shit. I know you're hurting, but don't think it's because you're not good enough…" He takes a deep breath and closes his eyes. "It's because you're too fucking good for me, and you deserve the world."

Clinging to him, I hold him to me, needing the comfort. "Nash is angry at me."

Bayou glances back at the elevator. "Why?"

"Because I brought up our father in front of Brianna. He slammed his fist on the table and yelled at me—"

"Fucker! I'll go slam my fist into his face for making you

upset like—"

I rest my hand on his chest and shake my head. "Just... please... take me home?"

Bayou places a tender kiss on my lips, and a spark ignites, sending a jolt straight to my clit. But I ignore it for now as he lifts me and heads back toward the car. He places me on the passenger side and does up my seat belt, then leans in, his lips gently kissing my forehead. Then he closes the door and walks to his driver's side.

He glances over at me as I peer down at my hands on my lap, and Bayou starts the car.

"Novah, you've been holding that in for a long time. I think you need to talk this out with someone who knows you better than anyone."

I furrow my brows. "What are you talking about?"

Bayou continues to drive, and he exhales. "I think you need to call your mom. Tell her what you've been feeling. About everything."

"I can't tell her about *everything*... that would mean talking about *you."*

The hesitation in his response makes me turn to face him, and I widen my eyes. "Bayou! What aren't you telling me?"

He exhales, his hand reaching out to rest on my thigh. "Ingrid knows..." he nods, "... about us."

"What! How?"

"I had a conversation with her when I was struggling with it all. Turns out she knew anyway."

My stomach churns, and I sink into my seat. "Holy shit!" My skin prickles in goose bumps. "What did she say?"

A slow smile crosses Bayou's lips. "Basically, she knew since we were young and said it was about time we realized it for ourselves."

"But is she okay with it?"

He glances at me with a smile, then turns back to the road.

"She's more than okay with it. She wants us to be happy."

A sense of excitement builds inside me. Bayou and I have been so concerned that everyone will be dead set against us being together that we never entertained the idea that anyone could be happy for us.

I'm not even sure how to process this.

I turn to Bayou and shake my head. "Mom's *really* okay with us?"

He chuckles, his fingers clench my thigh. "Yeah, beautiful, she is."

"Okay, I'm gonna call her now." Pulling out my cell, I make the call.

She answers on the second ring. "Hi, darling."

"Mom," it comes out like a whimper.

"Oh, Novah, what's wrong?"

My eyes shift to Bayou for that added encouragement I need, and he smiles at me.

So fucking gorgeous.

Exactly what I needed.

"I just had dinner with Nash and Brianna."

"Who's Brianna?" Mom asks.

"I am pretty sure she is Nash's new love interest. She's great, but Nash and I had a falling out. I think Nash is upset with me—"

"Fuck Nash! The asshole yelled at Novah," Bayou snaps out so Mom can hear.

Mom chuckles down the line. "I see Bayou is there with you?"

Taking in a deep breath, I try to relax my tight muscles. "It's okay, Mom. He told me that he told you."

Mom lets out a long exhale. "Oh, thank the Lord. It's been killing me not to talk to you about it. Are you happy, honey?"

I glance over to Bayou, who can't hear what Mom just asked, and I weakly smile. "There are things we need to work on, but for the most part, we're doing really good."

Mom sighs contentedly. "That is all I could ask for."

"Mom..."

"Yes, darling?"

"I kind of had a little breakdown about Dad."

"Mmm... you've been fighting your emotions on that for so long, Novah. When your father left, you were beside yourself. He was your hero, and he broke your tiny heart when he did what he did. It's okay to feel hurt by his actions. Lord knows Nash was hurt... I was hurt. What your father did was horrible, and the day he left, Novah, you clung to his legs, begging him not to go. That's not something a ten-year-old forgets. It's why you got into social work, darling, so you can help others with tragic stories. You want to be able to help those who need saving from a situation that seems unfixable..."

She lets out a long exhale. "You like putting this positive image out there trying to make everything shiny and peachy to make people think the world is an okay place, but Novah, the world can be *shit*. People are *shit*. And sometimes, you have to have a day where you grab your pillow and scream into it because nothing is going right.

"You can't put up that façade you always do and expect it not to crack every now and then. Just like Nash puts up his hardass businessman façade, yours is the exact opposite...

"Darling, you both had the same trauma but dealt with it very differently. Nash had the added problem of feeling like he had to step up and be the man and take care of you and me when your father left us. I think that's why he went the other way. But honestly, it could have been touch and go for the both of you."

She always has this way of making everything seem so much lighter, so much clearer. "I don't know why we haven't had this chat sooner. Thanks, Mom, for putting it all into perspective for me. I think talking this out is helping."

"I am always here for you, darling... you and Bayou, and Nash, and, of course, Hurricane too. I love you all equally. And just because I look at Bayou as my son doesn't mean that I find it weird that you and he are together. You're not related in any way, and like I've said, I've seen the connection between the two of you since you were about sixteen, Novah. This *isn't* a surprise to me."

"Thanks, Mom, thank you for understanding."

Bayou pulls into my garage, and I let out the weight I've been holding. "Thank you, Mom, love you."

"I love you, Novah Lee. I am here any time you need to talk. Any time. Tell Bayou I love him as well."

I grin and turn to face him. "Mom says she loves you."

Bayou smiles. "Love you, Ingrid," he replies.

"We just pulled in, Mom. You really are the best."

"I'll talk to you soon." She ends the call.

Bayou jumps out and walks around, opening my car door. Smiling, I take his hand as he pulls me to him and wraps his arms around me. "I just want to say how proud of you I am."

I snort. "What on earth for?"

"For facing your demons, for realizing you've been pushing them down. I'm glad I'm here to help you through them tonight."

"I'm glad you're here too." We walk inside my home, and I make my way to my bedroom to get changed when my cell rings. I glance down—Nash's name is flashing. I've had so much drama already tonight I'm not sure if I can handle anymore. So I pause, just staring at his name. But then guilt hits me, so I decide to answer.

Groaning, I swipe the call. "Hey," my tone is deflated, not filled with the usual spark that lights up the room.

"I'm a dickhead," he tells me.

A giggle leaves my lips, instantly feeling like a weight has been lifted from my shoulders. "You have and always *will be* a dickhead, that's never in question, but I will take that as your apology and run with it. I'm sorry too. I pushed too hard. It's only because I want to see you happy. You always seem so lonely."

"Being alone doesn't mean I'm lonely, Novah. I have a great bunch of friends. I have Lucas."

I laugh down the line at his allegiance to his best friend. "Lucas is a playboy. You do *not* need to be taking your cues from him."

"And why are you so invested in my love life? You don't see me forcing men down your throat."

Snorting, I glance over at Bayou, who is watching me intently. "Do you see me dating at all, Nash? I have you, Hurricane, and Bayou to deal with. Three older brothers. One... billion-dollar CEO. The other two... outlaw bikers. Do you think *any* man is going to get anywhere near me?"

Bayou smirks, folding his arms across his chest as he leans on the doorframe.

So fucking sexy.

"You're right. You can devote your life to Jesus. He's the only man for you."

Rolling my eyes, I groan. "See."

Nash laughs at my reply. "I shouldn't have let you leave tonight. I was angry, and maybe my ego was a little dented in front of Brianna. You're my sister, and I love you. I should treat you better than that."

"I overstepped... but I do think you and Bri are holding back. I know what I saw when I walked in on you two. I wish I hadn't interrupted."

Nash lets out a groan. "I don't know what that was, Nov—"

"So it *was* something?"

"It doesn't matter... Brianna is angry at me now too."

I grumble. "What the hell did you do?"

"Just gave her some home truths about Blake Branson."

Nash's arch enemy?

The guy who stole his clients?

The man who still works for our father, the father who walked out on us?

"What? Why does she give a shit about Blake Branson?"

Nash lets out a long, tired breath. "They grew up together. Apparently, they're best friends."

"Oh, for crying out loud, Nash. You hired the best friend of your enemy?"

"In my defense, I didn't know that at the time."

Rolling my shoulders, unease washes over me. "Hmmm… this complicates things."

"You're telling me," Nash mumbles.

I'm quiet for a moment, then I huff. "Well, she's too amazing to let Blake get in the way, Nash. He's taken up far too much of your life as it is. Don't let him win at *everything."*

Nash is quiet for a moment, almost like he's thinking something through, when suddenly he chimes, "Novah, you're a genius."

I giggle. "I know. You just tell me if you need any help with getting Bri to fall for you, and I… am… in."

"Thanks, sis. I don't deserve you."

"No… you don't. But I will always be here for you anyway. Now send me Brianna's phone number and I will message her about the gala and see if she says anything about you."

"No, Novah, we're not in damn high school."

I giggle. "Okay, but really… send me her number. I told her you were gonna send her my number so it's not crazy to think you would send her number to me instead."

"What the fuck for? I don't need you running interference for me."

I snort. "Not everything is about you. I need to talk to her about the gala, I have ideas."

"Mm-hmm… fine. I'll text it to you."

Nash is clearly hung up on Brianna, but I'm not going to meddle in his love life. I already tried that once tonight, and look what happened. All I am going to do is keep up the work with Brianna on the gala. But I like Brianna, and if she happens to fall for my brother in the meantime, then that's an added bonus. "It's going to all work out, Nash. The gala. Your company. Even down to whatever is meant to happen or not happen with Bri. Everything happens for a reason."

"That's very insightful of you."

"I have to be optimistic in my line of work. With the shit I see every day, Nash, your current situation is a walk in the park."

"I'm hearing you. I don't say this enough, Novah, but you're an amazing woman."

I widen my eyes. It's like he knew I was having doubts about myself and even our relationship tonight. Like he knew how much I needed to hear those words from him. Letting out a sigh, my eyes glisten with unshed tears, and I blink quickly to stop them from falling. "Thanks, Nash."

"Okay, love you, but I have to go. My apartment is a pigsty."

I chuckle under my breath. "Don't you hate it when dinner guests leave without helping to clean up?"

"Yeah, bastards."

I can't help but let out a contented laugh. "Send me her number."

"I'm hanging up now."

"Make sure you message her—"

"Goodbye, Novah."

"And don't forget to—"

He ends the call before I can tell him to freeze the leftovers of the dessert for me. But as Bayou chuckles, standing back, I glance up at him. "What?"

He smiles. "You're so fucking sexy when you're excited."

Rolling my eyes, I open my texting app and pull out Nash's number because the guy hasn't done what he is told and needs a nudge.

Me: *Number?*

I don't have to wait long before he sends Brianna's contact information, and I smile, knowing I have won that round with Nash. I walk over, plugging my cell into the charger as Bayou steps up to me. "You settle things with Nash?"

Nodding, I wrap my arms around Bayou, finally feeling like maybe the crazy of this night is starting to calm. "I don't want to think about Nash right now."

Bayou smirks. "Oh yeah? What do you have in mind?" His fingers trail down my hips, slowly hoisting my dress up and over my head.

Giggling, I step closer to him, planting my lips on his. That tingle spreads all the way down my spine, and my entire body comes alive. I don't know how Bayou has this effect on me, but I freaking love it. My tongue dances with his, the kiss becoming deeper, more heated. He lifts me, throwing me back on the bed. I smirk as he slides in, reaching for my panties to start pulling them down. "I'm gonna make you feel so damn good, beautiful."

I reach out, halting his movements. His eyes widen, looking at me in curiosity as I shift up, standing from the bed in front of him. He stares at me like he thinks I am about to reject him, but it is far from the truth. My fingers trail down his chest, and I move to his belt, making a move to undo it. "How about... I finally make *you* feel good?" I suggest, even though my fingers are trembling as I try to undo his belt.

Bayou narrows his eyes on me.

When I finally undo the leather, then slide down his zipper, his eyes don't leave me for a single second. "Have you done this before?" he asks, his voice gruff and husky.

Biting my bottom lip, I shake my head as I drop his jeans around his ankles, freeing his already huge and erect cock.

He groans like I couldn't have replied with anything better. He grips his cock in his hand and tugs. The sight making me tingle. "Fuck, Novah... are you sure?"

I drop to my knees in front of him, a smirk crossing my face as I take a deep breath. "Just remember, I've never done this before. So if it's bad, or if I suck at it—"

"You don't have to do this. In fact, let me—"

I grip his balls in my hand, not waiting for him to try and

convince me to let him take charge. Instead, I want to show him that I can do this. He hisses through his teeth, and I line my mouth up with his cock. "I shield my teeth, right?" I ask, and he shrugs.

"You wanna use teeth, baby, you use teeth." He grins.

I smile, licking my lips while I continue to massage his balls. His fingers slide into my hair, but he's not gripping tightly. Though I wish he would as I lean in, slowly edging his thick length toward my mouth. I dart my tongue out, not having a plan but just going with what feels right. I reach out with my free hand and grip his shaft, tugging a little while my tongue licks up the tip of his cock.

He inhales sharply, letting out a feral growl. "Fuck, Novah, don't tease me."

Smirking, I tug on his cock a little more. At the same time, I slide my lips over the edge of his head. He's so thick it's a little unexpected at how tight the squeeze is in my mouth. His fingers tighten in my hair a little, letting me know he's enjoying it. Saliva leaks out the side of my mouth, and I widen my eyes, wondering if that's normal.

Am I doing this right?

Then he groans, thrusting his hips a little more into my mouth, his cock hitting the back of my throat, making me gag a little. He stops instantly, his head snapping down to look at me. "Fuck, sorry." He pants, stopping all movement, trying to calm himself down.

But that is the exact opposite of what I want.

I want him to let go.

I want him to be wild and free.

So I push further, edging the tip of his cock down my throat, relaxing my muscles, and letting the tip slide down as deep as I can.

"Fuck, fuck, fuck!"

I massage his balls and send his cock down the back of my throat again. His fingers in my hair tighten, but I can tell he is still trying to hold himself back.

"Dammit, Novah! I'm trying to be good here."

I pull back, popping his dick out of my mouth. His body jerks with the force as I look up at him through my lashes. "Well, don't be. Don't treat me fragile, Bayou. I'm not going to break."

I see it, the second the hunger and desire take over in his mind. His eyes darken, and his fingers grip my hair, yanking my head back with force, making me stare up at him. "My cock is the only one those lips are going to touch… to suck. Period."

I smirk and nod my head. "Yes."

He inhales sharply through his nose. "Good girl. Now hold on because this is going to get rough."

His fingers hold my hair so tight, I let out a small whimper, but it's okay. I like the pain as he slams his cock into my mouth.

"Your mouth is so fucking tight. Use your teeth, Novah."

My eyes bug out of my face as I move my hands to his ass, needing something to hold onto. He wants teeth, I'll give him teeth. I unsheathe them, so they graze along his cock. Spit and slobber slide out the sides of my lips as he thrusts in and out of my mouth so rapidly my eyes begin to water, not from fear or sadness, but from friction. The slurping sounds, teamed with the saliva, is making this whole thing messier than I thought it would be. But it's only adding to the excitement and adrenaline. My clit is throbbing as Bayou hisses with the pleasure rolling through him. "Fuck, just like that."

We're both moving so fast I can hardly keep up. He is fucking my face, grunting animalistically, his cock slamming into the back of my throat. And with every thrust, my clit throbs, and an unbearable ache forms between my legs as my panties become soaked.

I didn't know sex—this kind of sex—could be this powerful or erotic.

He slams into me, my teeth running up and down his cock. My fingers squeeze into his ass cheeks while his grip in my hair is so tight my scalp has pins and needles.

"Fuck, Novah, I'm gonna—"

Then before I have a second to prepare, hot salty liquid bursts into the back of my throat. My eyes widen as he pants for breath and slowly looks down at me. My glistening eyes glance up at him when he withdraws his cock from my mouth. He leans over to grab some tissues, but I reach for his hand, making him look back at me.

His eyes meet mine, and I swallow, making sure he knows exactly what I am doing. A slow smile creeps up his face when he lets out a small laugh moving back to me. His finger wipes the excess drool from my chin. "So fucking beautiful." I smirk as he moves his hands under my arms and hoists me up off the floor. "Was I too rough?"

I loop my arms around his neck and let out a soft sigh. "Just fucking perfect."

"You sure you haven't done that before? It was *real* fucking good."

Laughing, I pull away from him and grab his hand. "No, but I am glad you liked it because I loved doing it."

He waggles his brows before I lead him to the bed. "Lucky me... now let me repay the favor. Get on your back and spread your legs."

BAYOU
The Next Day (Saturday)

Waking up wrapped up in Novah is the only way to wake.

Running my nose along the back of her neck, I inhale deeply as I place featherlight kisses along her skin while I spoon her from behind. She lets out a small moan in satisfaction as my cock begins to harden against her ass. She grinds back against me, so I slide my hand across to caress her breast. "Good morning, beautiful."

She brings her hand up, sliding her fingers into my hair, keeping my lips pressed to her neck. "I want to wake up like this every damn day."

Sliding my hand south, I move between her legs. "Pretty sure I can make it an even better morning for you," I say, then press on her clit.

She moans, rocking against my hand. "God, yes," she murmurs as my cell starts ringing.

"Ignore it. Just come for me, baby."

She whimpers, panting for breath as the phone rings out. "I'm so close."

"Good girl. Fuck my han—"

Suddenly, Novah's cell starts ringing. Her head snaps up, her movements stopping as we both look at the phone on the bedside table.

She pants for breath.

I groan. "Fuck!"

She pulls my hand from her, clearing her throat. "It must be urgent. We should get it." And she reaches for the cell before I have a second to stop her. "Hello?"

She sounds breathless and raspy.

I roll on my back, my cock hard as anything while I try to calm my racing heart.

"Oh, hey, yeah, he's here."

My eyes widen as I turn to look at her. "No, I just ran from the bathroom to grab my cell, that's all. I really need to do more cardio."

Rubbing my temple, I grit my teeth as she sinks back into the bed.

"Well, I was out at Nash's for dinner last night, and Bayou drove me there to keep an eye on me. It was late when we got back, so I told him to crash."

She widens her eyes like Hurricane is saying something amusing.

"Mm-hmm, I'll tell him to answer his *damn phone*." She smirks.

Hurricane interrupted us, and he stopped Novah from reaching her peak.

Well, I'm not going to let him keep that high from her anymore. So I move in, planting a kiss on her shoulder. She tenses as my hand slides down between her legs, but she squeezes them together, her eyes bulging wide in shock while she continues to talk, "No, everything is all good here. There's been no trouble."

I move in, pressing on her clit again, and she clenches her eyes shut, biting down on her bottom lip. "Mm-hmm."

She's so slick against my finger, so I circle faster, her legs part giving me full access.

"Good girl," I whisper in her ear. Her breath catches at the praise, a small whimper escaping her lips. Smiling, I circle faster, my teeth grazing against her neck as her hips begin to ride my finger.

"Yes, *I'm listening,*" she murmurs a little more forcefully than needed. Her fingers fist in the bedsheets, her head arching back in the throes of pleasure.

My cock is so fucking hard.

Novah tries to control her breathing. "I'll tell him."

"You're so fucking sexy like this, Novah. The things I want to do to you," I whisper in her ear.

Her hand slaps to cover her mouth as her entire body quivers. I circle on her clit faster, her body writhing with the climax rampaging through her. She drops the cell from her fingers. It lands on the mattress as she lets out a loud exhale, still trying to keep quiet, but a small whimper escapes her as she collapses against me. I race to pick up the cell and put it to my ear.

"Novah? Novah. Fuck! What's wrong," Hurricane blasts down the line.

I let out a mock laugh. "Sorry, brother, Novah just went down like a ton of bricks. She walked into the wall and stubbed her toe."

"Where the hell have you been? I need you back here. We've had word from the Baroness."

Novah is still coming down as I run my hands all over her helping her to descend from her high.

"Shit, okay. Sorry, brother, but when a man's gotta use the bathroom, you can't just stop mid-flow."

"Right. Help Novah with her toe, then get your ass in here."

"Will do. Be there as soon as I can."

Hurricane ends the call, and I throw the cell to the bed and turn to glance down at Novah, who is grinning from ear to ear.

"You're so fucking evil," she whispers.

Laughing, I press a tender kiss to her forehead. "You almost made it through the entire call too."

"Yeah, darn you and your magic fingers."

I laugh, leaning in to kiss her. "You think my fingers are magic? Wait until you feel what my cock can do."

She waggles her brows. "What better time than the present?"

My hand slides up, caressing her cheek. "Soon, beautiful... soon." I lean in, kissing her, then pull back with a low groan. "Okay, I better go before Hurricane becomes even more suspicious than he already is."

I move to get up, but she reaches out, grabbing my wrist to stop me. "Hey, there's something I want to ask you."

I sit back down and raise a brow. "Okay, shoot?"

She inhales. "So Nash is having this black-tie gala event for his work. I'm helping plan it with Brianna, the woman Nash is dating, even if he thinks he isn't dating her."

I smirk. "Okay, I'm following. Continue..."

"So anyway, Nash said I can go to this gala. The theme is black and gold, and I need a plus one."

My eyebrow raises as I look at her. "Is this your way of asking me to go to the gala with you, Novah?"

"Well... I mean, yeah."

"And it's black tie, so I have to wear a tux?" I curl up my lip.

"It's black and gold, so you'll need to wear gold on you somewhere."

Scrunching up my face, I groan. "Jesus, Novah."

She exhales. "Think of it this way... I'll be dressed up real nice, and... you'll be my... date."

A slow smile crosses my lips. "Are you asking me out on a date?"

She shoves my shoulder. "Don't make it weird."

A huge smile crosses my lips. "If you wanna go on a date, beautiful, you could have taken me to Whataburger. But you're going all fancy with a black and gold gal—"

"Shut up. Are you coming with me or not?"

I hesitate, narrowing my eyes on her. "You're gonna be wearing a sexy dress?"

She smiles, nodding her head.

"Do I have to dance with you?" I ask.

She nods her head again.

"Will there be food?"

She giggles. "There will be food."

"Free alcohol?"

She nods again.

Exhaling, I see desperation in her eyes, and I crane my neck to the side.

Fuck.

She really wants this.

"When is it?" I ask.

"Not this Friday but next."

An idea starts forming in my mind, and I nod. "Okay. I'll go to this gala with you. We'll tell Hurricane I'm going with you as your protection detail."

She rushes forward, embracing me tightly. "Thank you. We're going to have the best time."

"I'm going to be wearing a fucking penguin suit. Doubt I'm gonna be feeling that. I'll be out of my depth, but I will do it… *for you."*

"Thank you. This means a lot to me."

"You mean a lot to me, Novah. I only want to make you happy."

She kisses me again and then slaps me on the shoulder. "You better get dressed. Hurricane is so demanding."

Laughing, I nod because she's so right.

I get up and dressed. Then after spending way too long kissing Novah goodbye, I leave for the clubhouse feeling like I have an idea brewing in my mind. I want to make everything perfect for Novah. So when I arrive back at the clubhouse, I go in search of Grit. The one person I can talk to about all this, and I find him sitting outside lifting weights. I move in behind him and stand ready to spot him—the weight he's about to lift is far too much for him, especially with his collarbone still on the mend.

Grit breathes harshly out his nose as I stand with my hands out under the bar. He lifts the weight off the holder and brings it down to his chest, his face red. Instantly, I know he isn't going to make it as he starts pushing it back up, his arms shaking, and I rush in, grabbing the bar and helping it to the rack.

Grit lets out a grunt in frustration. "I had it, brother." He groans, and I let out a chuckle.

"You would have had a broken neck if I didn't come out here. So what the hell are you trying to prove?"

Grit groans again, sitting up from the bench and wipes the sweat from his face, throwing a towel over his shoulder. His head falls like he has a lot on his mind. "I feel like I always have to compete."

I furrow my brows in confusion. "With us? You kicked ass, got your patch because you stood out above the rest of us. You're not competing, you asshole. You're outshining us."

He shrugs. "Nah, I don't mean with you guys. You're all like family. I feel more at home here than I ever have with my real family."

I walk around, sitting next to him on the bench press. "You having family drama?"

He rubs the back of his neck with the towel. "Dad's being a dick, making me feel inadequate."

"You're giving him that power, Grit. You fucking threw a bomb to save us. You are *not* inadequate. What the fuck is he telling you?"

"He wants me to leave the club, especially considering I got injured. He thinks it's too dangerous. He wants me to get a real job. Be successful in a career of his choosing. All that bullshit I can't stand."

"Well, he doesn't have any say in what you do. It's your life. You live it, however the fuck you want."

He dips his chin, exhales, then he turns to me. "Was there something you want to talk to me about? I mean, you didn't come out here to hear my bullshit sap story."

"It doesn't matter. You got shit on your mind. You don't need mine adding to it."

He scowls. "Bayou, c'mon… you helped me. Let me help you if I can. What are brothers for, right? Is it about Novah?"

Glancing around to see if anyone's nearby, my stomach twists. Talking about this shit here is always a risk, but I need to talk to someone, and Grit is the only brother who knows about Novah and me.

So here goes nothing.

"Okay, Nash invited Novah to some fancy fucking gala. It's formal as shit, and she is excited about going. She's even helping plan some of it. So she asked me to go with her as her plus one."

Grit smiles wide, his smirk mischievous as he chuckles to himself. "You gonna have to wear a suit?"

I let out a long puff of frustrated air. "It's black and gold themed, so not only a suit but one with fucking gold on it."

He laughs but then quickly restrains himself. "Okay, sorry. Continue..."

"This night means something to Novah, so I want to make it special for her." I raise my brow, and he widens his eyes.

"How special are we talking here, Bayou?"

I tilt my head. "First time, kinda special."

He smiles wide, nudging my shoulder. "Fuck, man, this is big. You think she's ready for that?"

"Yeah… she's ready. But the whole reason I have been waiting is because I want to make her first time perfect for her. I want it to be special. I want her to feel cherished and adored. I don't want her to just feel like it's something that happens, and then it's over."

Grit widens his eyes and huffs. "Holy shit… you really have fallen hard."

That hits me right in the chest as I roll my shoulders from the tension in my muscles. "Can you help me?"

"I have some ideas. Okay, first, you need to…" Grit and I get lost talking about how to make the night perfect for Novah. We discuss back and forth exactly what I am going to do, and how the night will go to ensure she has the best experience.

Grit had a long-term relationship with his ex, Maddie. They were each other's firsts, so when it came time for them to take that next step, he planned a big evening for her too. Without even knowing it, Grit was the perfect person to come to for help with this shit. I've never had to plan something like this before, never caring enough to bother. So having someone on my side who could help me with the finer details of making this special for Novah was so helpful.

I'm not going to go over the top, but enough for her to know what she means to me.

"I mean, the hardest part is the self-control. Trying to calm yourself down to remember that Novah's gonna need you to go slow the first time. Especially when you're used to just taking control and letting loose."

Suddenly, Hurricane steps into the gym. "Fucker, where you been? I told you to come see me when you got here," he snaps as he steps up to me.

My heart leaps into my throat, and my breathing quickens at almost being caught talking about having sex with Novah for the first time.

But Grit pipes up breaking my panic, "Sorry, my fault. I distracted him with meaningless talk about my family," Grit covers my ass for me, and I thank him subtly with my eyes.

"Talk later. We got shit to discuss." Hurricane grunts, walking back inside, and I turn to Grit and dip my head at him. He knows I can't say anything, but he understands my thank you. Then I turn to follow my twin into the Chapel where City and the others are waiting.

My eyes widen as I jerk back a little.

I didn't realize they were all in here waiting for me.

Taking my seat at the table, Hurricane glares at me like he's pissed as he sits back in his chair. "So, the Baroness is coming to New Orleans to talk shit over. She should be arriving in a few days."

"What does this mean? Can she help with the Novikovs?" I ask.

"Don't know. She wouldn't discuss shit over the phone. We just have to wait."

I let out an obnoxiously loud scoff. "And in the meantime, Novah could be in danger."

Hurricane glares at me with his brows drawn like I'm saying something incredulous. "And Kaia and Izzy and Lani. *The fuck,* Bayou?"

Widening my eyes at how obvious I just sounded, I backtrack. "Of course, I fucking meant all of them."

Goddammit! I need to be more careful.

"We need to find a way to protect all the women of the club until we can handle the threat ourselves. Bayou, if that means you stayin' out with Novah more frequently, then do it."

I didn't see that coming.

"Okay, I can do that."

"We all need to be alert but not alarmed. They tried to attack, it failed. We're gonna go after them, but we need more information first. The Baroness is gonna help us with that. In the meantime, we keep our eyes peeled and be on the lookout. Now get the fuck out."

Everyone stands from the table.

Hurricane's obviously in a pissed-off mood as we all stand. "Bayou, you stay right where you fuckin' are."

Shit, here we go.

Everyone leaves the Chapel, Raid shutting the door as he exits, and I sit back down.

Hurricane glares at me. "What is happening with Novah?"

My stomach churns as I feel the color drain from my face.

This is it.

The moment he officially kills me.

"What do you mean?" I play stupid.

"Is she coping with what is goin' on? You're the one who's with her all the time. I need to know if she's okay out there or if I need to bring her back in."

Slumping my shoulders, I let out a long breath I didn't know I was holding. "She's doing okay, still going to work. She had a full-on disagreement with Nash last night, so she was rattled by that... but they figured it out."

"Do we need to go and pay Nash a visit?" Hurricane asks.

I smirk. "I said the same thing, but Novah assures me they're all good. But I am glad I was there to help her when she was that upset. It brought back up the memories of her father. She felt like she wasn't good enough... for everyone."

"Jesus! That man's an asshole for makin' her feel that way. I have a mind to go see him anyway."

"I got her to call Ingrid, and they talked it out. It's all good. Trust me. Everyone is fine now."

Hurricane growls under his breath. "Novah's too pure and innocent. No one is fuckin' hurtin' her on our watch."

Rubbing at my beard, I dip my chin. "You got that right."

"Okay, stay with her, guard her, and report back to me when you can. Keep in touch."

"Got it. I'll pack a bag. It'll be easier than riding back and forth."

"Good idea."

I'm going to be staying with Novah for the foreseeable future.

Now, I just have to keep my hands off her so I can bring my plan to fruition.

NOVAH
The Gala Night

My best friend, Xanthe, is helping me get dressed in my bedroom while Bayou is in the living room getting ready for the gala tonight. I picked out his tux, seeing as he had no idea what to get or how anything worked. Although, I have to admit I am looking forward to seeing him in it.

Xanthe plays with my hair, putting it up loosely off my shoulders to give the bodice of my A-line gown the full effect. The straps and the V-neck corseted area are all gold lace with black silk behind it. Then the floor-length black chiffon skirt flows out so gracefully, giving the whole outfit an almost Disney vibe as I walk.

Xanthe smiles as I stare in the mirror. "You look gorgeous, Novah. I'm so happy you are finally putting yourself out there with Bayou."

"I wish we would go further. I feel so ready, you know? I've waited twenty-seven years to be with him. I'm good to go."

Xanthe snorts out a laugh. "You horn dog, but there's more at play here than just your virginity. Babe, you guys have history. You have a future. You're, for want of a better word, family, so it's not like once you have sex, you can simply walk away from each other if shit doesn't work out. These are all the options he's got to be weighing up, you know?"

I sink in on myself. I was so caught up in being with Bayou that I didn't think about what would happen if this didn't work out. I understand his reluctance now. "Thanks for that insight. I think I needed to hear it."

"You're welcome, babe. But now you're ready, glowing, and perfect. We need to show you off to your man out there. You good to go?"

Taking one last look in the mirror, I nod. "Let's do this."

Xanthe opens my bedroom door and walks down the hall toward the living room. "Here comes the most beautiful woman you've ever seen," Xanthe calls out.

"Hardly," I reply as I step into the living room.

Bayou is standing in the middle of the room wearing a black-on-black tux, and his lapels are gold silk. He looks so fucking different that it knocks the wind from my lungs. I've only seen him in leather and denim, and it is crazy to think he can look this good in a tux. I am in awe as I stare at him, but he is staring at me too. All the while, Xanthe stands back, watching the two of us lost in each other's gaze.

"You both look amazing." Xanthe breaks the silence.

I step up to Bayou, his eyes wandering up and down me. "You are... *breathtaking."*

I can't help the blush moving up my neck and face.

The first thing I notice is the tie that he's massacred. So I undo it and retie it for him, his hands moving to my hips, obviously needing to touch me.

Xanthe pulls out her cell and starts taking pictures.

Bayou normally hates having his picture taken, especially while he is wearing this shit, but he's making an exception because this kind of memory is priceless.

"There, much better," I state, and he glances down at the tie.

"Perfect... shall we get going? Wouldn't want to be late. Nash would throw a hissy fit."

I smirk, placing my hand on his chest. "Be nice. But yes, let's go."

Xanthe hands me a sparkly black clutch. "You really look amazing, Novah," she states, leaning in and embracing me. "Now have the best night. Enjoy yourself, and don't do anything I wouldn't do."

Chuckling, I loop my arm with Bayou's as I finish my goodbyes to Xanthe, and we walk out to my car. Bayou opens the door for me, and I slide in, then he walks around to the driver's side and climbs in.

We pull out of the drive to a waving Xanthe and are on our way.

"She did a great job helping you get dressed tonight," Bayou states as we drive.

"She's amazing. I don't see enough of her."

Bayou smirks like something brewing in the back of his mind, but he turns on the radio and keeps driving. "You looking forward to tonight?" he asks, then plays with his tie. There is no doubt he's completely uncomfortable wearing it, but I know he's doing it for me.

"So much. It's going to be nice seeing all the work Brianna and I have put in bringing this gala together."

"I bet the place looks spectacular, knowing you."

I snort. "Brianna did most of the work. I just gave suggestions where I could."

Not long after, we pull into Ophelia Gardens and park around the back. Bayou's eyes wander over me up and down, and he shakes his head. "You are going to be the most beautiful woman in the entire room."

I shake the compliment off as he fiddles with his tie again. I smirk, knowing he is uncomfortable. "Thank you for coming. I know you don't like wearing this..." I wave my hand at his tux, "... but I want you to know you look so fucking good."

"Don't get used to me wearing this shit." He grunts.

"Noted." I can't help but chuckle at his crass tone.

Walking inside the ballroom, the gala is already in full swing. Bayou tenses beside me—he's on high alert as I watch his eyes dart around checking for any threats, but I ignore all that, soaking everything in, completely in my element.

The music, the lighting, the black and gold decorations, and the general ambiance is so thrilling that I can't help but feel the magic in the air.

Bayou places his hand on my lower back, making me feel secure and safe as we walk through the masses of people dressed elegantly in black and gold.

Honestly, it's like something from a fairytale in here.

I spot Nash standing with his COO, Lucas, at the other end of the ballroom. Nash has gone all out, it's so freaking beautiful, and Brianna has done a wonderful job of pulling this all together.

Bayou and I step over to Nash, with Bayou pulling at his collar constantly.

Nash and I both smirk. "Holy shit! I never thought I would see you at one of these things," Nash states.

Bayou glares at me. "Me neither. I still don't know how she managed to convince me to come. It's all kind of a blur."

I laugh as Nash dips his chin. "She has a way of ambushing you. Before you know it, you've bought her a puppy and convinced your parents that it was a stray and that if we took it to the pound they would put it down so we simply *had* to keep it."

Bayou turns his head to me as I grin. "That sounds too oddly specific to be hypothetical," Bayou declares.

"And to this day, I swear that Rupert was the best dog I ever had." I giggle.

Nash smirks.

Bayou shakes his head. "Why does this *not* surprise me?"

"Honestly, we just have to hold on for the ride when it comes to Novah at this point," Nash mocks.

Bayou rolls his shoulders while looking at me. "I still can't believe I let you drag me to this damn thing."

Leaning over, I straighten out his tie. "Oh, stop. You're going to have a great time."

"Yeah, like a hole in the head great time."

I grin, turning back to Nash. "You see Brianna?"

He shakes his head. "Not yet."

"I heard you guys were on shaky ground."

Lucas snorts, trying to hold in his laugh, and Nash turns to glare at him. "Oh, what?" Lucas snaps. "You guys are so focused on trying not to tear each other's clothes off that it's embarrassing. Just bone, get it over with, and then you'll be able to think more clearly around each other."

"It's not that simple. There are extenuating circumstance—"

"Fuck Blake and the Porsche he rode in on. If you two are into each other, then go for it," Lucas interrupts Nash.

"That's what I keep saying," I agree.

Lucas turns to me, his eyes wandering me up and down in a clearly sexual way. "Not just a pretty face."

"*No.*" Bayou and Nash both grunt toward Lucas.

He raises his hands in surrender as he backs up. "Okay, okay... I mean, Novah can make her own mind up. But—"

"Go near her, and I will cut your balls off with a toothpick and feed them to my pet alligator. It will be slow... very slow, and very painful," Bayou growls out.

Rolling my eyes at Bayou, I need to keep up the pretense. "And people wonder why I don't date anyone? This... *this* is why." I take off toward the bar, hoping Bayou will follow me. I don't want Bayou to get in a fight with Lucas over me because Nash will get suspicious, and right now, I don't want Nash finding out about us.

I take a seat on a barstool when I arrive, and Bayou quickly slides in beside me. "I went too far," he murmurs, making me turn to him.

I raise my brow. "You think? Cutting off his balls with a

toothpick and feeding them to La Fin? No, of course, that's not too far, Bayou. That's something any normal person would do."

He scowls. "You're mad at me for defending you when some stuck-up suit was trying to hit on you?"

"I'm mad because I could have handled it, and you didn't trust me to do it."

He raises his hand, tugging at his tie again with his other hand. "Okay… I'm just trying to find the right balance here, Novah. I want to be the right guy for you. But it's hard to be your guy when we're so secretive about it."

I exhale. "I know… we need to tell Nash and Hurricane."

His eyes light up, and he nods. "We'll do it together. Maybe have a family dinner. Tell them together. Rip off the Band-Aid all at once?"

"If we have Mom there to back us up, it might help," I tell him.

He nods. "I agree. We can do this."

I reach out, gripping his hand, then glance out to see where Nash is to make sure he's not watching. "Let's just enjoy the evening."

He groans, still messing with his tie—it's obviously annoying him. "I can't make any promises. These people are creeping me out."

Smirking, I try to hold in my laugh. "Because they're wealthy?"

"Because they're so fucking uppity. I knew Nash was different, but I didn't realize how upper crust he is."

"These people aren't that different to us. They just don't swear as much."

Bayou curls up his lip. "Fuck that."

I laugh, taking his hand and leading him toward the dance floor. "Then let's show them how bikers have fun, hey?"

He groans but walks with me to the floor and pulls me to him. We slow dance together for hours, spending the night together, enjoying each other's company. We eat our ridiculously pompous meal—though it was delicious—and watch the fundraising events and speeches. All the while, Bayou is quietly mocking everything under his breath. I giggle as Bayou's hand slides up under the table on my thigh. Not enough to be problematic, but enough to let me know what he is thinking and wanting.

Nash is in a whole other world than the one Bayou and I live in. It's not bad by any means, just so different to us. And as I watch him and Brianna slow dance, a rush of emotion washes over me. I bite down on my bottom lip that maybe, finally after all this time, Nash might be going to settle down with a woman who is actually worth his time.

The night is drawing to an end and Bayou and I are loitering about, but Bayou seems anxious to get out of here. So I cave and tell him we need to say goodbye before we leave.

I walk over to Brianna to say goodbye, Bayou casually walking behind me, taking his time. "Hey."

Brianna jerks back, like she is shocked from my arrival. "Oh, hey... are you enjoying your night?"

I stare at her incredulously. "You and Nash looked cozy together."

Brianna tries to fight her smile, but she can't hold it back. "We may have had a moment."

Gripping Brianna's hands, I giggle, bobbing up on my toes. "I am so happy for you, Bri. You're perfect for him. You'll keep him on the right path."

"I don't know about that exactly."

"You will. I'm sure of it."

Bayou steps up, finally undoing his tie, leaving it hanging on each side and looking pretty damn disgruntled. "Seriously, can we go now?"

"You're so grumpy." I frown. "Yes. Let's go get some ice cream or something?" Rolling my eyes, I smirk at Brianna but then loop my arm with Bayou to walk me out.

"Let's skip the ice cream and head back home. We can have something there," he grumbles.

"Why are you in such a rush to get home? We're having a night out on the town? We're dressed up, we look amazing, don't you want to live it up?"

Bayou looks me over, and he exhales. "Don't get me wrong, beautiful. You *do* look amazing, but we have been out for hours, and there is still the threat of the Bratva out there. I want to keep you safe, and I can do that better at your house."

I frown but understand what he is saying. "Okay... we'll head home."

I have to admit, I'm a little disappointed as we get in the car, but at least I had a good night, and Bayou was on his best behavior. I can't ask for much more than that. I turn to him as he pulls out of the parking space and starts driving, resting my hand on his thigh. He rests his hand on mine and interlaces our fingers.

"Did you see Nash with Brianna tonight? There is definitely something going on there. They're so going to be a thing—"

"Can we not talk about Nash tonight? He's such a mood kill."

Furrowing my brows, I glare at him and his attitude. "What is wrong with you? You're so on edge right now?"

He exhales as he pulls onto my street, not saying a word, his eyes focused ahead.

I huff, folding my arms over my chest, but as we pull into my drive, the driveway is lit with tea light candles. I sit taller, my eyes widening in shock, when I see twinkling lights lining the path to the door. "What in the?"

He pulls the car to a stop and relaxes his shoulders. "I've wanted to come home all night because I knew what was waiting for us."

I snap my head to him, letting out a small giggle. "You did all this?"

He shrugs. "I've been planning it since we knew about the gala."

Excitement bubbles through me as I bite on my bottom lip and turn, jumping out of the car. Bayou walks around to meet me, and as I glance down, the path is covered in rose petals. My hand snaps to my chest while tears well in my eyes. Bayou takes my hand, leading me to the front door.

"Bayou," I murmur, and he presses his lips to the side of my head.

"C'mon, let's go inside," he suggests, taking my hand and leading me through the front door.

As we walk inside my home, the twinkling lights cascade around the ceiling—the entire house looks like a wonderland. Bouquets of flowers are sporadically placed all over my living room, sending out a beautiful fresh floral scent, making all my senses come alive. Petals lead toward the hall and to my bedroom. I widen my eyes, turning toward him. "You mean?"

He smiles, pulling me to him, wrapping his arms around my waist. "I want tonight to be special. That's all I have ever wanted for you, Novah. You deserve to be treated like the queen you are."

My bottom lip trembles as I lean up on my toes, pressing my lips to his. That spark ignites in my soul, rushing through me like never before.

Bayou is taking care of me like I could never have imagined. He made me wait so he could plan something epic, and if this is anything to go by, tonight will be something spectacular. And as I run my fingers through his hair, my tongue dancing with his, I don't know if I can wait for one second longer.

NOVAH

Simply needing his lips against mine, I thrust my fingers in his hair. Our tongues collide roughly as he pushes me back against the hallway wall. My back collides hard, and I smile against him at the use of force. He's always so gentle with me, and I like that he's being a little more possessive right now.

A low growl reverbs from his chest as he kisses me passionately like he is having trouble controlling himself, but I love every second of it. His hand slides up, caressing my breast, and there is no way I can hold back the soft moan. Then, almost instantly, he stalls, resting his forehead on mine while taking a deep breath.

We pant, my fingers sliding up his thighs and around to his ass, pulling him closer, needing him near me. I don't want him to back out of this now.

"I need this to be right for you, Novah."

I grin, my hand sliding up to his cheek. "Then stop overthinking and just go with it." I press my lips to his again, more forceful this time, and immediately the hesitation in him cracks. His arms loop around my waist, then he hoists me up and carries me into my bedroom. I can't help the soft giggle that escapes me with his brute strength. It's so fucking sexy as we kiss all the way to the bed. Gently sliding me down his body, he places me at the edge. The move so damn sexy it makes my breath catch in my throat. He's so freaking gorgeous, lit up by the shimmering candles.

He couldn't have made this any more perfect if he tried.

Bayou takes a step back from me, rubbing at his beard. "You're so fucking beautiful, Novah. I'm going to take my time with you."

Nerves begin to creep in—I have waited for this moment for so long.

Dreaming of Bayou being the one.

Waiting for him to be the man to take my virginity.

It's why I held out because I *wanted* it to be him. Because I think deep down, I knew we would always end up here. It just took us a little longer than I had hoped.

But I always wished.

I kept the thought alive, and now here it is, and he is doing *everything* right.

"Don't take too long, though," I quip, and he smiles, taking a step toward me.

"Yes, ma'am." He saunters up to me, the swagger sexy as hell as he leans in, pressing his lips to my neck. Tingles prickle all the way down my body. I let out a breath when his hands grip my biceps and begin turning me. I widen my eyes as I move with Bayou and spin in his grip, turning my back to him.

Glancing over my shoulder, his hands slide from my biceps to the back of my dress. He grips my zipper, his lips moving to the back of my neck and pressing firm kisses on my skin while he tantalizingly slowly pulls my zipper down. My breathing comes slow and heavy as I lick my lips with the chemistry in the air. His teeth graze my skin, making my clit throb with need.

Bayou loops his fingers under the straps of my dress and gradually slides them over my shoulders. The dress cascading to the floor at my feet.

One of his hands slides around my stomach, the other to my

collarbone, holding my back to him as he grinds his erection into my ass. "See what you do to me?"

Biting my bottom lip, I push my ass back into his cock, grinding on him, enticing a growl as he slides his hands to my waist and spins me to face him. His eyes take me in, devouring my body. The way he is looking at me makes me feel like a goddess as I stand in my black panties and a strapless bra.

"I see you've taken to wearing black lingerie again?" He salaciously beams.

Giggling, I smirk. "I think you like it," I tease, running my hands along his shirt and sliding in, pulling off his suit jacket.

"I think maybe I do, but I like it better like this," he says, then he grips the edges of my panties and tears them away from my body.

My eyes widen in shock as I gasp, and he stares at my bare pussy. "So fucking beautiful."

If he wants to play that game, then I'm willing.

So I quickly grip his shirt and yank at the edges. The buttons pop off in quick succession. The shock on his face that I would do such a thing almost makes me giggle, but quickly they fill with lust instead. He shrugs out of his now ripped shirt and lunges for me. I let out a small squeal when he picks me up and throws me onto the mattress. Bayou's lips devour mine as he leans over me, his hard cock pressing into my bare pussy through his slacks.

Wrapping my legs around him, I pull him closer, needing the friction. I moan into his mouth as he grinds, making me whimper.

His mouth leaves mine, letting me finally take in some much-needed air. My lips are swollen from the intense kissing as he trails kisses down my neck, his teeth grazing all the way. My clit throbs so intensely that I might explode if he doesn't touch me soon.

Bayou sits back on his knees, his erection clear in his slacks. He stares down at me. "You're driving me crazy."

"Then do something about it," I tease.

He groans, moving off the bed. Undoing his belt, he kicks off his shoes and slides his slacks down, freeing his cock while I sit up a little and pull off my bra, flinging it to the floor with the rest of our clothes.

Being completely naked with Bayou feels natural.

You think I would feel nervous.

A little tense.

But right now, staring at his glorious form, all I feel is calm.

Because this is right.

He steps to my bedside table, and I raise my brow in curiosity when he pulls out what looks like a bullet vibrator. It certainly wasn't in my drawer before I left for the gala. *He planned for it to be there.* And I am excited about it. He also pulls out a condom, his eyes meeting mine. Almost like he is trying to gauge my reaction, so I smile wide, and he exhales like he's relieved. He tears open the packet and slides the condom onto his cock—the move so fucking sex—then he steps back to the bed, moving in next to me.

He brings his hand up to caress my cheek. "You sure you wanna do this? I won't be mad if you—"

"Bayou, I want you to fuck me," I interrupt, my eyes pleading with him.

"Then I'm gonna make you feel so good."

Butterflies dance in my tummy. Is it nerves or excitement? Maybe a little of both. But as he moves between my legs, he flicks on the vibrator, placing it on my nipple, and I let out a gasp feeling the movement send an instant jolt straight to my clit. I had no idea the nerve endings could come alive like this. I let out a breath while he glides the bullet vibrator down the center of my body ever so enticingly slowly. The sensation makes me shudder with anticipation. My clit throbs with need, want, and desire for him to touch me.

He edges the bullet down, slowly circling my belly button.

I whimper impatiently. "Bayou, please."

"That's it, beg for me."

Throwing my head to the side, my hands fist in the sheets wriggling against his touch. He's teasing me, sliding the bullet further toward my pussy. I arch my hips up, aching for him to reach the final destination and when he finally presses the bullet on my clit, the instant shockwave pulsates through my entire body, making my back arch high off the bed. "Jesus, Bayou." I pant.

"I know, baby... just ride it out like a good girl."

I let out a moan—hearing him call me that does something to me. I don't know what it is, but when his deep voice rasps like that, it's so fucking sexy.

As he intensifies the pressure of the bullet on my clit, he bites down on my nipple, pulling at the bud. My whole body throbs so hard, I feel like I am dripping from the pleasure rolling through me.

"You're so wet for me already. My cock is so fucking hard, Novah." He grunts as the sensations of the vibrator work on my clit. It's so intense it has my breathing rapid and stuttered, I can hardly catch my breath. While his tongue ring circles on my nipple, he pulls my bud into his mouth, sucking hard then he blows on the hard nipple sending a jolt surging right through me.

My fingers clench, needing something to hold onto as this massive high starts to roll through me. "Bayou, I'm so close."

"Come for me, Novah. Come... *now*." He growls, then sucks on my nipple, his teeth clamping down, biting my skin. It's enough to have my senses going into overload. My skin prickles, coating me in a fine mist of sweat. My breathing hitches while lights dance behind my eyes, and just as my muscles tense so tight preparing for my climax to rock through me, Bayou lines his cock up at my entrance.

My eyes widen when he presses his lips to mine and thrusts up inside me at the same time my orgasm pushes me over the edge. The sensation is an overload as I climax around his cock. He fills me to the brim, the pain of him taking my virginity is overwhelmed by the pleasure rushing through me. I pant against his lips and moan into his mouth. The sting of the moment is not lost on me. He's just taken my virginity so he stills for a brief moment as I come down from my high with him inside me.

My eyes meet his, so full of devotion while he tries to control his breathing as he places the bullet to the side. My eyes begin to glisten, not from pain but from sheer joy. He widens his eyes, but I bring my hand up to the side of his face and caress him. "Keep going... don't stop."

He presses his lips to mine, softer this time. My fingers slide into his hair, just needing him. My legs wrap around his ass, pulling him closer to me as he starts to slowly move. He pulls back, and I gasp, feeling his huge girth sliding in and out of me. It is more than I had expected. It doesn't hurt so much, it's simply an adjustment. But something I have never felt before, and it's a little strange.

But good strange.

Very good strange.

My nails dig into his back while we rock together slowly. Bayou buries his head into my shoulder like he's having trouble keeping himself under control, his teeth digging into my shoulder as he grunts with his slow, languid thrusts.

I don't want him to hold back.

I want him to be himself with me.

So I run my fingers into his hair, gripping tight, and yank his head back to look at me.

His lust-filled eyes meet mine, and breathlessly, I begin to move my hips quicker. His nostrils flair, looking at me as I yank his hair harder. "Novah, I don't want to hurt you."

"I'm not fragile... fuck me, Bayou... please."

A guttural groan erupts from his chest, and his eyes darken. And fuck if that doesn't turn me on even more. He yanks my hands from his hair and slams them up above my head by my wrists. "You drive me fucking crazy."

Smirking, I roll my hips against his. He brings one hand down, hoisting my right leg up and over his shoulder. I widen my eyes at the new position, but I go with it as he thrusts deeper inside me. The push makes my insides ache, my eyes well with the intense feeling, but I welcome it as he slams his lips to mine while bending my leg right back.

My tongue dances with his frantically as he thrusts inside me, the feeling so fucking powerful it has me seeing stars almost instantly. If I had known I was missing out on this all these years, I would have made a move on Bayou sooner.

He kisses me strongly, his cock sliding in and out of me, filling me completely.

It's the most natural, beautiful feeling in the world.

And I want to do this every day with him.

Bayou thrusts again. His fingers on my wrist are so tight I'm sure they will bruise, but I don't care as his kiss deepens, and I sense he is close. He thrusts again, hitting just that right spot, making my back arch off the bed. Lights flash behind my eyes while my body trembles, adrenaline surging through me. My breathing is rapid and fast as we kiss frantically. It hits so furiously that my muscles constrict, and even though he's wearing a condom, the pulsing of his cock has my pussy clenching around him so tightly it causes him to pause as he unloads inside me.

"Fuck!" He groans as we still, both panting for breath, then he relaxes, still on top of me but letting my leg down while I look into his lazy eyes and smile.

I breathe for a moment, simply staring at him, then finally whisper, "That was utterly amazing."

He rests his forehead against mine, like I couldn't have said anything better in this moment, and he presses another kiss to my lips. "I needed everything to be perfect for you."

I stare at him as he continues to come down, and I furrow my brows. "Why? Why was it so important?"

He hesitates like he is debating whether he wants to tell me or not. Then he licks his lips, looking right in my eyes, nothing but adoration staring back at me. "Because… I'm in love with you."

My heart leaps into my throat, and my chest swells with warmth.

Then I kiss Bayou passionately.

I've waited to hear those words from him for so many years, and now I have.

He couldn't have made this night more perfect if he had tried.

Pulling back, I gently caress him. "I'm in love with you too."

He kisses me again but then slowly pulls out of me, the feeling strange and a little painful, so I wince. He runs his hand down my arm. "You feeling okay? Are you sore?"

"I mean, it wasn't as painful as I was expecting, but I think you had a little something to do with that with the way you started the whole thing."

"Just wanted you to be comfortable and relaxed, not tense."

"I certainly wasn't tense."

"Oh, I know." He grins wide like he is proud of himself as he pulls off the condom and throws it into the trash.

I bite down on my bottom lip. "Was it… good… for you?" I ask, nervous that I didn't make it as memorable for him with my lack of experience.

He growls, pulling me to him. "Baby, that was fucking incredible. I'm never going to forget that. I'm so glad I shared it with you. But right now, I need to get you into a nice warm bath."

I glance at the small amount of blood on the sheets and grimace. "Okay… a bath would be nice."

He stands and places his hand out for me. "Then let's go relax."

Taking his hand, my muscles ache in ways they never have before, but I welcome it as we make our way to the bathroom. When we walk in, it too has been decked out with candles and petals. He had this part of the night planned too. I smile as I stand back and let him take care of me. He really has gone above and beyond tonight. I couldn't have asked for anything better—definitely worth the wait.

As the water fills the bubbling tub, he turns to me, wrapping his arms around my naked body. "You mean everything to me, Novah. I hope you know that."

My eyes well with tears, and I nod. "I do now. Thank you for making this night so amazing for me. First attending the gala in a penguin suit, even though I know you didn't want to be there, and now all this. I know it's out of your wheelhouse, but I appreciate it all."

He leans in, planting a kiss on my lips. "I'd do anything for you."

My chest squeezes as I stare into his beautiful eyes. "I love you."

He smiles wide like he can't believe he's hearing me say that. "I fucking love you too. Now get in the water before it turns cold."

I smirk at his bossiness when he places his hand for me to follow, and I step in between his legs. The hot water stings my skin as I turn my back to him and ease into the water, sitting on his lap. The flickering of the candles holds a romantic hue, and as I sink back, I relax into him completely. Gently he runs the washcloth over my skin, and I close my eyes, loving the delicate way he's taking care of me.

He washes my body, taking special care between my legs. It's tender but not like I was expecting from some of the horror stories I have read. *Takeaway—don't believe everything you read.* But, honestly, he did such a good job of ensuring I was taken care of that I want to try this whole thing again.

But I know I need time to recover.

He does too.

If I wanted to push my luck, he won't allow it.

Sinking back, I let his hands glide up and down my body as a burning question lingers in my mind. "Hey... how did you get all this done when you were at the gala with me? The candles, the flowers?"

He chuckles. "I had some help... Grit and Xanthe. I told them what I needed, and they pulled it off."

"They certainly did." I bring his hand up to my lips and tenderly kiss the back of his hand. "Thank you for going all out like this. I have never felt so special in all my life."

He wraps his arms around me tightly, kissing my shoulder. "You are special, Novah Lee. You always have been."

My heart beats faster, pounding with giddy excitement for how amazing this night has panned out. I love the way my body is feeling right now, but I know I am not done with Bayou just yet. However, for now, we will unwind.

We spend at least forty-five minutes in the tub, getting cleaned up and relaxing until the water starts to go cold.

I am feeling an itch that surely needs to be scratched.

And Bayou is the only one who can deal with the need.

We hop out of the bath, and he wipes me down with the fluffiest of towels, obviously bought especially for tonight. He pays special attention to between my legs. I smile, somehow feeling like a new woman. Like a part of me has been unlocked, and I want to explore every single part of who that woman is, so I blurt out, "I want to go again."

He chuckles. "You need to rest and recover—"

"We can rest and recover tomorrow. Right now, I want to take charge."

He furrows his brows. "I don't think that's such a good idea, Novah. You'll be too sore."

Huffing, an idea springs to mind, and I smirk. "Fine... you dry off. I'm just gonna grab us some drinks from the kitchen."

He dips his head while I have a plan I need to put into action. Making my way out to the kitchen, I rush to the pantry and grab some chocolate sauce. Grinning wide, my mind flashes back.

Kaia giggled, shaking her head and she stood, reaching out to grab the chocolate sauce from the pudding. She dipped her finger in and shoved it in her mouth. "Still warm," she chimed as she sauntered off toward the hall for the bedrooms.

Hurricane growled under his breath and took off after her.

Bayou shook his head.

Biting my lip, my legs were clenched at the thought of all the sex they were having, and I was not. But, I so desperately wanted.

Bayou leaned into my side and whispered, "When the time comes, I can arrange for chocolate sauce to be available... if you think you'd be into that kind of thing?"

My eyes widened, and I snapped my head around to Bayou, trying to fight the massive grin on my face. "Bayou, people might hear," I whispered quietly so no one else could overhear.

Chuckling, he sat back in his seat, licking his bottom lip. "Mmm, I love chocolate," he teased, and I reached out, slapping his arm with a giggle.

Placing the chocolate sauce into the microwave for a few seconds, a wicked grin forms on my face. I know Bayou wants to wait until tomorrow to continue this, but it's after midnight, and I am ready to keep this party going.

The microwave sounds. I pull out the sauce container, walk over to the kitchen table, and hoist myself on the end. "Bayou," I call out.

"Yeah?" he calls back.

"Could you come here for a sec?"

His heavy footsteps thump on the floorboards, and I begin to pour the chocolate sauce all over my torso. Bayou steps into the kitchen, his eyes bug out of his face as he lets out a small growl, his cock instantly hardening. "Novah?"

"Remember Christmas Day... and the chocolate sauce talk?" I ask, dipping my finger into some of the sauce on my breast and then sticking my finger in my mouth.

He inhales sharply and nods. "I remember."

"You said you *love* chocolate... so why don't you come take a bite?" I gnaw on my bottom lip, waggling my brows as he rolls his shoulders and saunters into the kitchen.

"You're not being a very good girl right now, Novah."

Shrugging, I slide my finger in the chocolate on my breast again, then press it to his lips. He takes my finger into his mouth and sucks the chocolate in an incredibly drop-dead sexy way while I smirk.

"Maybe I don't always want to be good?"

He growls, his hands gripping my thighs and forcing them apart to step between them. "You're playing with fire here, Novah."

Smiling, I pick up the sauce container and start pouring it down his chest. He flairs his nostrils as I move in, licking the sugary treat from around his nipples and bite down.

"Fuck!" He groans, his hand moving out and sliding into my hair, gripping tightly and yanking my hair back, forcing me to look up at him. "You want to play?"

Smiling, I nod my head. "Remember how you owe me one do-anything-I-want token? I'm cashing it in."

He inhales long and hard, craning his neck to the side. "Dammit, Novah, you're gonna be the death of me." Then before I have a chance to think, his hand splays out on my chest, pushing my back to the table. I gasp at the same time as he grips my legs and hoists them up over his shoulders. Finally, he squats at the edge of the table.

Wriggling with anticipation, he grabs the sauce and starts pouring it over my clit. I tense at the feeling, but the second his tongue lashes against it, sucking and licking, I let out a moan. "Yes, God, yes."

His hands squeeze my thighs while his tongue works my clit, circling and sucking. My hand grips my hair needing to relieve the pressure as I writhe on the woodgrain table. "Bayou, just like that."

He chuckles against my clit, which only heightens the friction as I feel more of the warm chocolate pour down my folds. My back arches, his tongue laps it up, tasting the combination of me and the chocolate. Bayou flicks his tongue ring in that special way that he does, sending me over the edge. My arm flies out, knocking a fake potted plant off the center of the table. It smashes to the floor, but I don't even care. My body inflames so intensely as my orgasm rampages through my body.

"Bayou, fuck," I scream.

He reaches for my scarf hanging off the back of the chair and starts wiping me down. I pant while falling from my high. As I lay in a blissful haze, I notice Bayou stepping up to my side with the scarf in hand. I widen my eyes when he pulls it out into a long thin line.

"Do you trust me?"

I nod, and he moves his finger in a come-hither gesture, so I stand.

"Do. You. Trust. Me?"

Nodding, I smile. "With my life."

He doesn't say anything else, just spins me, turning my back to him. My breathing quickens as he grabs my wrists and ties them together with the scarf. I gulp. When he said he wanted to play, he meant it. But I started this, and I am ready for whatever he brings my way.

He wraps the scarf around my wrists, yanking them tightly behind my back. "You look so fucking beautiful like this."

Smirking, I like this side of Bayou as he moves me back to the table, and he presses my torso onto the surface. I lean down as he grabs my thighs and yanks my ass off the edge, then he steps his knee between my legs, using it to spread my legs wider.

He has all the control right now.

Well played, Bayou.

Well played.

I lay with my face squished against the wood, my chest heaving with desire. Bayou's hand slides up and down the center of my back, giving me goose bumps. "You want me to taste the chocolate, Novah?"

"Mm-hmm," I mumble, wriggling my ass in the air at him.

He chuckles, picking up the container of chocolate sauce. "Good fucking girl." Then he pours the sauce across my ass, drizzling the warm liquid all over my skin. I bite my bottom lip as he lets out a panty-melting growl. "So fucking sexy." Then he sinks, his tongue gliding over my ass cheeks, lapping up the chocolate. I writhe against him needing more, and he dips his finger inside my pussy as his tongue glides around my ass.

I let out a moan, these feelings all so new, but so intoxicating as I experience them for the first time with Bayou. My body wriggles against the table while he pumps his finger in and out of me. I moan, needing more. "Bayou, fuck me rough."

He stalls his movements, pulling his finger from me, his breathing heavy and hard. "You sure you're ready for rough?"

I wriggle my hips trying to angle them toward him, but he really does have all the power right now as he holds me, positioning his cock at my entrance. My clit tingles with the possibility of him fucking me. "Bayou, fuck me like you mean it. Give me rough and dirty. Don't hold back."

He chuckles. "That's the single sexiest thing you've ever said. Hold on, baby."

Bayou's fingers clench my hips as he pulls me hard and deep onto his cock. We both hiss through our teeth at being joined again within a short time, and this time doesn't feel anything like last time. It's so much better, even though last time was amazing. I let out an animalistic moan as I push back, needing more of him. "More."

Bayou doesn't hold back, thrusting up so deep inside me it makes me gasp. He's not worried this time like he was before. He's not scared about hurting me, making this so much better. I didn't even think it could *be* better, but this… this is next level.

"You're so fucking tight like this." He grunts as he pulls back and thrusts.

My body slides up and down on the table. The friction makes my nipples pebble and harden while my clit rubs on the smooth polished wood.

He pounds into me, and the feeling of the binds on my wrists makes this even more intoxicating. I moan, making a noise I have never heard before as he fucks me hard, dirty, primal. The table creaks and groans with our frantic movements. The sensations rushing through me are like nothing before. My entire body comes alive. My face flushes, my skin breaks out in goose bumps, and lights flash behind my eyes.

"That's it, good fucking girl." He growls that unmistakable sexy noise, and it is my undoing.

My muscles tense, and then the euphoria explodes inside me, making every sensation wash over me. "Bayou," I scream, but just as my climax rampages through me, the table makes an almighty crack, and I feel myself beginning to fall. He doesn't give me a second to panic as he holds my wrists tight, preventing me from going anywhere. I let out a small squeal when the table crashes to the floor, breaking apart under our frantic movements.

He doesn't waste time turning me, pressing my torso down onto the countertop. The shock of the cool surface makes me shudder. "Now you're really going to take it like a good girl."

Biting down on my bottom lip, he spreads my legs, his hand gripping my hair tight. It sends an ache through my head, but I fucking like the pain as he fucks me from behind.

Fast.

Unrelenting.

Resolute.

My body slides up and down on the counter. The friction making goose bumps blister on my skin.

He's working me to the brink again as he pulls me by the hair upright, his mouth next to my ear, his heavy breath making me even wetter for him. "I own your pussy. My cock is the only one you will ever know. Do you understand?" He growls the words with so much intensity into my ear I shiver.

I nod because I simply can't form words right now.

Bayou's hand slides around my throat, gripping it tight, forcing my head back as he drives deep into me. "Do. You. Under. Stand?" he says succinctly with each thrust.

"Yes." I moan as a wave of ecstasy hits me so intense I can't see. Then, everything goes black while I zone in and out for a moment with the intensity of the pleasure rolling through me.

Gasping as I come to, I can't help but smile.

This is so much fucking sexier than I could have ever imagined.

Being tied up with him like this—I fucking love it.

He pushes me back down on the counter. His hand sends a slap across my ass. The sharp sting reverberates throughout my entire body. I let out a whimper, more because it felt so good than anything else.

"Next. Time. I. Tell. You. To. Rest. You. Fucking. Do it." He grunts out each word with every thrust, then slaps my ass again.

My breaths are coming as breathless pants. Bayou's muscles tense, his body jolting with his impending climax. He slams against me, his cock jerking dramatically. "Fuuuck!" He moans as hot cum flows inside me.

Slowly, he rests his hands on the counter on either side of my body. "Jesus, Novah."

I can't wipe the smile from my face as I glance back at him, and he slowly pulls out of me. Then he gently undoes the binds and helps me from the counter while I giggle, which makes him shake his head.

"That was—"

"Me letting myself go. I'm sorry. I was out of contro—"

"Fucking amazing. Bayou, we need to do that again."

He widens his eyes, taking the scarf from my wrists and rubbing the red welts, which are of my own doing because I couldn't keep my arms still. "What? Now?"

I bounce on my toes. "Now, tomorrow, the day after… I fucking need that every day of my life."

He chuckles, bringing his hand up, caressing my face. "I've created a monster." He plants a kiss on my lips. "We will, but you do need to rest." He looks down at the chocolate covering our skin. "And now we need another bath."

I lean and kiss him.

Because this night has been perfect, and I couldn't have asked for anything better.

Except maybe to just keep doing this all fucking night long.

BAYOU
The Next Day

Waking up with Novah in my arms like this, after last night, I can't remember a time I felt this fucking good. It's like my life has been a puzzle up to this point, all the pieces floating around, and last night it all came together. I haven't felt this whole, this together in as long as I can remember.

Leaning in, I gently kiss her shoulder. I want more than anything to fuck her again this morning, but I know, even though she won't admit it, she will be sore. So as much as it kills me, I need her to have a break. *We have the rest of forever to fuck like rabbits.* I chuckle at the thought.

Novah glances over her shoulder at me, her sleepy eyes blinking. "Something funny at this time of morning, sir?"

I gently kiss her skin, my fingers running up and down her naked flesh. "Just thinking about how fucking surreal this is."

She spins in my grip and faces me, her hand sliding up to cup my bearded cheek. "Thank you… for making me wait. For making last night so amazingly special."

My chest squeezes. *That's all I wanted for her.* "You know now that I've had you, no other man is allowed within ten feet of you.

You're mine... only mine."

She widens her eyes. "Is this your way of claiming me, Bayou?"

My stomach tightens as I think of the repercussions this will have. Novah means more than the shit I am going to be in with Hurricane and Nash, so there is no question about it. "Yeah, Novah, I'm claiming you."

Her eyes light up. "Oh God, this is going to get complicated and messy."

I dip my chin. "I know, but we will handle them together. We'll make a day with Nash and Hurricane, maybe have dinner so they're together, and I will tell them I have claimed you. Make sure we're all in the one room so the fallout can be contained. I think it's the only way to keep the carnage to a minimum."

Novah groans out a sigh. "I think you're right. We tell everyone together, but today is about us. I only want to think about you today and have copious amounts of wild sex with you tonight before I have to go back to work tomorrow."

Grinning, I lean in, planting a kiss on her lips. "I like this plan. Today we relax. Tonight I'm going to show you what I am really made of."

Her eyes light up, and she giggles. "You mean there's more than what you did last night?"

Chuckling, I slide over the top of her pinning her to the bed. "Oh, beautiful, there's so much fucking more."

The Next Day

Nothing could burst the blissful bubble Novah and I are in right now. I love the fact that I get to stay with her at her house and escort her to work. Being with her twenty-four-seven sounds like pure fucking bliss if you ask me. I love watching her work—she is in her element here, helping people, families, children, and women out of shitty situations. She was born to do this job. I couldn't be more proud of her if I tried.

Sitting back on the sofa in her office with my feet propped up on the coffee table, I sit reading a book while she taps away on her computer. My cell rings, and I glance down seeing Hurricane's name flashing. Swiping, I answer the call. "Hey, what's happening?"

"The Baroness is due here in the next hour or so. She didn't give us any warnin'. I need you here."

My eyes shift up to Novah, and I grimace. "What about Novah? I can't just up and leave her here on her own."

"I got Omen headin' your way to take over. But I need you here when she arrives, Bayou. She's Texas fuckin' royalty. We gotta welcome her with open arms if we wanna reap the benefits of havin' her on our side like Houston does."

Groaning, I nod. Because I completely understand, but I hate leaving Novah. "How long 'til Omen gets here?"

"He's walkin' out the door. You leave Novah now… she'll be on her own a matter of ten minutes."

Scrubbing at my beard, I crane my neck to the side.

I don't like it.

But I've got to do what my president says.

At the same time, he's my brother, and if I put up too much of a fight, he will know something is up, and I'm not ready to tell him just yet. "Okay, I'll pack up and be on my way."

"Bring your A-game, brother. We gotta impress her."

"Got it." Ending the call, my eyes shift to Novah, who's looking like she is pretending not to be listening, but she clearly is. I smile and stand, walking over, then planting a kiss on the top of her head while rubbing her shoulders.

"Important call?" she asks, trying to sound blasé.

"Hurricane needs me to go in. Wants me to leave now. Omen is on his way. It will leave a gap where you're on your own for a few minutes."

She glances up at me with a genuine smile. "Bayou, I'm more

than capable of looking after myself for a few minutes."

Squeezing her tense muscles, I nod. "I know you are, but—"

"Go. Remember, we need to butter up to Hurricane as much as possible. You need to get on his good side before we tell him about *us."*

Groaning, I know she's right. "Fuck… fine. Just stay in your office and wait for Omen, okay?"

"Where am I gonna go? I have work to do. I'm gonna be here at my desk, sifting through paperwork all day."

Leaning down, I press my lips to her forehead. "Good girl, I'll see you when I get back, okay?"

"Raise hell," she jests.

Laughing, I step off toward the door looking back over my shoulder, knowing I don't want to leave her.

She blows me a kiss, and I smile.

Tapping the doorframe, I turn and walk out of her office, feeling all kinds of guilt for leaving her. But I know I don't have much of a choice. I have to go when the club calls, and right now, we might have someone who can help regarding the Bratva, so we need to take the help with both hands.

No matter the cost.

Hopping on my ride, I make the journey back to the clubhouse. All I can think the entire time is Omen getting his fucking ass over to Novah. When I pull up, Hurricane walks out to greet me as if he's been waiting on my arrival. "Apparently, the Baroness is comin' with an entourage. So we gotta be prepared for her soldiers to be with her when she arrives."

"Is she really as fucking amazing as Houston makes her out to be?"

He shrugs. "There's only one way to find out? Get your ass off your ride and get ready. She'll be arriving' here any second."

Throwing my leg over, Raid rushes outside with City and everyone else. "They're pulling down the street now, Pres."

Hurricane tilts his head at me. "Just in time."

Grit opens the gate, and the rolling entourage of the Baroness' camp drives in, followed by a few bikes we weren't expecting.

Hurricane, City, and I all raise our brows as we see Houston Defiance riding in alongside the fancy cars driving in the Baroness. Smiling that our brother chapter has come for an unexpected visit, we all chuckle among ourselves. It's always a good time when Houston rides into town.

Six, Chains, and Wraith all step off their bikes, and the rest of us move in instantly, pulling them to us with back-slapping man hugs.

"The fuck. We had no idea you were all comin' here to help with this situation?" Hurricane states toward Six, and he smiles.

"When the Baroness told us you reached out, I discussed it with the guys, and we agreed that we wanted to come and offer our support. You helped us when we needed it... we're here to do the same," Six offers.

I glance down at his president badge. While I think it's great Six has been able to step up into the role, I hate what happened to Zero.

"Sorry to hear about Zero. He doing all right?" I ask as the rear door to the fancy car springs open.

"Zero's doing just fucking fine," he snaps as Zero slides out of the car's rear and holds out his hand to someone.

A woman takes his offer, and she exits the car, standing in all her glory. She's wearing an all-white business suit, her hair in short blond waves to her shoulders as she glances around the clubhouse parking lot.

She screws up her face and turns to Zero. "Fences could do with a lick-a-paint."

Hurricane widens his eyes as Zero chuckles. "Now, now, Connie... play nice."

Smirking, I dip my chin to Zero, the ex-president of Houston Defiance, Six's older brother, and one of the best men I have ever known. He was injured severely in a club battle. Some fucker took to him with a baseball bat to his hands. Completely fucked all his tendons and knuckles—did a real number on him. The problem is you can't be a biker club president if you can't ride a bike. So he handed the reins to his younger brother, Six. But Zero is still around to help, to mentor. He may not be able to fight, but his brains are still intact, and some of the best battle plans have come from his mind. Guy's won some of the most epic biker fights I have ever seen.

Just unfortunate he lost the one that counted the most.

"Fine, but let's go inside. You know I do not like talking business out in the open," she states and starts walking toward the clubhouse without any introduction. Nothing.

She's fucking taking charge like she owns the place.

She may own practically all of Texas, but this is Louisiana, and you're not completely in charge here—yet. My eyes shift to Hurricane, who is clearly thinking the same thing.

He curls up his lip as he moves across to Six. "A little warnin' that you boys were comin' would've been nice, Six."

Six smiles cockily. "And ruin all this fun?" He slaps Hurricane's shoulder then we walk inside and straight to the Chapel. We take up our usual seats, but press in tight to include our brother charter and the Baroness.

"Welcome to NOLA Defiance, Baroness. Thank you for takin' my call and comin' over to see us about our Bratva problem," Hurricane states.

"You're welcome, but nothing comes cheap, and *everything* comes at a cost. I do you a favor, you do one in return. My relationship with Zero and Six works well this way. They know having me in their corner is beneficial, isn't that right, boys?"

Six and Zero both chuckle. "I think we've helped you as much as you've helped us, but yes... we know the score. And the Baroness has helped us out of some damn tight spots," Six states.

"The thing is, and I mean no offense by this, but isn't all your pull, power, and persuasion in Texas? This is Louisiana. How are you going to help us here?" I ask.

She grins. "And *you* are?"

I raise my brow as Hurricane glares at me. "Bayou, Sergeant-at-Arms."

"Well, *Bayou, Sergeant-at-Arms,* I may own Texas, but my arms and abilities have a long reach. I have many people working under me and *for me...* I have one such person that I believe you are already aligned with."

We all jerk our heads back in confusion.

"Who?" Hurricane asks.

"Marcel Laveau? Brilliant man, devoted to his work, his bar, and to his boss... *me.* You think he got to where he is in New Orleans on his own? No. I helped him get there. I have subordinates all over the country working for me."

Jesus Christ.

This woman is a powerhouse.

I'm surprised she isn't running for president.

Give her time.

"So if Marcel is our link to you, what do we need to do in the meantime? What are we gonna do to deal with this Bratva problem?" Hurricane asks.

She sits forward, resting her hands on the table. "You're thinking is too narrow-minded, Hurricane. You see the Bratva as a problem. A puzzle piece to solve."

We all furrow our brows.

"They're a direct threat to us, to the people we love. We can't find anythin' on them, and yet, they keep comin' for us."

"Well, that's the thing, isn't it, Hurricane? You keep looking for the Bratva while they *know* you're looking for *them."*

Raid widens his eyes before he dramatically opens his laptop and starts typing.

Six chuckles, shaking his head. "Neon does that too when he's figured something out."

Raid shakes his head. "You're a fucking genius, Baroness. We've been so focused on finding the Bratva that we never thought for a second they would be hiding and working under something different."

Six smiles with a shrug. "This is why we use her. She knows how the underworld works. She knows the inner workings of every-fucking-thing. You need a problem solved, the Baroness can solve it."

She chuckles. "Quit the accolades, but unless… Raid, was it?" Raid nods. "Unless Raid can figure out what the Bratva are disguising themselves as, my tip may be useless."

Raid types a couple more things into his laptop, then he laughs, shaking his head. "I've found a set of cabins rented out to an Olek Vokivon, about an hour away from here. Looks like there is a little commune of about six cabins and maybe a warehouse right near it with only one major road leading in and out of the area."

The Baroness smiles. "I like you, Raid. I tried to poach Neon for my team, but maybe I can poach *you* instead?"

Raid widens his eyes.

The rest of us glance around, unsure if she is joking or not, when Zero laughs. "Connie, leave Raid alone. Does that name mean something, Raid?"

He grabs a piece of paper and starts writing the name down. I narrow my eyes on him, trying to figure out what he is attempting to tell us. He points to the first word. "Olek. When I was studying Anton's files, his middle name was Olek. Now, if you look at this, he points to the surname and starts writing it backward.

Vokivon—N.O.V.I.K.O.V.

We all widen our mouths.

The Baroness simply smiles like she knew this was coming.

Hurricane reaches across, grabbing the piece of paper. "Olek Vokivon *is* Anton Novikov. We've been lookin' for his details all along, and he's been hidin' with his name fuckin' backward."

The Baroness sits forward. "Now you just have to decide what to do with this information…" She smiles. "Do you sit on it and gather as much intel as you can, build as many forces as you can, and go in when the time is right? Or, do you strike while you know the iron is hot?"

We all turn to Hurricane, and he sits back in his chair, rubbing at his beard like he is thinking it through. "My initial instinct is to storm in there with what we have and burn everythin' to the ground. But, we did that once before, and while we did a lot of damage, we didn't get everything. And *that's* why we're in the position we're currently in. I think we have to wait... gather as much information as we can and then hit with *every... fuckin'... thing* we got. Takin' every damn thing out and leave it in our wake."

Six pats Hurricane on the shoulder. "Houston's got your back when this goes down, brother. You let us know when you need us. We'll be here, guns at the ready."

Hurricane dips his chin to the young president. "Appreciate that, Pres. We're gonna need all the help we can get."

"In the meantime, I can have my men dig into Olek Vokivon. I'm assuming Raid will search too, and we will see precisely what we find. I will help where I can, but like I said, everything is for a price, and so you know, I don't always collect immediately," the Baroness states, and I glance at Hurricane wondering if we *really* want to get into bed with this woman.

But Zero and Six seem to trust her.

They work well with her.

So I guess she can't be *all* bad.

The problem is—I hate owing anyone anything. It always comes back to bite you in the ass when you least expect it.

Hurricane scrubs at his beard, his eyes shifting to Zero, maybe searching for guidance, and Zero dips his chin in reassurance. Hurricane turns back to the Baroness and huffs. "Okay. You've already helped us. Now we owe you a debt. We *will* pay that when you come to call."

She smiles wide, it is menacing. *I'm not sold on her.* I think we need to be careful with this one.

"Excellent, I am glad to hear that. For now, though, how about we celebrate this union by having a drink?"

Hurricane dips his head and moves to stand. "Couldn't think of anythin' better. Dismissed. Let's drink."

We all stand and head out into the main room.

Wraith chats with City while Hurricane is busy with Zero and Six. The Baroness is chatting with the girls, and I spot Chains over by the bar grabbing a drink. Nodding my head, I walk over, slapping him on the shoulder. He turns to me with his big goofy grin. "Hey, brother."

"Hey… can I have a word?"

"Yeah, what's up?"

I gesture with my head for us to move outside, away from curious ears. "Can I talk to you discreetly?"

Chains furrows his brows. "Everything okay?"

Craning my neck to the side, I grimace slightly. "I wanna talk to you about Chills and your relationship."

Chains places his drink down and stands. "Ahh, okay… let's go." He walks with me outside, my heart fucking racing in my chest. Besides Mom and Grit, I haven't spoken to anyone about Novah and me. It will be good to see what another brother thinks about this situation.

Chains and I pull up a seat outside, and he nods. "Okay, hit me?"

"You and Chills were foster siblings, right?"

Chains exhales but nods. "Yeah, we practically grew up together. It was so fucking strange when we finally admitted our feelings for one another, but I tell you, now we have our kid, I wouldn't want it any other way."

I'm quiet for a moment. Obviously, Chains can read me because he grips my shoulder. "There someone in your life you're nervous about, brother?"

"Nervous about, no. Her… I am absolutely sure about. It's everyone else that has me concerned."

Chains hums under his breath. "So it's controversial?"

Inhaling, I lick my bottom lip. "She's my stepsister."

Chains chuckles, nodding his head. "I see. It's making more sense now. Look, brother, it took me and Chills fucking forever to get our shit together. We wasted so much time wondering what our parents would think, what the club would think, when the only people caught up on the issue were ourselves. You'd be surprised how many people here will have already picked up on your chemistry and just not said anything to you."

I let out a small laugh thinking of Grit. *He was onto it in no time.* "You're right, brother. I am concerned about how Hurricane is going to take it, and that's stopping Novah and me from living a full life. We need to just tell him."

Chains sighs. "Knowing Hurricane like I do, he'll probably be pissed at first, but he'll want you to be happy in the end. Both of you. And if your feelings for Novah are real, then you gotta go for it."

"Oh, they're real, so real it scares me."

Chains chuckles, gripping my shoulder. "Then, brother, you gotta grab that shit by the balls and twist it for all it's worth. Because something real doesn't come along all that often, and when it does… you gotta grip hold of that like it's your lifeline."

"Yeah… I'm feeling that."

"We need another fucking drink," Chains states, and I let out a small laugh.

Yeah, we really fucking do.

CHAPTER 22

NOVAH

Omen should be here any moment, and I know I should stay in my office, but I *really* need a coffee. Bayou has been gone maybe all of ten minutes, so it should be fine if I go to the kitchen. It's not like I am leaving the building.

Glancing to my door, my eyes feel heavy. The need for caffeine is real as I tap my foot anxiously on the floor. "Oh, fuck it." Rolling my chair back, I stand and walk out of my office toward the kitchen. Making my way over to the coffee machine, I pick up a mug and turn to see an out-of-order sign plastered on the machine.

My shoulders slump as I let out a loud groan. This is Bayou's fault for keeping me up all night. Not that I mind, my pussy is still throbbing just thinking about it, but I shake my head from those thoughts and place the mug down. I'm having a serious crash right now and need a pick-me-up. The coffee vendor is literally at the end of the street, and it will take me all of one minute to walk there. I know I shouldn't, but I need caffeinating.

I rush back to my office, grab my purse and cell, and take off for the coffee shop. If Bayou knew I was leaving the safety of this building, I know he would seriously kill me, but he isn't here right now, so caffeine wins.

Walking out of the building onto the street, the sun shines in all its glorious hues. The New Orleans' city streets are bustling with people. A child busker stands on the sidewalk next to a hydrant playing blues on his guitar as I walk past, noticing his money tin sitting on a crate of red apples on the sidewalk.

Why does he need so many apples?

I giggle as I stroll past, dipping my chin to him. He smiles, and I keep walking toward my destination. The smell of the coffee lingers in the air, and I inhale feeling happiness creep into my soul at just being near the nectar of the Gods.

Approaching the door of the shop, I go to push it open when someone grabs my shoulder, pulling me back a little, pressing something long and pointy into my back. *Goddammit!* I'm pretty sure it's a gun.

"It's so good to finally meet you. Let's go for a walk."

My heart rate skyrockets as I try to look over my shoulder at the man, but he nudges the gun further into my back and grunts in my ear. "Keep your eyes forward," he demands, leading me toward the trashcan. "Drop your purse and cell inside."

Fear rolls through me like a tidal wave so furiously, I feel sick. Letting out a whimper, I don't want to make a scene out here in front of everyone, so I do as he says, even though I know this is the only way Bayou can trace me. I drop them into the trash, and he leads us off around the corner. My skin prickles at who this could be and what the hell they want. My immediate thought is that it's the Bratva. They're coming after me because of the club. Coming to finish what they started on New Year's. My body trembles while he leads me to a car parked in an alley, and he presses my front to the side of the car. "Keep still," he demands as tears well in my eyes.

"Who are you?" I demand.

He chuckles, as he yanks my hands around behind me. "Shut up and keep quiet or I *will* shoot you. Though that's not what I want to do, Novah, so don't force my hand."

My bottom lip trembles as he wraps cable ties around my wrists and yanks them so tight they cut into my skin. I let out a small whimper when he finally spins me around to face him.

My eyes bug out of my head when I take in the man before me.

It can't be.

Bayou said he took care of him.

But he's here.

In the flesh.

"Johnny?"

He chuckles. "Unfortunately not. I'm Arsen. Johnny's twin. And you're the bitch who took my brother away from me."

My eyes widen. I never knew Johnny had a twin. It never showed on any of his records. But here he is—the spitting image of Johnny standing right here waving a gun in my face.

"I don't know what happened to Johnny."

"Yeah, see, I don't believe that... you took Johnny away from Morgan, away from his kids. That destroyed him. He went to prison because of *you,* Novah. I was without him for *three months* because of you. And now he's gone for good... *because of you."*

"I-I don't know w-where Johnny is," I tell him truthfully.

"I believe you, Novah, but I also know *you* have to suffer for my greatest loss... and suffer you will." He suddenly brings up a rag and shoves it over my mouth, the chemical fumes invading my senses instantly. I scream as I struggle in his grip and fight the best I can, but my energy is fading, becoming harder and harder to move.

Everything feels like I am floating, like the entire world is weightless as my voice disappears, my eyes roll into the back of my head, and everything turns pitch black.

My mouth is dry when my eyes slowly blink, trying to find some equilibrium. I'm dizzy as all hell, a metallic tang in my mouth that I can't seem to shake.

Suddenly, the memory of the alley slams full force back into my mind, and I open my eyes, jerking upright. My entire head swirls in a fog while I try to steady myself, my hand gripping onto something long, thin, and cold. I close my eyes, taking a few deep breaths, just trying to slow my breathing and to stop my head from spinning.

Once the fog clears a little, I open my eyes, attempting to take in my surroundings. My fingers are wrapped around a wrought iron bar, part of a cage locking me in a tiny cell. My eyes snap up as my chest squeezes, and my head shoots around to see a tiny bed with a tatty mattress and a sheet for a blanket. The room smells of mold, and as I look through the bars, it's clear that the cell is located smack dab in the middle of someone's living room in some creepy house.

My breathing is labored, like I can't get enough oxygen. My fingers tingle, going numb as nausea rolls through me so intense that I dry heave. Chills sweep over my skin and cause goose bumps to stand tall on my arms and the hairs to raise on my neck. I stand and race to the bars pulling at them as hard as I can, trying to find a way out. But nothing is working because I am so physically weak. I don't know what Arsen has done to me, but I feel godawful as the panic overcomes me.

I burst into tears, racing around the cell, trying everything and anything to find a way out, but nothing is budging, and that's when I hear footsteps. I turn to see Arsen step in from another room holding an apple, peeling it with a blade and taking a chunk out, then shoving it into his mouth. I stand still, staring at him while he walks over to the cage with a slight smirk on his face. I'm shaking all over while I desperately try to think of a way to tell Bayou I am here.

I don't know how I know, but I do know he *will* find me.

Arsen sits at the edge of the cage staring at me, eating the apple, and not saying anything but in the creepiest of ways. It's unnerving.

I should say something.

What the hell do I do to break this weird tension?

I need to know what the hell he has in store.

"What do you plan to do with me?"

Arsen chews on his apple, slowly saying nothing until he swallows, and then he smirks. "We're going to play a game."

The hairs on the back of my neck stand up straight like soldiers. "What *kind* of game?"

He tilts his head, narrowing his eyes on me. "You'll have to wait and see."

He stands, walking off without another word, leaving me utterly terrified at what he's just said.

I can't leave it at that. "Arsen, please. *Please* let me go," I plead with everything I have.

But he simply chuckles and exits the room, making every ounce of hope I had leave with him. I collapse to the floor, pulling my knees up to my chest, cradling them to me.

I'm in a world full of trouble, and I have *no idea* how I am going to get out of this one.

BAYOU

As I sit drinking and generally having a good time with Chains and the other guys from Houston, Omen comes running into the clubhouse, and Novah is not with him. I stand abruptly, grabbing Hurricane's attention when Omen rushes toward us, out of breath.

"Where is she," I demand.

He tries to catch his breath, but I storm toward him, my hands reaching out, gripping his leather cut, and yanking on him aggressively. "Omen, I swear to God… you better start talking."

He swallows the lump in his throat. "When I got to her office, she wasn't there. Her phone and purse were gone, so I asked around, and they said they saw her heading for the coffee shop. So I pulled up the tracker app and pinged her cell…" I hold my breath as he holds it out along with her purse. "They were dropped in the trash outside the coffee shop."

Turning, I run my hand through my hair, trying to figure out just what the hell she is playing at.

Hurricane grunts as he steps up to me. "She say anythin' to you about this?"

I glare at him. "You think I'd be this uptight if she fucking did?"

Hurricane narrows his eyes on me, then turns back to Omen. "Anythin' look suspicious?"

Omen shakes his head. "Not that I saw, and I checked everywhere."

My chest squeezes so fucking tight as I try to think of all the various scenarios that could have happened.

Did she ditch us of her own accord? *Not likely.*

Did someone call her and blackmail her? *Possibly.*

Or has someone got her and is holding her against her will? *More likely.*

And my bet is on Anton fucking Novikov.

"Raid," I call out, and he steps up to us. "I need you to hack into security footage outside the coffee shop near Novah's work."

He nods, pulls up his laptop, and starts typing as we crowd around the screen. He zooms in and we see Novah come into the shot.

"There!" I snap.

He slows the footage down, and we watch as a man moves into view, though he clearly knows where the cameras are and is hiding his face.

"Can we get another angle?"

Raid checks but shakes his head. "It's all we've got."

"Dammit!" I grunt, making Hurricane narrow his eyes on me, but right now, I don't care. *Some asshole has my Old Lady.* "Keep following him," I tell Raid, and he does.

We watch them get into a car, and the number plate has a reflective coating, making the cameras ineffective against it. Whoever this guy is, he knows what he is doing. It's not Novikov, but it could definitely be one of his minions.

And as they drive off, the cameras lose tracking, and then just like that—*she is gone.*

My heart hammers in my chest as I stare at the footage ending, and my skin prickles in a fear so intense I want to kill everyone and anything in my path. "Tell me there's more, Raid," I snap.

He shakes his head. "The footage runs out here... we've lost her."

My blood ignites in a rage so hot, sweat trickles down my temple as I turn, picking up a beer bottle and hurtle it across the room. It smashes into the wall, fracturing into tiny pieces, then beer runs down the wall. I spin around glaring at Omen. "You had one job. *One. Fucking. Job.* And you fucked it up."

Omen narrows his eyes on me. "She left before I got there, brother. What was I supposed to do?"

Running my hand through my hair the realization hits me. "This is my fault. She's gone because I left her there without any supervision."

Hurricane steps up to me, furrowing his brows. "We'll find a way. We will get her back."

Shaking my head, I grunt. "You don't understand. I love her. I can't lose her—"

Hurricane waves me off. "Yeah, man, I feel the same. She's our stepsister."

Letting out a long pained groan, the emotion hits me all at once. There's no way for Hurricane to understand how important this is unless I tell him everything. So I spit it out in frustration, "No, you don't fucking get it. I'm *in* love with her. I made her my Old

Lady. We were waiting to find the right time to tell you because it's such a fucked-up situation. I know you're gonna hate me for it, but I can't help it. *I. Fucking. Love. Her."*

Hurricane widens his eyes as he shakes his head. "She's our sister. We've grown up with her almost all our lives. *What the fuck, Bayou?* We've been the ones warning men off her when I should have been warning her off you all this time?"

"Out of all the men in the world she could have chosen, she chose *me.* You know I'm going to treat her right. I'm not an asshole who's gonna use and abuse her, Hurricane. I'm going to love her like no one else fucking can... as long as we can get her back."

He shakes his head. "It's fuckin' wrong, Bayou."

Chains steps forward. "So... is what Chills and I have wrong too?"

Hurricane scrunches up his face. "That's different. You and Chills are perfect for each other."

Chains chuckles. "How is it any different for Bayou and Novah? They might be perfect for each other too. Chills and I are foster siblings... that's not much different from stepsiblings. Just because you don't have that kind of connection with Novah doesn't mean she can't have it with Bayou. It's not wrong or immoral, Hurricane. It's chemistry like you have with Kaia. You can't help who you fall for."

Hurricane groans. "We will talk more about this, but right now, we need to find Novah."

"Couldn't agree more," I snap, my anger still seething inside me.

The Baroness steps forward. "How can I help?"

"We need resources to figure out who the hell has her and how on earth we can track her down. Without her cell, we can't trace her," I say.

And she nods. "Leave it with me. I'm going to make some calls."

My eyes meet Hurricane's. He's clearly annoyed with me, and this wasn't how it was supposed to go down, but I need him to know how imperative this is. I need him to know that he's not just looking for our sister but my Old Lady too.

The woman I love.

More than anything in this world.

I just need her to be okay.

NOVAH

It's been hours and the day is fading into night. I've been alone with this guy who isn't talking to me, merely going about his business like I'm not in the middle of his living room trapped in a damn cage.

Truth is, I am terrified, but I know if I am going to make it out of this, I need to build a rapport with this asshole. Make him feel like he needs me to stick around so he won't hurt me. Taking a deep breath, I move to the edge of the tattered mattress and straighten my shoulders.

Time to make an effort.

"Is this where you live?" I murmur in a quiet voice.

He glances over, eyeing me up and down. "She speaks."

Weakly smiling, I try to play nice house guest. "I wasn't sure if you just wanted some peace and quiet or whether you wanted conversation?"

Arsen shrugs, continuing with whatever he is doing on the other side of the counter. "Not one for lengthy discussions myself."

Biting down on my bottom lip, maybe I need to try another approach. "Do you live out here on your own?"

His head snaps up, a hard glint in his eyes. "Stop fishing for answers, Novah."

Okay no talking about the house or why I am here, focus on him instead. "Talk to me about Johnny. What was it like growing up together?"

Suddenly, he races up to the cage, slamming into the bars, his eyes hard on me, staring into me like I am his latest meal. "You don't get to talk about Johnny. You're the reason he's gone."

My heart races so fast, but I can't show him that I'm scared right now. I have to meet him on his level. So I slowly step up to the cage next to him, my eyes somber, showing sympathy. "I don't know what happened to Johnny, Arsen… but you have to know how he treated Morgan wasn't right? He was hurting her."

Arsen scoffs, turning and starts pacing. "Morgan… insignificant. Little. Morgan. All she did was take Johnny away from *me.* Johnny was *my* anchor. *My* left hand. And when she came along, she became *everything* to him. His obsession. I didn't matter anymore. Women do that, you know? They take and take until you're a shell of who you once were… you're like Morgan too, Novah. You took Johnny away from me, but this time it was for good… and I *can't* let that go unpunished."

My entire body begins to shake at his words as I take a large step away from the cage. "W-what are you going to do with me?"

"Not *with* you, Novah… *to* you. And I told you, it's going to be a game. Once I have everything prepped and ready to go, we will begin."

"What kind of game, Arsen?" I say quicker than I should have, showing my fear in the moment.

"Well now, *that* would ruin the surprise, wouldn't it?" Arsen walks off to the other side of the room as I sink back onto the tattered mattress feeling deflated.

That didn't go at all how I had hoped.

Then he steps up to the cage with something in his hand and chuckles. "Have fun with your new friends." He slides a box into the cage and lifts a lid. I gawk as a couple of scraggly looking rats come running out racing right for my feet. Gasping, I lift my legs onto the bed.

This guy is crazy.

Bayou better find me soon because I honestly don't know what Arsen has in store for me, but by the small games he is playing right now, I don't think his big games will be very good.

Bayou
The Next Day

I haven't slept a wink.

All I wanted to do was go out and search for Novah. But without any leads, I didn't even know where to look. I have Raid and the Baroness' people searching to try and find out who the hell this person could be who took her. But in my mind the only option is the Bratva. The only course of action we can take is storm the Novikov cabins and try to find her.

Sliding out of bed, I make my way to find Hurricane. I need to make some big moves, and I need to do them *now.*

We have waited long enough.

This inaction shit is bullcrap.

We have to move.

Making my way to Hurricane's room, I don't even knock, just walk straight in. I don't give a shit about his privacy or his Old Lady right now, not while mine is out there fending for herself.

Kaia is cuddled into Hurricane's chest obviously naked under the covers because she pulls them up to cover herself, but I don't give a shit about her fucking privacy.

"Bayou, the fuck, man?" Hurricane grunts, his eyes glaring at me.

"While you're in here loving it up with your Old Lady, mine is out there having God knows what done to her. We need to storm the cabins, Hurricane. We need to find her."

Kaia shifts off Hurricane, and he sits up in the bed, making sure to cover Kaia from me. *Like I give two shits about that right now.* "I'm concerned for Novah too. And goin' into the new Bratva camp without knowin' all the facts is a risk, but this is Novah. If they have her, if they're hurtin' her, we need to fuck those bastards up."

"Exactly. We need to do this *now,* Hurricane. I can't stand the thought of them holding her captive. Of them *hurting* her. I know if this backfires, it could be building a rod for our own backs. This battle with the Bratva is minimal at the moment, but *if* they have taken her, they kick this into a fucking war. And I'm *not* scared to bring in the heavy artillery."

"Go get the rest of the brothers. We make a plan and we ride out today."

Nodding my head, I don't hesitate, and I walk out into the hall, banging down heavily on everyone's doors to wake them. They all step out into the hall looking sleepy, including our brothers from Houston who are still here. "Everyone mount up. We're going to the Bratva camp to get Novah back."

City dips his chin at me, and they all turn back into their rooms to get ready as Chains steps up to me, gripping my shoulder. "We're gonna get her back, brother."

My stomach churns with anxiety as I nod my head. "Yeah, we fucking better."

Hurricane steps out into the hall, his eyes finding mine. "Right, everyone to the Chapel. We got shit to discuss."

My feet don't fail as I take off straight for the Chapel, following my twin and president. The rest of our brothers not far behind us. The Baroness making an appearance as well. We all take our seats, making room for the Houston boys.

Hurricane bangs his gavel. "Right, we let this sit, we waited for information that isn't comin'. Novah is out there, and there can only be one group who took her, the Bratva. We think we know where they are, so we have to take the chance and go in. We can't hold back."

Omen sits forward. "We can take some explosives for those cabins and whatever that warehouse is. I suspect that is where they are holding Novah."

"Good idea... Raid, you need to make sure you bring your tech shit to hack into whatever security feed they may have as we approach."

Raid cracks his knuckles. "On it."

"I will do what I can on this end," the Baroness adds.

I don't know what that means, but if she can help, we will take it. "Thank you," I tell her, and she dips her head.

"We move fast. We get this shit done. I don't care how many Bratva we take out. Fuckin' all of 'em if we have to, to get Novah back unharmed. You hear me?" Hurricane states.

Tension rolls through me at the thought that we may already be too late.

But I can't think like that.

I must go in with a clear mind, or I won't be any good to anyone.

"Any questions?" Hurricane asks. No one says anything. "Good... let's ride."

He bangs his gavel, and everyone slides their chairs out, rushing for the armory. The weight of what we're about to do weighs heavy on me. I'm about to attack the Bratva on a hunch that they have Novah.

If we're wrong, it could be catastrophic.

Grabbing what I need for protection and defense, I load myself up, then head for my ride. My muscles are tense, so I try to relax them, but I can't seem to let go of this impending doom sensation.

We jump on, start our rides, and take off in formation. Riding in a group is one thing, but riding with members of a brother chapter is an all-new high. It's that added layer of protection. Knowing these men will stand by you and fight for you—there's nothing like it.

The ride takes longer than I would have liked, but as we pull up at the long road leading down to the cabins, we park our rides behind the brush and take off on foot. There's greenery down the long drive, so we duck in and out of the brush, trying to keep inconspicuous. The smell of burning wood fires and something delicious cooking wafts through the air as the log cabins come into view.

Hurricane halts us. We try to be as stealthy on our approach as possible. No one says a single word. Hand signals only as Hurricane signals to Omen to *let it rip.*

Omen rushes forward toward the nearest cabin, hurtling off a smoke bomb. It detonates, sending a plume of white smoke through the air, and that's our cue. Bringing our guns up, loud coughing comes from inside the cabin when we start racing straight for the warehouse. Our aim is to find Novah. But just as we thought, Bratva comes out of the other cabins and begins raining bullets at us as we run.

Defiance scatters as we duck and weave past the many cabins, bullet spray going everywhere. I slide onto a porch, ducking down behind the railing for cover as a bullet lodges into the wood sending splinters spraying off in all directions. I let out a heavy breath, pulling a grenade out of my pouch and hurtling it toward the group of Bratva marching through the camp. "Fire in the hole," I scream out, more for my brothers in case any decide to run out, as the grenade lands right in the middle of a bunch of Bratva.

They all glance down at it, then move to run, but it's too late, it explodes, and they fly through the air in pieces, blood splattering across the cabins closest to them. I duck down avoiding the spray narrowly, smirking as I enjoy the show.

Screams filter through the air when I race out from the porch, more of my brothers following me, just needing to get to the warehouse, but as I do, more men from the cabins race out, trying to block our path. I raise my gun to shoot them, when a couple of kids suddenly race out from inside the cabin. My heart leaps into my throat, and I raise my hand toward my men.

"Hold your fire," I scream.

The guys behind me all stop as we pant heavy breaths, the roaring sounds of gunfire and grenade blasts all dull down, only the crackling of fire can be heard and the whimpering children as we stare off at each other.

We may be assholes, but we *don't* hurt children.

Even if they are Russian Bratva.

The other cabins open, and more women and children step out onto the porches as we all lower our weapons.

My heart races so fucking fast at the sound of cars racing up the drive behind us comes into focus. The Bratva all look at us like they're shocked we stopped, almost thankful. We turn to see Marcel stepping out of the black SUV with a bunch of his men, and he strolls up to us with a group of people now heavily outnumbering the Bratva who are here. His guns are aimed at the Bratva, who are standing with their arms up in surrender. "Heard you could do with some reinforcements?"

I smile at Marcel as Hurricane cranes his neck to the side, and the cabin door to our left opens. None other than Anton Novikov steps out, two young children at his side as he holds them close to his legs. "How did you find us?" he grunts.

"Olek Vokivon... *not* very discreet," Hurricane states.

Anton ushers the two children to a woman and cranes his neck to the side. "You think you can come here, try to take out the place where our families are living, and it *not* have repercussions, Hurricane?"

"In all fairness, we didn't know there were women and children here. It's the only reason I'm not shootin' you where you stand right now."

"It's the *only* reason we're *not* returning fire," Anton snaps.

I step forward, my teeth gritted together so tight, I fear they might chip. "Where is she?" I grumble.

Anton snaps his head to me and then tilts it. "Who?"

I go to race forward, but Hurricane places his hand on my chest.

"Novah, where *the fuck* have you got her?"

Anton smiles so wide it's almost disturbing as he lets out a chuckle and folds his arms over his chest. "Someone has taken your little sister?" He nods. "A bold move."

"A fucking stupid move for the cunts who took her. And if they don't give her back in one piece, we will tear their limbs from their body and force them up their asses with razorblades attached," I growl.

Anton jerks his head back, his lips turning up in the brightest smirk. "Oh... I see.... one of you has a little kinky side with your sister, huh?"

I go to rush forward again, but Hurricane grabs me by my cut and glares at me. "Keep your shit together."

He shoves me back, and I take a deep breath to keep my cool.

Anton chuckles, rolling his shoulders. "Okay, while taking your precious Novah *would* have been a marvelous plan, and yes, I agree, on New Year's, we did try to take your girls. But, on *this* occasion, it was not us, I'm afraid... you must have a *lot* of enemies." His mocking tone isn't missed on us as we all look at each other.

We can't take his word on this.

We need to make sure.

"You'll forgive us for not believin' you," Hurricane states and signals us to enter the warehouse.

Anton waves us through. "Go for it. You won't find Novah in there. In fact, I think you will be surprised at what you do find."

We all walk toward the warehouse, cautious not to be taken out by booby traps. But as we walk in, my eyes widen when I see it decked out like a school and communal eating place. They've made it a sanctuary for their families, and we've just come in here and blown up half their cabins.

They're going to have to rebuild.

These kids won't have homes, which doesn't sit right with me.

I feel like shit. *Even if they are Bratva.*

"What will you do for the kids?" I ask.

"Right now, you outnumber us, and it seems you have *plenty* of allies to help you. We need to focus on our families and getting everyone situated again. But when the time comes... when we have rebuilt... we *will* come for you and your NOLA Defiance. We have plenty of reason to seek revenge, and you have supplied it all. An eye for an eye. And trust me, it will be when you *least* expect it."

A cold shudder runs over my body, and I glance at Hurricane.

He gestures for me to step to the side and whispers in my ear, "You want to keep lookin', or are you satisfied she isn't here?"

"She's not here. We've looked everywhere. I have no fucking clue where she is. We're back to square one. And now we've dug ourselves a huge fucking hole with Anton."

"We'll figure it out. We gotta get back to the club and continue the search for Novah."

"Agreed. But we gotta go before they don't let us leave."

Hurricane turns back to face everyone. "I'll send you some money and supplies to help with the rebuild. If we knew this was for your families, we would never—"

"Too little too late, Hurricane." Anton grunts and turns, walking inside a cabin with the two children.

Taking a deep breath, we walk with Marcel and his crew back to his cars, and Hurricane slaps our friend on the shoulder. "Thanks for the save, man. If you didn't show up, this could have turned out a hell of a lot differently."

Marcel rolls his shoulders. "Anton would have wanted some form of revenge. He couldn't do that because he was so heavily outnumbered. You can thank the Baroness for calling me in. That's two favors you owe her. *Her words, not mine.*"

Six chuckles shaking his head. "Typical Connie." He slaps my back. "You'll get used to how she works. She grows on you, trust me. She can do a lot of good for the club when you get her to work with you. You just have to know how to work her."

Groaning, I turn up my lip. "I'll keep my reservations for now."

Six smirks. "Fair enough. Took us a while to warm to her too."

Hurricane gestures for us to head back to our rides. "All right, brothers, let's return home and reassess."

We fucked everything up.

This was nothing but a complete fucking failure.

And now I am still without the woman I love.

Where are you, Novah?

Where are you?

NOVAH
Three Weeks Later

Time is like a foreign concept to me right now. I have no clue how long I have been here, but it feels like weeks. I am beginning to lose all sense of hope. The fucking rats run around my feet constantly while Arsen is hardly ever in the cabin, leaving me locked in this cage with nothing to think about but my own demise. He goes out all day like he is preparing something. The wait is killing me. He's barely feeding me or giving me any water, the dehydration alone is making me nauseous and dizzy, but I have never been so hungry in all my life. I can tell because I have thought about picking up a rat and taking a bite multiple times.

Rocking on the mattress, my arms wrap around my legs, and I wonder if I might be starting to go a little crazy.

I was sure Bayou would have found me by now…

… but I am definitely not giving up hope.

I just feel so damn weak.

Like my body wants to give up.

My eyes begin searching around the cage for something to take the edge off my insanity, just something to make me feel anything other than the numbness creeping through my soul, when Arsen walks through the door. With a pep in his step, he smiles so wide it makes me want to punch him with the little energy I have left.

Instead, I'm going to finally find my voice. *What the hell do I have left to lose?* I'm not getting out of here, that much is obvious, so why not make as much noise as possible on my way out? Standing, I walk to the edge of the cage, glaring at him. "Why are you doing this."

He steps up to the cage, his eyes narrowing on me. "You hurt my brother, so I've been planning this for a long time. I've been watching you, studying you." He steps over to the refrigerator and pulls out an apple, peeling it with a blade, and grabs a jar of apple sauce and brings them over to me, placing them both down on a plate and offering them up. "You should eat. You're going to need your strength for this next part."

My eyes fall to the apple.

Something clicks.

The sauce on my desk.

The apples in a crate outside my work.

The apple at my house.

"The apples I've been seeing everywhere, they were all you?"

He smirks. "So you did notice? I've been leaving plenty of hints that I was coming for you."

My eyes widen at all the signs I missed.

I should have known.

He grins. "But now, it's finally time to play our little game."

He grabs a key, unlocking the door, and widens it. "You familiar with hide and seek?"

A chill sweeps over my body as he glances at the door. "You better find a *real* good place to hide out there. I'll give you a minute's head start, though... just to be fair."

My eyes widen as I gasp. "What are you talking about?"

He glances down at his watch. "Tick-tock, time's a-ticking, you're losing your advantage. Better get moving."

I glance for the door, wondering if this is a trick and whether he's going to stab me in my back or something equally as horrifying if I turn and run , but if I don't, and that minute runs out, I'm not sure I want to wait to find out what he has in store for me.

I need to try.

So I take off for the front door, and he bursts out laughing as I yank it open, and the second I do, a bunch of rats run across in front of me like they were let out of a cage specifically to scare me. But I ignore them, and take off, my eyes taking in what's around me.

Nothing but a misty old swamp.

Full of mud, mosquitos, animals, and things I don't even want to think about. I hesitate for a brief moment.

"Tick-tock, Novah," Arsen calls out, and it's all I need. I don't have time to waste. I take off, barefoot through the mud at the water's edge, then into the dense tree line. Sticks and God knows what dig into my feet, making me want to scream out in pain, but I keep quiet as my heart races so frantically fast, I have no clue what in the hell I am going to do.

All I do know is that I need to get to Bayou.

With the lack of food, my head is a fog, swirling with the adrenaline surging through me. It's hard to focus as I wade through the murky water, fearing for whatever lies in the depths below. The water is freezing as I wade in up to my knees to cover my tracks and keep rushing through the water, my feet running across stones and sticks which are digging and cutting into my flesh, making rivers of tears flow down my face.

If I have a chance to get to Bayou, I'm going to take it.

Suddenly, a loud squeal reverbs through the swamp, making me block my ears. A mass of birds fly out of the trees with the intrusion of sound. I stop dead, still clenching my eyes shut from the intensity of the noise—it's so loud it rattles through my bones and the frequency is so high it churns my stomach. I have no clue where it is coming from, but I know that it is Arsen playing games.

I hunch over, trying to block out the constant noise. It's almost crippling when it suddenly stops, and a crackling follows, then a throat clearing like someone is talking through a microphone. My eyes snap open as I spin around, looking everywhere. That's when I glance up into the trees' foliage and see speakers everywhere.

What in the hell?

"Welcome to our game, Novah. I have been setting this up since you got here. I think you will find you'll have a great time out there. I will be watching you, hunting you, so… you better get moving. Tick… tock."

My skin crawls.

The speakers crackle again, then the sound of classical music blasts over the swamp so loud I can hardly think. One I am very familiar with, but the sound of the loud operatic chorus sends a chill right through my bones. Carmina Burana "O Fortuna," the cantata booms through the trees, shaking the leaves, even some Spanish moss falls from the branches into the muddy water.

My muscles begin to tremble with fear and what that music means—a lament about the inescapable power of fate—instantly courses through me. The cold seeps through my veins, and the music heightens the fear inside me. But the one thing it does more than anything is make me want to run.

So I take off.

Fast.

Spooked.

Terrified.

Arsen's manic laughter echoes over the music.

Alarm.

Anxious.

Petrified.

Tears flood my cheeks as I race through the swamp, mud rushing up my legs, splattering all over my dress. My hands push branches back as I swerve in and out of the debris. This place is a maze, and I have no idea which direction to head. I stand circling as the drumbeat hits, and the mass of orchestral voices start frantically singing again, making my heart rate spike. If this was Arsen's intended effect and why he has this song playing, then it is working. Bringing my fingers into my tattered hair, I pant for breath, looking out into the endless swamp, trying to figure out my next move.

Finding my strength, I take a deep breath and surge forward just as a wild pig races out in front of me, its tusks aiming right at me. I let out a scream. and the only choice I have right now to get away from the animal is to dive into the murky water. So I jump, narrowly missing the pig. It grunts and continues running like it too is disorientated by the loud music.

As I wade through the water, something brushes past my leg, and I jump. *Jesus, what was that?* Turning, I rush as fast as I can to get back to land. The water is freezing anyway, and I know for a fact that gators lurk in those depths. Hoisting myself out of the water, my hands slip on the mud, my body sliding, and I cringe finally making it to my feet.

Wiping my face, I sniffle, trying to make sure none of the putrid water goes in my mouth. *Who the hell knows what kind of bugs are in that backwater?* My eyes snap around, trying to gain my bearings. I need to keep moving, so I take off further into the swamp. Otters and turtles float in the murky depths, and I shake my head at just how full of life this place is and how badly it wreaks of death—it's pungent in the air, and I don't know whether I am imagining things or whether I am just so close to my own that I can sense it coming.

Death is all around me right now.

It is in every tree, every drop of water, and every molecule of air.

And it's terrifying me.

It seeps into my bones like a noxious weed spreading through my system and soaking my blood. It invades every crevice of my being, making the fear inside me ignite with such terror I'm not sure I can control it.

I rush past a tree, and I hear a loud click.

Suddenly, an arrow flies past, and the blade's tip scrapes my bicep. I let out a loud yelp while clinging to my bleeding flesh and slam back against the tree. "Fuck!" I grunt as the arrow lodges into an old decaying trunk behind me.

I glance down at my arm and see it's just a scratch, but if I were standing a foot to the left, it would have gone straight into my chest.

Panting, I shake my head and dart around the other side of the tree, making my way in the other direction.

I can't believe Arsen has fucking booby traps out here.

The music reaches another peak, and I begin to feel like there is no way I am going to make it out of this alive because, quite simply, Arsen is a crazed lunatic. Bursting into tears, I keep pressure on my arm as I hobble through the swamp, trying to find my way out.

I just need to hold on long enough for Bayou to find me.

He's going to find me.

He has to.

Suddenly I turn, my leg catching on a wire, and I trip, falling. A hatch releases as I slam down on my ass, and as the hatch opens, four snakes slither out toward me. My eyes widen, I rush backward, mud and sticks ramming up underneath my fingernails as two snakes slither into the swamp, but one snake hangs back, lifting and hissing at me, the other not waiting and coming right for me.

Panic washes over my entire body as my bleeding hands rummage around for something, anything. Grabbing a rock, I will only have one chance at this, and if I miss, I'm a goner. So I wait until the snake is close enough as it slithers toward me, and with everything I have in me, I slam the rock down on its head. The squelching sound makes my skin crawl as the other snake quickly turns and slithers away while I continue slamming the rock up and down on the attacker to ensure it is dead. Blood and guts splash out all over the swamp ground, and I can't seem to stop myself. It's releasing my frustrations when suddenly a red laser narrows in on my chest.

I glance down at it, my eyes flashing up as I see the laser shining from deep in the swamp, but I can't see where it is coming from. *All I know is it is* not *a good thing.* So I drop the rock and get up as quickly as possible, ducking out of the way before a huge flame thrower ignites, scorching everything in its path.

I pant, running as fast as I can as the Spanish moss ignites in flames, lighting a portion of the canopy in flames. I duck, running faster to avoid the heat. My skin was covered in goose bumps from the bitter cold of the water, and now I am prickling in heat from the flames above. But somehow, I manage to rush out, beating the inferno, smoke making me cough as the trumpets and flutes flurry manically over the speakers, heightening the moment's tension.

It's like he knew this music would suit everything that was going to happen out here. I'm having trouble catching my breath, but I continue running, though with the lack of food and water and everything up to now, I am having trouble maintaining my strength.

But I have to keep going. I *have* to keep going.

I have to find my way back to Bayou.

I *can't* give up now.

A loud blast echoes from behind me, and while I'm running, I turn to look, but I can't see anything, and as I turn back, a branch from a tree starts collapsing right in front of me. I skid to a halt, but the branch slams against me on the way down. I let out a yelp as I drop to the ground, the branch slamming against my knee. I lay on my back for a moment. Just one moment staring up at the swamp's canopy, wondering if I should just let Arsen win. Even Mother Nature is against me right now. But my eyes shift to the tree where the branch came from to see the remnants of C4 taped to the tree.

Letting out a small, crazed laugh, I shake my head.

I should have known this was Arsen. Sorry, Mother Nature.

Somehow finding my inner fight, I lean over, shoving the branch off me, seeing my leg sliced and cut up, my knee instantly swelling. Gritting my teeth, I shake my head. "You want me, Arsen? You come and fucking get me," I scream at the top of my lungs as I fight through my pain and hobble to my feet.

My leg hurts like a bitch, but I am not letting this motherfucker beat me. I haven't come this far to be taken out by him. No, sir.

Arsen chuckles down the microphone, the sound is ominous and alarming. But he doesn't say anything, so I straighten out my shoulders, even though I am bleeding practically everywhere, and I take off again. I may be hobbling, but I am going to fight for my life because I want to get back to Bayou.

I find my way to the edge of the water to what looks like a path. All the while that fucking song is playing on repeat and driving me absolutely crazy. My breathing is labored, my eyes darting everywhere as I try to keep my wits about me. Every single inch of me is screaming in agony, but my eyes land on something ahead on the path. I stop for a moment, knowing it is probably a trap, but I hesitantly step toward it, seeing it is a hole dug out in the shape of a grave. At the top of it is a cross with my name written on it.

My head begins to spin.

Chills sweep up and down my body.

I can't seem to gather enough oxygen to breathe.

My chest squeezes so tightly that my heart feels like it will explode from the fear crippling me right now while my eyes snap around to see if Arsen is close by. I can't see him, but I am not taking any chances.

I don't want to end up in that ditch for all eternity.

No way.

No how.

Spinning, I race toward the water. I don't want that asshole to know where I have gone if he tracks my footprints. I slide into the gloomy depths, and as I slowly and cautiously wade into the swamp, shifting through the moss, trying to be discreet, something slides past my leg. Something scaly.

My heart leaps into my throat as I glance behind to see a fucking alligator swimming toward me, and I gasp. My flight instinct kicks into full gear. I swim as fast as I can to get away, tears stream down my face when full panic sets in.

I make it to the bank, climb up the edge and race onto land just as the alligator opens his mouth and chomps. The loud smack of his teeth slamming together while he tries to attack me makes me scream out as I run, the giant reptile narrowly missing me. I run as quickly as possible on dry land while the alligator tries to take chase, but on land, he is too slow, and I am not stopping for anything.

I take off into the trees again, leaving the alligator behind, my eyes fogging over so much I can hardly see. How Bayou can have an alligator for a pet is beyond me. *They're fucking terrifying.*

Snakes hang down from the trees causing me to duck and weave, avoiding them.

Feeling like I'm running in circles.

Like I am losing my mind.

Will I ever get out of this hell hole?

I run my fingers into my wet, knotted, and tatty hair and let out an almighty scream, and as I turn, the ground collapses beneath me. I fall, my legs giving out as I land on something that doesn't feel like ground—not to mention the smell. The ditch isn't too deep, so I glance up. I can climb out of here, but it might take me some effort with my hands and feet more cut up from landing on whatever is in the bottom. Taking a deep breath, I glance down at whatever the fuck I am standing on, and I let out another scream as I fall back with the shock, landing on a pile of dead bodies in various states of decomposition. My hand snaps to my mouth to cover it from hurling as I see every single woman has had their stomach torn open like the rat on my front doorstep.

My body trembles with such an innate fear that I can hardly move.

I feel like I am frozen to the spot.

"Tick-tock, Novah," Arsen calls over the speakers, and it's enough to snap me out of my daze.

I spin, scurrying for the edge of the ditch, racing to get out of this mass grave.

This is so much bigger than I realized.

Arsen has killed before.

He killed all these women.

He killed them like he killed that rat, and this is his plan for me.

I have never been more terrified in my life.

I am so physically weak.

I feel like there is no way out of this.

But then I think of Bayou.

That he would want me to fight.

That he *needs* me to fight.

So I push through the pain and hoist myself up and out of the ditch, racing off from that horror to find a tree to hide under.

I need a second to decompress.

Sliding down, I pant, shaking from the cold, my body all banged up and bruised as tears cascade down my face. My mind shifts to Bayou and the life I could have had with him. We were only just starting, only just getting our act together. We wasted so much time hesitating when we should have jumped in the second we felt our connection.

We waited, and we missed out on our life together.

I am trying to hold my shit together.

Trying to keep my mind focused on Bayou.

On my need to find him.

To keep going for him.

I must be strong.

I need to fight.

So I try to dust myself off, and as I stand, I turn out from behind the tree, and Arsen is standing there, waiting.

I gasp as he brings out a taser, slamming it into my collarbone. The volts surge through my system so intensely I can't see or think straight. It's like a thousand knives are jamming into every part of my body simultaneously.

I can't breathe.

I can't think.

A vision of Bayou crosses my mind before everything goes black.

BAYOU

These last three weeks have been the most draining and painful in the history of time.

There are no leads.

No hope.

Absolute despair.

We have no idea where Novah is located, and it's killing me more and more every day she is away.

And with each passing day, there's less hope of getting her back.

We've been holding off telling Nash and Ingrid. Though, I'm sure Ingrid will have noticed something is up, especially as she has not heard from Novah for three weeks. Nash will be too caught up in his own drama to even realize she's missing.

But the main outcome in all this...

... I have failed her.

I am the one person who was supposed to keep her safe.

The one person she could and should rely on.

So as I sit at the bar drinking, Hurricane steps up to my side and slaps my back. "I thought I was the raging alcoholic in the family?"

Snorting, I throw back the last of my bourbon and tap the bar for another. "The burn helps."

Hurricane sits next to me and crosses his arms over his chest. "This is killin' me, brother. I have Raid workin' round the clock tryin' to figure this shit out…" He sighs heavily. "We're gonna find her. We have to."

"Goddammit! I should be out there looking."

"And where are you gonna look, brother? We have zero leads."

"Random fucking places. It's better than sitting here hoping for a damn miracle?"

"Sometimes, all we need is a miracle, Bayou. We have the Baroness and Marcel lookin'. We're gonna be owin' favors out the ass for this one. But in the end, someone is gonna find somethin'."

"I feel like I should be doing more."

"When the time comes, you will be there for her."

Dipping my chin, something on the television catches my attention. "Hey, Frankie, can you turn that up?"

She grabs the remote turning up the volume. We all turn around to the late-night news report.

"The New Orleans PD is declaring they have no official leads. Missing women reported strange sightings before each of their disappearances. In the twelve instances, the women spoke to friends and family about spotting apples or variations of apple byproducts in their day-to-day life. The victims also found disembodied rat carcasses on their front porches. In each of these cases, not long after this, they would go missing and have not been heard from or seen since. Detective Tyler Cain, the lead detective on the case, suspects that each woman may have met with foul play. So far no bodies have been discovered, but if bodies *are* recovered, New Orleans may very well be dealing with a serial killer, the biggest since the 'Storyville Slayer' back in 1996, and if this is the case, they have already named him the Core Ripper due to the connection to apples. Detective Cain has no leads on the Core Ripper, but let's hope he doesn't have another victim in waiting."

My head snaps to Hurricane as my stomach falls through the floor. My mind flashes back to Novah finding the apple with the blade through it and the rat on her front doorstep. "You don't think... *do you?"* I whisper the last few words breathlessly, not wanting to think the worst.

Hurricane is as white as a sheet. "We thought the rat and the apple were Johnny. Everythin' stopped, didn't it? Did she say anything else about more apples or rats?"

I spin, turning to face Raid. "Raid, I need you to tap into Novah's work cameras... see if you can find anything to do with apples."

Raid dips his head, pulls out his laptop, and starts typing. He digs and digs, and finally, after what feels like an hour, he lets out a small, "Hmm..."

"What?" I spin to him.

"Okay, so here, look... someone delivered apple sauce to her office."

We crowd in over Raid's shoulder to watch the footage of a delivery driver dropping off the jar of sauce.

"Keep searching." My whole body goes tense as my teeth grind.

Raid sifts through more footage. Then he stops, pulling up cameras from outside her office. "Here... there's a crate of apples outside her work."

"Jesus! Fuck! What if Novah has been taken by some fucking serial killer? What if we're too fucking late."

Hurricane shakes his head, his brows pull so tight they are a single line. "Why the hell would a serial killer come after Novah? This shit don't make sense. There must be more to it. Raid, who delivered the apples outside her business?"

Raid scans the footage and zooms in on the man. He pauses on the image, and we all jerk back in shock.

"I saw you feed Johnny to La Fin, right?" Hurricane asks me.

"Absolutely. I sliced that asshole through the meat cutter myself," I reply in confusion.

"So then... who the fuck is that guy?" Hurricane asks.

Raid starts a different search pattern. "I can't find anything using normal channels. Let me dig deeper."

He hunts through the dark web and finds that Johnny has a twin, but his mother gave Arsen away at birth. Their names are different, and there's no record of them being brothers because the adoption agency changed Arsen's name. Records show he's been in and out of psych wards all through his life, because his mother couldn't look after two kids, so she gave him away and kept the one, Johnny. Apparently, that was a trigger for him.

Once he was over eighteen, he went in search of Johnny, and they found each other. Their biological mother went missing, presumed murdered, but they never found her body or her killer.

"Because Arsen killed her…" Hurricane mumbles.

"Jesus Christ! This lunatic has Novah? And because we killed his brother, he took her from us in some sort of retaliative move. Raid, I need you to find him," I demand.

"Already searching."

"Search fucking faster. He's had her for three weeks. *Dammit!*"

"You yelling at me isn't gonna make me go faster. If anything, it will slow me down. Fuck off somewhere and let me work, brother."

Turning, I pace the clubhouse floor not having one clue what else to do.

Hurricane steps up to me. "We'll figure it out. She's gonna be okay. She has to be."

Fear almost cripples me. "If he's—"

"He hasn't. She's gonna be fine. I feel it in my bones. Novah's strong."

The problem is that killing only takes a minute, and Arsen's had three full weeks.

Too much time has passed.

I should have pushed harder.

Novah's probably been murdered.

And it's all *my* fucking fault.

CHAPTER 26

NOVAH

The harsh sting of frigid water splashes on my face, jolting me awake. I gasp as the freezing water sends a chill deep into my bones. I can't gather my bearings being half zonked out from the taser to my chest. But as I go to lift my hand, I soon realize that I'm strapped down to a surgical table. My head snaps down to see I am completely naked, and that's when a wave of tumultuous terror runs through me while I struggle in the restraints trying to break free.

Arsen's maniacal laughter breaks my panic as he stands at the end of the table with the brightest smile on his face.

Tears flood my eyes, and my bottom lip trembles. "So, this is where you do to me what you did to those other bodies out there in the swamp?"

Arsen runs his hand along my thigh, revulsion wracks through me at the thought of him touching me, but all he does is continue to smirk. "You all deserve it, you know. Thinking you're better than me. That I don't belong."

I need to stretch this out for as long as possible, so I have to get him to talk. "Why the apples, Arsen? What draws you to them?"

He chuckles. "My mother, my *real* mother, gave me away when

I was born. She chose Johnny over me, and that's okay because he was great, but she didn't want me. She gave up on me. She sent me to that place where I lived in a rat-infested hell hole. The only way I could stop the rats from invading my bed was to cut open one of their friends and place them around my bed on the floor as a deterrent. That was the squaller I was living in… that's the *hell* that bitch sent me to."

My body shakes not only from the cold but sheer terror, though somehow I pull out the courage to continue, "I'm sorry you lived through that, Arsen. It must have been horrifying."

"*Horrifying?* I was just trying to survive. So when I finally met my bio mom at eighteen, and she was standing there in all her perfectly made-up glory, slicing an apple with a blade like I meant nothing, something inside me clicked. I wanted to see what *her* insides looked like. Just like how I cut open those rats, I wanted my mom to be flayed open and to let that be a deterrent to any other woman who would treat me like I meant *nothing* to them."

"So that's what this is? You kill the women who treat you badly?" I ask.

"Kill them? No… I set them free."

He's fucking insane.

"But what if they don't want to be set free? What if by hurting these women, you're making the same mistake your bio mom did all those years ago?"

He twists up his face. "You don't know what you're talking about. I am *nothing* like her."

"It sounds like she had detachment issues, which made it easy for her to remove herself from the situation she was in and the people she was close to…" I pause before continuing, "Isn't that exactly what you do, Arsen? Detach yourself from the women you intend to set free?"

His eyes dart around the room like he's trying to maintain his thoughts, but then he walks over to a large blade and picks it up—similar to the one stabbed through the apple at my home. He raises it in the air, the light reflecting off it around the room while he stares at the sharpness of the blade. "You're trying to psychoanalyze me, Novah… I don't like it. I've been building my anticipation, waiting for weeks to get to this point. We played our game, and you lost. Now I get to claim my victory prize."

My stomach churns, a chill sweeping across my skin as I shake my head from side to side. Tears flow down the sides of my face while I wriggle against the restraints.

That's when he brings the blade down in between my breasts and presses lightly.

"Now, Novah, I like it when my victims scream."

He presses the blade into my flesh, it burns, ripping apart my skin, and I can't help the ear-piercing scream that leaves me.

My eyes close when he drags the blade downward.

This is it.

This is how I am going to die.

Pain.

Agony.

Despair.

Then I fade to the memory of Bayou's face.

CHAPTER 27

BAYOU

My pulse is racing as the guys and I wade through this thick swamp to get to Arsen's cabin.

Raid had a ping from Arsen's cell, which led us here, but it was fucking hard to find. The ping only popped up for a minute, if that. Like he forgot for a brief moment he could be tracked, then he remembered and turned it off. But it was enough for us to get a location. And as we rush through the swamp, getting mud and shit all over us, we're on guard rushing toward the cabin.

An ear-piercing scream echoes through the swamp.

We all halt.

My stomach somersaults, knowing in my heart that scream came from Novah. I don't wait, taking off faster than my feet can carry me. I don't give a shit about anything other than the monster hurting my girl.

Finally, I spot the cabin as Novah's terrifying screams continue.

Hurricane calls out to all of us. "Okay, let's all approach via the—"

Fuck that. I am not waiting to hear his orders.

I rush for the door, turning and slamming my shoulder through the rickety old wood. It smashes apart as I race inside, my brothers following behind me.

I spot Novah bleeding profusely, her body shaking on some fucked-up surgical table. Arsen's standing over her with a blade in his hand and a shocked expression on his face like he wasn't expecting us.

But honestly, I don't care about this asshole as I bolt straight for Novah.

"You can't come in here and ruin this," he screams, aiming his bloody knife at me menacingly.

But Hurricane reaches for a broom nearby and without hesitation, sideswipes it into Arsen's forearm making him yelp. The knife drops from his fingers as Hurricane rushes forward slamming his fist into Arsen's face, and he keeps on hitting him.

I tune out Hurricane beating the living shit out of him and slide in next to Novah, taking in the bloody sight before me. My hand reaches out for her face, cupping her cheek. "I'm here. Sorry it took me so long, but I am here."

Novah's eyes roll around in her head, her tortured body shuddering as she goes into shock. My breathing quickens when I glance down to her stomach, seeing the deep gash from the base of her breasts heading toward her belly button, and I can't help but let out a small sob. I don't know how deep the cut goes, but she is losing a lot of blood. I reach for her hands and untie her.

Grit grabs a blanket from somewhere, and wraps it over her naked body. I lean in, running my fingers through her matted hair, undeniable panic overruling me right now. "You're gonna be okay. You have to be okay, baby."

She moans, her head turning to me as she licks her parched lips. "M-mass g-grave in the s-swamp—"

"It's okay. Save your energy," I tell her as Hoodoo steps up.

"I called an EMT. I can't help her... this is beyond me. I also called NOLA PD. Cain needs to come out here and check this shit out thoroughly."

"I'm gonna take Arsen and get him out of here, so *we* can deal with him. We're not handin' him over to the PD," Hurricane grunts, then walks off, pulling Arsen by the leg and dragging him along the ground.

Every inch of me is trembling as I stare at Novah and stroke her hair, fear seeping into my veins that she might not make it. That we're too damn late. "You're gonna be okay," I tell her, but she is turning paler, shaking, and is so freaking cold. "You gotta hang on. Look at me, Novah. Just a little longer. You can't quit on me now."

She's zoning in and out of consciousness when the sounds of people approaching alert us, and a whole bunch of police enter, including Detective Cain.

"Get on the ground," the heat yells out at everyone, who reluctantly fall to their knees, but I shake my head, not moving a single inch.

"We said… *Get. On. The. Ground. Now,*" a cop states, aiming his gun in my face.

"I'm not leaving her side. Arrest me all you want, but I am not fucking letting her go until the EMT arrives to help her. *You. Got. Me?*" My voice leaves no room for misinterpretation. My monster is about to unleash its fury if these cunts don't let me stay with Novah. I will rip them all new assholes before they know what's happened.

Cain steps up and waves at his men. "Stand down. Send in the EMTs. Who's in charge here?"

City steps forward. "That would be me."

"What the fuck happened?" Cain asks.

City starts talking to Cain about what went down with Arsen and Novah, telling Cain that Arsen fled on foot while we were helping Novah.

The EMTs rush in.

My hand is tightly gripped onto Novah's as the EMTs move in beside her and start assessing.

"She's lost a lot of blood. These wounds need to be stabilized before we can move her to the hospital… right now, her blood pressure is incredibly low."

Novah's eyes meet mine, her body visibly shaking as she mouths, *I love you*.

My heart constricts as I tighten my hand in hers.

Then her eyes roll into the back of her head, and she lets out a breath.

"She's coding." The EMT shoves me back out of the way as they get to work on her.

My breathing is stuttered.

My mind is blank.

My heart is breaking.

Grit grabs me, trying to pull me away, but everything in me needs to be near her.

"Novah," I holler and try to race forward.

Grit and City both lunge, pulling my arms back behind me, stopping me from getting any closer to her. I struggle in their hold as I watch the EMTs working frantically.

"Novah. Fuck! C'mon, baby." Panic washes over me so intensely that my stomach empties all over the floor.

The EMTs charge the paddles, my body feeling as though I'm going to feel the shock at the same time as they yell out, "Clear!" Novah's body jerks up with the force of electricity flowing through her. I let out a groan, watching them trying to restart her heart, then they check for a rhythm that simply isn't coming.

I roar like some wild animal, turning and yanking out of City and Grit's hold and start pacing, frantically trying to find some strength to send to Novah.

"Clear!" They shock her again.

I turn to see her body jerk with the electricity, and when I see it, I pick up a fucking apple sitting in a fruit basket and hurtle it across the other side of the cabin. "Fuuuck!" My eyes take in her lifeless body as they check her over while I rub at the base of my neck. I lean against a beam, my back sliding against it, needing the support to keep me upright as the EMT checks for her pulse. But ultimately, I can't stand anymore, and my knees give out as I slump down the beam.

My breathing is nonexistent while I wait to hear what he says. My eyes fog so much I can hardly see, grief slamming into me full force. It's like a tidal wave so fucking fierce I can't stop the emotion from overwhelming me.

"We have a pulse," the EMT calls out.

I snap my head up.

Startled.

Surprise.

Hope.

"It's weak, but it's there."

Letting out a heavy sob, I sink onto my ass, my head in my hands as I let fucking tears I never cry overcome me. I don't care that my brothers are seeing me like this. Grit rests his hand on my shoulder for support as they work on getting her stable for transport while I try to pull my-fucking-self together.

Novah needs me to be strong.

I *have* to be strong for her.

Swiping at my face, I let out a long exhale and make a move to stand. Then, walking over to the EMTs, I dip my chin as they prepare her for transport. "Thank you... for saving her."

"She's not out of the woods yet. We have to get her to the hospital *right now*. We have no time to lose."

"I'm going with her."

The EMT nods, and City steps up to me. "We'll meet you. You gonna be okay till we get there?"

"Yeah. But you're gonna need to call Ingrid and Nash... they need to know what's happened."

City nods. "I got you."

I grab hold of Novah's hand and walk with her out to the waiting ambulance. She's loaded inside, and I sit in the back with her as we start our ride to the hospital. The EMT is trying his best to work on what wounds he can, and I shake my head at how much damage this asshole did to my girl.

"Is she going to be okay?" I ask him outright.

He looks at Novah, then glances at me, not saying anything in reply.

And his response is utterly terrifying.

CHAPTER 28

NOVAH
Two weeks Later

A tightness on my hand makes me want to open my eyes, but I can't seem to find the strength.

"C'mon, beautiful, today's the day. I know you can do it. Open your stunning eyes for me." Bayou's voice is close by, and it makes me want to go to him. Though it's hard to focus and make my body do what I want it to.

"Novah, I can't do this without you. I need you... please. Please open your eyes." The desperation in his tone tears my heart to pieces. So I fight through the fog, I fight through the pain, and I will myself to open my eyes.

I blink a few times, trying to gather my bearings. Bayou sits at the edge of my bed, his head resting on my lap as I slowly smile. "Hey," I murmur.

His head snaps up like he's heard a ghost, his eyes meeting mine in an instant, and he smiles so wide. His fingers gently caress my cheek. "Oh God, I've missed that voice." He leans in softly, kissing my parched lips, and my fingers run through his hair, just needing to feel him.

He slowly pulls back, his glistening eyes meeting mine. "I was so scared I'd lost you."

"I was scared too... so fucking scared."

"I failed you. I couldn't find you. I let you down, and you got really hurt—"

"But you *did* find me," I tell him, caressing his cheek. "You *found* me," I reiterate.

"That asshole was gonna kill you, and he almost succeeded."

I shift up a little on the bed, my stomach pulling and burning as pain rushes through me, and I grimace. "But you stopped him. You stopped a serial killer, Bayou."

He shakes his head. "I don't know what I would've done if he—"

"I'm alive... thanks to you."

"Yeah, you are..." He finally smiles. "The doctors had to do a surgery to repair all the muscle and blood vessels that lunatic cut through. We were lucky he didn't get any vital organs. You lost a shitload of blood, and because you were covered in filth from the swamp, you got an infection... it's why you've been recovering for so long..." He tightens his grip on my hand, his eyes never leaving mine. "But, they say your markers are all on the up. You're healing, and you're going to make a full recovery. You're just going to have one hell of a battle scar."

I glance down and slowly pull my bedsheets back.

Bayou moves to stop me. "Maybe you shouldn't," he warns.

But I keep pulling them down to see myself dressed in a hospital gown. I shift it out of the way to see a long patch of gauze down the center of my stomach.

I should be grateful if a scar is the worst thing to come out of this.

I place the sheet down and get comfortable back in bed. "So, how long am I in for?"

Bayou smiles. "At least another couple of weeks. They want you to be awake before they'll give me an exact release date."

"Is the food good?"

Bayou laughs. "Terrible."

Curling up my nose, I sigh. "Guess you'll have to smuggle me in some beignets then."

"Beautiful, I'm not leaving your side. Not for nothing."

Letting out a small exhale, a sense of calm washes over me. "Good. Because I don't want to be alone right now."

Bayou stands and moves to the side of my bed grabbing my hand. "I'm right here."

Sniffling, my eyes meet his. "Could you lay with me a while?"

His eyes shift to the door, then he glances back at me furrowing his brows. "I don't want to hurt you."

Slumping my shoulders, I shake my head. "I just need you to hold me right now, Bayou."

He nods his head. "All right, let me help you," he offers and then leans over, gently easing me as my muscles pull and ache when he aids in shifting me in the bed. I wince, but it will be so worth it.

Letting out a long exhale, I move to the edge of the bed. He smiles, kicks off his boots and climbs up beside me. He wraps his arm behind my head, and I finally feel like I am safe for the first time since I left that damn swamp. "I'm not going anywhere," he whispers against my ear.

My eyes begin to well as I lean into his chest, my bottom lip trembling while I try to wipe the memory of Arsen's face from my mind.

Bayou tightens his arm around me and holds me close. "It's okay, Novah, you can let it all out."

That's all I needed to hear to let the floodgates open. I burst into a river of tears while clutching to Bayou. He doesn't say anything, just lets me cling to him, needing his support. My heart hammers in my chest, feeling like it might explode as I cry harder than I ever have.

For the innocent girl I once was.

For the woman I was becoming.

And I cry for the Novah who was left back on that surgical table, cut open and bleeding all over the cabin floor.

Because *this* Novah will never be the same again.

BAYOU
A Month Later

It's been a long and painful road, but Novah is almost healed, and the boys and I are throwing a crawfish boil welcome home party for Novah. I brought her home to the clubhouse from the hospital this morning, so Hurricane and I thought it was a good idea to celebrate. Unfortunately, she needed to stay in the hospital so long because of the multiple surgeries and the endless antibiotics for the infections.

A long and painful road—but we got there.

The party is starting. Heavy rock music thumps through the sound system, letting us all relax and unwind after a tumultuous few weeks.

Ingrid is already here as she stands with Hurricane and Kaia.

Novah and I stand together, taking this all in. "You sure you're ready to tell Nash when he gets here tonight?" I ask her.

She nods. "Everyone but Nash knows about us. He's my brother, Bayou, and he deserves to know. I can't keep this from him anymore."

Smirking, I groan. "You know he's gonna murder me. I hope you've taken a good look because this is the last you're going to see me alive. We should check to see if my life insurance is up to date."

She rolls her eyes and giggles. "Dramatic much. We thought Hurricane was going to kill you... he didn't. I'm sure Nash is going to be fine too. In fact, here he is now."

Nash walks in, Brianna by his side. It's her first time coming to the club. The poor woman won't know what's hit her. But if she is going to be in Nash's life, we're part of it. She's got to get used to us and our lifestyle choice. They step up to Hurricane and Ingrid as I roll my shoulders. "At least he looks like he's in a good mood... right?"

Novah cuddles into my side. "Right... so let's go do this. Now or never, babe."

Inhaling, I crack my neck to the side. "Okay... here we go."

We step up just as Nash asks, "Is anyone actually going to tell me what's going on?"

Mom glances at Hurricane, and they both turn to Novah and me.

Nash furrows his brows, rolling his shoulders. "Why the hell is everyone being so weird. *What's going on?*"

Novah reaches out, grabbing my hand, probably for support. My eyes lock with hers, sending her nothing but encouraging love and adoration back, letting her know she has got this.

"Nash... with everything going on with me, with you, with the club... we were trying to find the right time to tell you," Novah mumbles out the words.

Tension rolls over Nash's shoulders as he tilts his head. "Tell me... what?"

Now or never Bayou.

Time to be a man.

I step forward and just get it out there. "Novah and I... we're together."

Brianna slowly smiles as I see the cogs turning in Nash's mind, his face turning redder and redder by the second. His nostrils flare, the vein in his neck begins to pulsate with every beat of his heart.

"No!" he simply grunts out, his hands balling into tight fists by his sides as he tries to control his breathing.

I take another step forward. "I love her, Nash."

His eyes glaze over—it's like Nash leaves his body as his anger takes hold. He brings his fist up, slamming it into my jaw. The pain shoots through my face so intensely that I drop to one knee.

Ingrid instantly steps up, placing her hand on Nash's chest. "Nash."

"No, Ingrid, don't interfere. I deserved that," I state, rubbing my chin and making a move to stand.

Nash steps forward, getting right up in my face. "All this time you were with her, making moves on her, and you never once thought to break it to me that you were into *my* sister?"

I sigh. "I told Hurricane without Novah being present. I thought she should be here when her blood brother found out."

"You could have called me any... *fucking*... time. I would have come right over. How long has thing been going on for?"

I hesitate and Nash glares at me. *"How long,"* he growls through gritted teeth.

"A while."

Turning, he runs his hand through his hair, pacing back and forth. "She's *my* sister."

"I'm aware."

"She's *your* sister," Nash snap back at me.

I huff. "She's my *stepsister.* We're *not* related, Nash."

Relaxing his stance a little, he tilts his head. "Okay, fair play... but if you hurt her, especially now, *I* will be the one you have to worry about. Don't think I'm not scared to come after you because you're a damn biker. She's my sister and I will destroy you if you even so much as make her cry."

I can deal with that.

Hurricane slaps Nash on the shoulder. "Right there with you, brother. If Bayou hurts her, he's in for a world full of hurt."

Ingrid snorts. "Leave Bayou alone, you two."

Novah smiles as she leans in, cuddling my side. "We never expected this to evolve the way it has, Nash. But when you fall, you just fall."

Nash turns to Brianna, and she weakly smiles at him.

Yeah, he gets it.

"As long as you're happy, Novah. You're my sister, and that's all I want for you... happiness."

She rushes forward, pulling Nash into a tight embrace. "I love you, Nash."

"Love you too." He wraps his arms around her body and plants a kiss on her head.

She pulls back and her eyes shift to Brianna. "Sorry about that, Brianna. That was not the welcome to the club we were hoping to give you," Novah states.

Brianna smiles. "I've met the family and seen a club fight in the space of fifteen minutes, I think it's the perfect initiation into club life."

Everyone chuckles as Nash pulls Brianna to him.

Hurricane gestures to her. "C'mon, let's get you introduced to the rest of the club."

"I'd like that," Brianna chimes.

Nash eyes Novah, dipping his chin, "I just have to say one more thing, then I'll let it go," Nash states.

Novah gnaws on her bottom lip, and I tighten my grip around her. "Okay?"

"All that time I was visiting in the hospital, I thought something was up. You were far too upset at Novah's condition. Now you tell me the *whole time* you were together... and you never fucking said anything, Bayou."

I nod my head. "Novah wasn't in any kind of fit state to deal with the fallout. We needed to concentrate on her recovery. That was the priority, Nash. Not telling you what was going on behind the scenes."

Novah steps forward reaching out for her brother's hand. "But we've told you now. We never wanted to hide it for this long... okay, maybe we did a little, but I'm glad you know now."

Nash pulls Novah to him for a gentle hug. "I'm just glad you're safe... and if Bayou makes you happy, who am I to stand in his way?"

Novah pulls back, tears glistening in her eyes. "You mean that?"

He cranes his neck to the side. "I'm going to have to get used to it, but yeah... just, don't kiss in front of me. It's weird."

We all laugh as he reaches out for Brianna, his eyes meeting mine, a mutual respect flowing through them, then he walks off with his woman and Hurricane.

I turn to Novah and roll my shoulders. "That went as well as can be expected?"

Novah places her hand on my chest. "I'm proud of you."

I go to reply, but my attention is suddenly taken by Grit storming past me on the phone, seeming like he is having a hard time. Everyone looks at him as he yells down the line, and I turn to Novah. "I'll go check it out."

Novah smiles, nodding her head, and I make my way over to Grit as he ends his call, pacing the clubroom floor. But as I approach, Lani beats me to it. "Hey, you okay?"

He turns, his eyes hard then he snaps at her. "I'm fine. Just back off, Lani." Then he storms off for the back door. Lani jerks her head back in shock as I rush up to her, watching the tears form in her eyes.

"Whatever that call was..." I quickly wrap my arm around her shoulder and sigh. "I know Grit didn't mean to go at you like that. It was stress. You know he adores you."

She sniffles and nods. "Yeah, but he's never spoken to me like that before."

The clear hurt in her tone means I need to fix this. "I'll talk to him, figure out what's up his ass, okay?"

She weakly smiles, and I send her off to chat with Kaia.

I walk out to the gym, where Grit slams his unwrapped fists into the boxing bag. Raising my brow, I step over, grabbing the bag and spotting for him. "You working off some tension?"

He thumps his fist into the bag, then turns, and starts pacing off his frustration. "He's such a fucking asshole, you know?"

I don't know.

"Who?"

"My fucking father. It's always Jones this, Jones that. Why can't you be like Jones. He's so fucking productive, and..." he turns back, slamming his fist back into the bag, "... he's so much better at every. Fucking. Thing." He slams his fist again, and I huff.

"Jones is your brother, right?" I ask while he continues to pummel the bag.

He stops and stares at me. "I mean, I get it. I know Jones is older and wiser than me. He's a successful tour manager for some band, and Dad is all about how Jones has made something of himself. But doesn't he understand the more he tries to make me like Jones, the worse it makes me feel, and the more it makes me want to do what I want."

"He doesn't like that you joined the club?"

Grit snorts. "I joined the club *because* of him, to *spite* him. He wanted me to go to college and be this fucking superhuman that I'm just incapable of being. I'm not Jones. I'm just *not.*"

I dip my head. "I get it. Out of everyone, I get it. I have a twin, who is the president of this club, and everyone expected me to step up and be his VP, but that isn't who I am... I'm not that kind of guy. I'm too laid back to be the man throwing out orders. So when Hurricane was on my back, riding me constantly, I felt that pressure. That constant disappointment you feel when you aren't rising to the occasion. I understand, Grit. But at the same time, I also know you can't let your father dictate your life to you. You gotta stand up for what you believe in, for what *you* want. This is *your* life. *You* make the rules..." I sigh. "But also, in the process, don't hurt or alienate those you care about in the process. If the past couple of months has shown me anything, it's that time is short and precious as hell. You never know when you're gonna lose the people you love the most."

He scowls. "Lani… was she upset by what I said?"

I dip my chin, and he curls up his lip. "Fuck! I'm an asshole. See… my dad's always fucking everything up."

"Then don't let him. Take your power back, Grit. There's a reason we gave you that road name. It's time you used it."

He slaps me on the shoulder and inhales deeply. "Thanks, and for what it's worth, I think you'd have made a great VP. But I get the whole *you not wanting it*, and I respect that."

Chuckling, I walk with him back inside the clubhouse, where he takes off to find Lani.

My eyes instantly check for Novah—she's sitting with the other girls.

She's so beautiful, like a damn angel.

How'd I get so lucky?

The party continued on, and Novah and I celebrated with everyone, just having a damn good time. Then, we spent the night cuddling in bed.

In the light of morning, we get up and walk out, ready for breakfast.

But Hurricane steps up to me before I even have a chance to sit, with a fire lit in his eyes. "Now that Novah is home, we've had our celebration, and everythin' is back to normal. Do you think it's time?"

A slow smile lights up my face. I've waited *so fucking long* for this moment. My skin is crawling with the need.

Novah raises her brow in confusion. "What's going on?"

I turn to her, inhaling, preparing to tell her what I've been holding onto all this time. "We still have Arsen here on the property. We were waiting for you to be fit enough in case you wanted to play a part in how we repay *him* for what he did to *you.* In case you need to witness that he's gone for good."

I watch her reaction closely. She's been doing so good, the last thing I want is for her to take a gigantic step backward, but she nods. "I want to do it."

Hurricane and I both jerk our heads back.

"What? Absolutely not. You can be there but not take him out," I snap.

She rests her hand on my chest and looks in my eyes. "You don't know half the shit that bastard put me through, Bayou. You can do whatever you want to him first, while I watch, but I want to be the one to *end* him."

I turn to Hurricane, I don't know if I'm seeking guidance from him or just some kind of moral support.

Hurricane shrugs. "If Novah is gonna be your Old Lady, Bayou, she's gonna have to get in tune with the club and how we do things. She can't stay innocent and pure forever. You're gonna have to taint her soul just a little."

"Fine. But the second it gets too much for you, you say, and I will pull you out of there."

She nods, and I reach out for her hand. "You sure you're ready to see this side of the club?"

She exhales. "Bayou, you can't protect me forever… let's do this. He deserves it."

Hurricane chuckles, nodding his head. "I knew you were a badass underneath all that sweetness, Novah."

She grins as we walk toward the Chamber where Arsen is being held. Making our way through the soundproof shed, Novah's eyes widen, taking in every little detail. As we approach the Chamber and the door is unlocked, she holds her breath, then says, "Time to make this asshole pay." The venom in her eyes is pure and full of hatred.

I didn't think she was ready for this. Maybe I was wrong. Maybe she is more ready for this than I am.

As we enter the Chamber, Arsen is tied to the Silver Chair, a cage strapped to him, a mangy rat inside the cage running rampant. The smell of rotting flesh lingers in the air, and it's clear the rat has been scratching and eating at Arsen's body.

A small smile lights up Novah's lips as she steps in front of Arsen, instantly setting me at ease. She's not put out by the torture scene in front of her or the blood leaking down his naked body, she's encouraged by it.

I don't leave her side as she narrows her eyes on his while they roll around in his head. He's weak and delirious, probably from an infection. He has been here for just under two months, and during that time, we have practically starved and continuously tortured him. He's pale and gaunt, and Novah looks his pathetic body over like she's happy as a pig in shit.

She steps right up to him. My adrenaline spikes as she leans down so her face is in line with his, and she narrows her eyes on him. "Look at you. You're nothing. No one is going to remember you. No one will glorify you and the heinous things you have done. Your mother was right about you, wasn't she? You *are* a worthless sack of shit. It's no wonder she chose you to give away."

Arsen struggles in the grips but says nothing.

Hurricane pulls the cage away, showing Arsen's stomach skin torn to shreds, the smell of the infection like a rotting corpse.

He groans, finally turning his ire toward Novah. "My mother was a worthless whore just like *you.*"

Stepping forward, I slam my fist right into the middle of Arsen's ugly face, a loud crack resounding through the small space, his nose clearly breaking, and he yelps with the pain. Blood pours down his face before he spits out a line of blood.

Arsen chuckles, his head bobbing from side to side like he can't control it, but he ignores me, focusing solely on Novah. "I should have killed you when I had the chance."

She doesn't back down, her eyes hardening with anger. "You spent too long playing your games, you idiot. So now, we're going to play games with you," Novah quips.

Arsen curls up his lip as I step forward, grabbing a pair of gardening shears. "See if we can guess which finger I am going to cut off first for touching my woman?" I step in and usher Novah to the side.

She smirks, and I know I don't have to worry about her thinking differently of me for mutilating a man in front of her. She's into this, and for some fucked-up reason, that kind of turns me on.

Arsen wriggles in the chair, his hard eyes firmly on me as he shakes his head. "You wouldn't?"

Chuckling, I bring the shears in line with his left hand, but he tries to ball his fingers into a tight fist. "Eeny, meeny, miny..." I dance between his fingers even though he's pulling them in tight, so I can't get to them.

"No. Stop! Please," he begs.

I land on his middle finger and smile wide. "Moe!" I grunt.

Arsen clenches his eyes shut, pulling his fingers in tight so I can't get to them, which I knew he would. So I drop to the floor, grabbing his big toe between the shears and snapping it off before he even has time to think. The click of the shears snaps shut, and blood spurts out as the toe flops on the floor. He lets out a loud wail, screaming out his agony. For a man who is used to causing it, you would think he would be a little more tolerant of pain. *Apparently not.*

My head snaps back to look at Novah to check she is okay—she is completely fine.

If I didn't know better, I would say she is thriving right now.

So I turn back to continue. Standing, I move over to the bench and grab something I purchased especially for him. Walking over to the tray of apples, I grab the apple corer and stab it into the middle of an apple. "You know, Arsen, these apple corers really do work well when used with a little bit of grunt." Twisting the corer, I yank it out of the apple and then slide the core onto the bench. I don't need it. This is all just for show, to draw this out and make Arsen wait. Placing the now coreless apple on the bench, I walk over to him, corer still in hand.

Arsen's eyes widen as he watches me. I hold it up, the juices from the apple glistening in the light.

"The fuck are you going to do with that?"

Smirking, I shrug. "You have an obsession with apples. Let's see if they're in the very core of you?"

Bringing my hand up with as much force as I can muster, I slam the apple corer into his thigh, then twist down. The metal pushes through the muscles and sinew as I push the corer into his flesh. I have to use all my force to do it, but the corer cuts through his muscle, and then I twist and pull out a core of his muscle and flesh.

Arsen gasps for breath as I walk over to the rat cage and drop the hunk of flesh into it. The rat goes crazy for the chunk of meat while the asshole hazes in and out of consciousness.

I turn to Novah to check again, but she is shining brightly, glowing from excitement. I need to stop worrying about her as she stands back, watching with the brightest smile on her face.

So I step forward with a blade and hand it to her. "You want to do the honors?"

She smiles and nods. "Hell yes," she replies, but she doesn't step up to him. Instead, she walks over to where I placed the apple core and picks it up. Furrowing my brows, I stand back and watch as she steps up to Arsen. "You killed countless women… you tried to kill me. You *are* evil, and I *won't* think about you again after this. You won't occupy a single thought in my mind. You *are* nothing. You *mean* nothing. You *accomplished* nothing. You *amount* to nothing. And in the end, you will *be… nothing.*" She slams the apple's core into his mouth, ramming it down his throat.

He begins to choke, and she stabs the blade into his chest. The asshole tries to scream, but he is choking on the apple core at the same time as Novah drags the blade down through the middle of his stomach. His innards fall out all over her feet, and I move in, wrapping my arms around her waist to hold her, so she knows she isn't alone in this. She's gasping for breaths when she reaches the bottom of his stomach, then she drops the blade.

Arsen gurgles, blood and guts oozing out everywhere while I hold her tight in my arms. She rests back against me, needing my support right now.

"I got you," I whisper in her ear.

Pulling her back a little from the scene, we all stand back and watch as Arsen shakes violently, his body giving in to the lack of oxygen and the tremendous wound his body has taken on. I hold Novah to me tight while she pants rapidly, watching Arsen as he shudders. Then his body stills, his head flops to the side, and the room goes eerily quiet.

No one speaks.

No one moves.

Not even a pin dropping could be heard.

We all stare at the man who took so much from this world and nearly took my world from me.

Novah suddenly spins in my arms and slams her body against mine. I wrap my arms around her, holding her to me, my bloodied hands sliding into her hair. "He's gone, beautiful. He's gone."

She lets out a heavy sigh. "Thank you for letting me do this." She pulls back, looking from me to Hurricane and back to me. "I honestly am not sure if I would have been able to move on if I wasn't able to do this. If I couldn't watch the life drain from his eyes and to know he is no longer in this world, how would I know I am safe?"

Hurricane steps over, pulling her to him in a tight embrace. "We got you, Novah. We've always got you."

She steps back, letting out a heavy exhale. "I love you both, in slightly different ways, but still... I love you."

Hurricane scrunches up his face as I pull her to me, planting a kiss on the top of her head. “I love you too, beautiful.”

Hurricane chuckles, shaking his head. “I’m never gonna get used to that.”

I smirk. “Well, you better because this is happening.”

Hurricane groans, turning back to face Arsen. “You want to do the honors, Bayou?”

“You wanna come feed La Fin with me?” I ask Novah and she giggles.

“Oh, fuck yeah.”

EPILOGUE

NOVAH

I've never felt that kind of power before, holding a man's life in my hands, then taking it with one fell swoop. If you had asked me even six months ago if I were capable of such a thing, I would never have thought so. But Arsen irrevocably changed a part of me.

Maybe it was for the better, in a way.

Because to be with Bayou, I need to be strong. I need to be fierce. I can't be that meek and sweet little girl he has always known. Sure, I am still me, but I know now, with everything I have endured and with what I have just done, that I can stand by Bayou's side and be the Old Lady he needs to fight with him.

Not hide behind him in the shadows.

As we stand in the shower, the scorching water running down our bodies turning the bottom of the drain bright red, Bayou's hands run all over me comfortingly. He is so attentive right now that it soothes me in a way only he can. His hand comes up, running his fingers through my hair as I soak it under the water, washing remnants of blood out, and he leans in, planting a tender kiss on my collarbone.

Peace.

I finally feel like I am at peace.

My hands slide up his naked back as my eyes meet his, the blood all but gone while I stare into his eyes. "Thank you… for letting me do that."

He leans in, pressing his forehead against mine. "You needed it. He hurt you, and I know I could have sought your vengeance for you, but seeing that calm in your eyes now is why I let you in the Chamber with him and let *you* take the lead. You deserved to let your demons free, Novah. Just because I didn't want to let what we do to taint you doesn't mean I have the right to stand in your way and hold you back."

My chest squeezes at how thoughtful he is. He definitely could have said no. Made me stay out while the men took care of business, but I am glad he was there to hold me when it all went down. My wounds are practically healed, and now mentally, I feel like I am in a good place.

Leaning in, I press my lips to his, and that incredible spark ignites all around me. Just being with him right now is all the proof I need that I am where I'm supposed to be. While the water pummels down on us, my tongue dances with his, his tongue ring making me smile against his lips as I deepen the kiss.

I miss him.

I need him.

I want him.

Moving my hands between us, I wrap my fingers around his giant cock and start moving up and down. He hardens instantly, but he pulls back from the kiss. His eyes burn with lust as he stares at me like he is unsure. "Novah, you're still recovering. I don't want to hurt you."

Letting out an exhale, I begin tugging on him faster, making him groan a little. "I've been aching for you for over a month. I need you."

His hand comes out, grabbing my hand around his cock, stopping my movements. My eyes widen as he edges me back against the wall. "Then let me make this about you. I want to make you feel good."

I slouch my shoulders. "Bayou…" I sigh, and his eyes darken as he pulls my hand from him and lifts it to sit on his shoulder.

"I'm not asking, Novah. Now spread your legs."

Biting down on my bottom lip, I nod, shifting my right leg to the side while my back rests against the wall. The water cascades over Bayou's torso, making his abs glisten and shine like some damn marvel, and my clit throbs already from simply looking at him. His hand darts out, sliding in against my folds as my breathing hitches, finally feeling him again after so long apart. He nips just under my ear. His teeth graze my skin as his finger presses on my clit.

I let out a gasp at the feeling. My eyes close, my head falling back against the wall as I rock my hips against his hand. "Bayou. Oh, God."

"Do you want it faster, Novah?" He growls into my ear, his tone so deep and gravelly it almost has me coming undone on the spot.

All I can do is whimper as he continues to circle on my clit. The pleasure rolling through me. He slows the pace, making my eyes snap open. I glare at him, making him smirk. "If you want it faster, Novah, you're gonna have to tell me."

My fingers on his shoulder dig in, my nails clenching into his skin. I know I'm going to leave marks as I let out a frustrated groan. "Fuck, yes… faster Bayou. Faster," I beg.

Instantly, his finger circles so fast it sends a flourish through my body. My skin comes alive, pebbling with goose bumps as I pant for breaths I can't seem to catch. "Fuck, don't stop."

He chuckles, his teeth clamping down on the sensitive skin behind my ear. I let out a gasp as the sensations roll through me. "Don't think, Novah… just let it go."

Bayou circles on my clit faster, bringing me to the edge as I clear my mind from everything that has happened and focus on us. Right here, right now. The pleasure rolls through me while his tongue slides out, licking all the way up my neck. I let out a moan as the cool metal of his tongue ring sends a sensation overload through me while he circles on my clit.

My back arches off the wall, and my skin flushes red hot. I clench my eyes shut, feeling my muscles contract and tense all over with my impending orgasm. I gasp, the pressure building, and I explode with one more rotation of his finger. My climax has my entire body relaxing as the wave of euphoria hits so intensely I see stars.

But I don't have even a second to recover before Bayou wraps his arms around my waist and hoists me against the wall. My languid arms wrap around his neck, my fingers threading in his hair as he thrusts up inside me, pushing me against the shower wall.

"Fuuuck!" He groans.

Feeling him inside me is so fucking amazing, I will never take this for granted.

His eyes lock with mine, and he stills for a moment, just looking at me.

I see it, the realization in his eyes.

Knowing we could have lost this.

We could have lost us.

It came so scarily close.

As we stare at each other, finally joined again after all this time, so much being said by not saying anything, I lean forward and kiss his lips tenderly, letting him know that no matter what, I will always fight to keep this.

To keep us.

He kisses me back and starts to move inside me, pushing me back up against the wall. He's hitting me at such a deep angle, I pull my lips from him, needing to breathe. Rocking my hips against him as we fuck in the shower, he hisses through his teeth.

The water cascades over his back, falling between us, making the sensations all the more heightened. We've never had shower sex before, but knowing how good this feels, it's going to become a regular thing for us.

Bayou's fingers press into my skin, his grip tight on my ass. So tight, I am sure they will leave bruises as he holds me up against the wall while he fucks me. I can tell he's taking it easy with me because of my injuries, so I guess that is to be expected. While this feels so damn good, I've missed him too much. I need him. And I want him to know I can take this. So I reach up, pressing my fingers around his throat and holding tight, restricting his airway.

His eyes bulge as he glares at me. He pushes me harder against the wall, one hand moving to grab mine, and he peels my fingers back then slams my wrist against the wall above my head, all the while still thrusting inside me. "What game are you playing at, Novah?"

Panting at the dominance he is finally showing me, I push back a little. "Bayou, I need you. All of you. I'm tired of you holding back, doubting what I want or can handle. Isn't what just happened in the Chamber evidence enough that I am stronger than you think?"

He growls, pulling out of me, and turns to the bench seat attached to the wall, flicking the chain to release it. It falls into position, and he sits on the wooden slats. "You want it rough? Sit on my fucking cock, and I'll show you rough."

I can't help the smile forming on my face as I move to sit on him, but he grips my arms and spins me around. I widen my eyes as he lowers me onto him, my back to his front. I slide onto his cock, he fills me completely, and we both moan at the filling feeling. "You're gonna take it like a good fucking girl."

His hand slides around as I try to grip the wall beside me for stability, but his fingers instantly wrap around my throat, pulling my back toward him. His grip around my throat tightens as my head falls against his shoulder, and he starts thrusting inside me. I let out a moan at the feeling while his other hand slides down, pressing on my clit.

This is definitely rough. He has complete control over my body as he fucks me. His fingers tighten more on my throat, my airway becoming narrower and teamed with the mist from the heated water, it's really hard to breathe. But all it does is intensify the sensations rolling through me.

"Your pussy is mine, Novah. And I take what's mine." He thrusts up, the force making me let out a moan while the pressure builds inside me.

"Yours," I rasp out, unable to say more because what breath I have hitches from the pressure on my clit.

"Come for me, Novah," he demands. His grip tightens on my throat until he cuts off my airway completely. I gasp as my muscles quiver with the emotions running through me. My body wriggles against him when he growls against my skin and orders, "Come, Novah."

I let go of my fear when he circles on my clit once more, letting the pleasure run through my body like a typhoon. It hits with such an intense force it feels like the scar on my stomach is ripping itself open, but in the most delicious way as I scream out my breathless orgasm. My pussy clamps down around his cock, and as he releases his grip on my throat, I suck in a long gulp of air.

Bayou's body jerks. His fingers clench into my thighs, then his breath catches, and he releases a stuttered groan, burying himself deeper into me while holding me in place.

"Novaaah!" He moans out my name as he detonates inside me.

We both pant frantically, coming down from the insatiable high. I relax back into his body, my head leaning back into the crook of his shoulder, his hand sliding down and running slowly up and down my scar in the most loving way. You'd think I'd be embarrassed about him touching it like that, but I can see he's doing it out of love, and because of that, it makes me feel undeniably cherished.

Turning my head, I gently kiss his cheek, and he languidly smiles at me. "We're so fucking good at that."

"I thought all our other sex was amazing, but that... that was something else." He chuckles, still running his fingers along my scar. "Thank you for not treating me with kid-gloves anymore."

He kisses my shoulder, then exhales. "I won't lie... it's fucking hard. All our lives, I've had to protect you. So just letting you step into yourself and be this badass woman you're growing into is difficult for me. But as long as I am here by your side, helping you, being there if you fall, I am okay watching you grow."

I glance down at his fingers trailing up and down my scar and bite my bottom lip. Reaching out, I touch my scar. "And what about this?"

His other hand slides in, pressing against the scar as well. "You're fucking beautiful, Novah. They're a part of you. A part of us. I'd love you regardless of what you look like, regardless if you had scars all over your body. And even then, you would still be as beautiful to me as you are now. Because I see what's in here..." he presses his hand against my chest, "... as well as the outside."

My insides tingle with warmth. I don't know what it is about Bayou's words, but they feel so genuine and honest.

I believe him.

And that makes me feel like the luckiest woman on earth.

Turning to look at him with watering eyes, I smile. "I love you."

"I fucking love you." His hand comes up, caressing my face. "Actually, there is something I want to ask you." I raise my brow, and he continues, "It's more like tell you... I need you to move into the clubhouse. You can keep your house and rent it out, but I want you here with me."

A slow smile creeps across my face as excitement bubbles inside me, and I slowly nod my head. "Yes... of course. Yes."

He grins so fucking wide. Suddenly, he lifts me off him and stands, taking me with him. Then he pushes me back against the shower wall, forcing his lips to mine. His tongue collides with mine as he kisses me so passionately, I wonder if we're going to start this whole thing up again, but then he slowly pulls back, his hand sweeping some hair away from my face. Then he lets out a small laugh. "You make me so fucking happy."

I widen my eyes. Out of everything, I wasn't expecting him to say that. "You make me happy too. So fucking happy."

He leans in, kissing my lips briefly once more, then reaches over, turning off the shower. "C'mon, I think we better make an appearance for dinner. We need to tell everyone you're moving in."

Giggling with excitement, we hop out of the shower and dress then make our way to the dining room. I have a pep in my step. I'm feeling the most content I have felt in my entire life. It's nice that even after everything I have been through, I feel like maybe it was all worth it to get to this very place in time.

To be this person I am right now—a painful way to get there, a traumatic way to get there, but one I have grown and learned from.

We move over to Grit and Lani, who seem to be back in the good books with each other. Everyone knows they're doing this will-they-won't-they dance. No one can figure out what is stopping them from taking that plunge and being together.

But I guess everyone has their reasons for doing things their own way.

Bayou and I sit, and Grit and Lani both look up, smiling at our arrival. "You look happy. You feeling good?" Lani asks me.

Nodding, I exhale, relaxing my shoulders. "The best I have in years. It's amazing what can change when you do something you never thought you could do. I don't know if that says more about me as a person or more about the person I used to be?"

Lani raises her brow. "Well, seeing as you're talking in cryptic language, not sure I can help much there. But I can say I like this version of you."

"Me too," Grit agrees.

Bayou wraps his arm around my shoulders.

"So, what's on the plan for everyone today?" Bayou asks.

Lani smirks. "Grit was gonna take me out for a ride. I haven't been out since Hurricane took me in the sidecar on his bike, but

Grit has added it to his bike. I'm so excited."

Grit chuckles with a roll of his shoulders. "It's nothing. I like seeing you smile."

I can't help but smile as Lani bumps into his side. "I know I'm a pain in the ass having to modify your bike for me because of the seizures, but I do appreciate it."

Grit waves his hand through the air. "You keep making me that mochiko chicken, and I'll do anything you ask of me."

Lani waggles her brows. "Oh, well, now you're just asking for trouble. I'll have you as my personal slave in no time. You'll be my errand boy, my drink maker, my personal masseuse, my pool boy."

Everyone laughs.

Grit smirks. "Pool boy? We don't have a pool?"

Lani waggles her brows. "But you can still stand around shirtless and pretend?"

Smirking at the obvious chemistry between them, Grit smiles, picks up his drink, and takes a sip, seeming more than a little happy with Lani's attention. "Only if you sit around wearing a bikini."

Lani nods her head. "Deal."

"Hey, Pres, we got visitors." Omen calls through the speakers from the gate outside.

We all snap our heads up as Hurricane reaches for the radio for the gun turret.

"Who the fuck is it?" He grunts.

"They say they're here for Grit. Family or some shit." We all turn to Grit as he furrows his brows, then he stands walking toward Hurricane.

"All right, let 'em in."

We all sit in silence, watching as an older man and a younger, gorgeous woman step inside the clubhouse doors. Grit stops dead still like he sees a ghost. His eyes widen, his mouth drops open as he gasps. "Maddie?"

She races forward into his arms, and he sweeps her up, swirling her around in a circle, embracing her tightly.

He obviously knows her *very* well.

Everyone turns to Lani, her eyes dropping to her lap as she swallows hard.

"What? I don't? Where the *hell* have you been?" Grit asks in quick succession.

She giggles, pulling back from him, but her hands stay on his. "My parents took me away to this crazy cult they got themselves ingrained in. Your father found me and helped pull me out."

Grit turns to his father, slumping his shoulders. "You never stopped looking for her? All these years?"

"Despite what you think, Grey, I do care about you. I know how close you and Maddie were. I know what she meant to you. I know what her vanishing did to you. It led to you coming... *here.*" His father glances around at all of us with his lip curled up.

Yeah, fuck you, asshole.

Grit tenses his muscles. "There were many reasons I joined the club, Dad. Maddie was only one of them. But fuck. I thought you were dead."

"It came close a couple of times. I'm so glad I'm here with you again, Grey." She leans in, planting an intense kiss on his lips, and everyone widens their eyes as he stands stock still like he is in shock.

Lani stands abruptly and starts walking toward the bedrooms.

Kaia subtly follows her sister as Grit pulls back, and instantly his head snaps around to find Lani, but she is gone.

He grimaces, turning back to Maddie and his father, then shakes his head. "I'm so glad to see you, Maddie, but I have a life here. I have people I care about. I can't just pick up where we left off."

She nods her head but keeps her grip on his.

Grit's dad steps forward, placing his hand on his shoulder. "This is your chance, Grey, to have the life you were meant to have.

Come home with us. Get reacquainted with Maddie. You can be the man you were always meant to be."

Grit stares at Maddie, her beautiful blue eyes glistening back at him.

And the fact he hesitates lets us all know that he's considering their offer.

Holy fuck, Grit. Don't do it!

NEXT FOR K E OSBORN

Incinerate

The NOLA Defiance Series Book Four

Want to read more about Hurricane's stepbrother, Nash?

Hostile Hearts

An enemies to lovers billionaire romance.

Want to read more about Nash's friend, Lucas?

Guarded Hearts

A Secret Baby Billionaire Romance.

If you liked this book you may also like:

THE HOUSTON DEFIANCE MC SERIES
Books 1-8 – The Complete Set

THE CHICAGO DEFIANCE MC SERIES
Books 1-9 – The Complete Set

THE SATAN'S SAVAGES MC SERIES
Books 1-6 – The Complete Set

First and foremost, I would like to thank my mother, Kaylene Osborn. Thank you for always helping me with my words in the author industry and everyday life. Your help and guidance in all situations make everything just that little bit easier. I couldn't do this without you. So thank you.

To Cindy, Diana, and Kim – Thank you for always helping my books shine. You find all the little idiosyncrasies I miss and show me how to improve. I am so glad to have you on my team!

To Chantell – The way you help me with 'the spicy scenes' in my books makes them come alive. I am so glad we found each other and that you help me bring my characters to life. Thank you from the bottom of my heart. Thank you!

To Nicki – Thank you for everything. I'm always so happy to have you be one of the last people to look over my work because I know you will find the flaws we all missed. You polish my manuscript and make it shiny and bright, and for that, I thank you so deeply. My books are so much better for having your eyes look over them. You're the best!

To all of my awesome beta readers – Thank you for once again putting your thoughts into this book. I appreciate all of your energy and ideas, and together we make a great team.

So thank you!

To Jane – Love you to the ends of the earth. Thank you for always being there when I need an ear or someone to run ideas by. You're the BEST!

To Dana, I say it a lot, but I adore this cover. I think Hesitate is one of my favorites. It is so striking and captures Bayou at his finest. Thank you for working so hard to get it just right for me. You're so talented, and I love the team we have built together.

To Golden and Dylan Horsch – This gorgeous cover wouldn't be as amazing as it is without the two of you. Golden, thank you so much. Your photo of Dylan perfectly depicts my character, Bayou, and you nailed exactly what I was after. Dylan, thank you for being the perfect muse for my cover. I am so thrilled we are able to work together. I think, with the help of Dana, we have all created something utterly stunning.

Thank you to The Hatters PR and Grey's Promotions for helping me promote Isolate and for the provision of PA services. You all work tirelessly to support me, and I am honored to have you as part of my team.

To my beautiful, playful, and utterly adorable pup, Bella – You're starting to show your age. You are going deaf, which is a fun time for all of us now, but you're still full of energy and excitement—which I adore about you. I love that you sit under my desk when I write. Those little snores keep me smiling as I type. You light up my life, little Boo. Love you to the ends of the earth.

Last of all, I want to thank YOU, the reader. Your continued support of my writing career is both humbling and heartwarming. I adore my readers so much, and honestly, I couldn't keep going without the love and support you all show me daily. Thank you for believing in me, and I hope I can keep you entertained for many years to come.

Much love,
K E Osborn

On a more serious note:

This book is a work of fiction, but some situations discussed are of a sensitive nature.

If you or anyone you know is in emotional distress, suffers from substance abuse, or any sort of abuse, please seek help or assist them to obtain help.

Crisis hotlines exist everywhere, so please don't hesitate.

If you live in:
USA call RAINN - 1-800-656-HOPE
Canada call 1.888.407.4747 for help
UK call The Samaritans 116 123
Australia call Lifeline Australia 13 11 14

Check these links for more books from Author K E OSBORN.

READER GROUP

Want access to fun, prizes and sneak peeks?
Join my Facebook Reader Group.
https://goo.gl/wu2trc

NEWSLETTER

Want to see what's next?
Sign up for my Newsletter.
http://eepurl.com/beIMc1

BOOKBUB

Connect with me on Bookbub.
https://www.goodreads.com/author/show/7203933.K_E_Osborn

GOODREADS

Add my books to your TBR list on my Goodreads profile.
https://goo.gl/35tIWV

AMAZON

Click to buy my books from my Amazon profile.
https://goo.gl/ZNecEH

WEBSITE

www.keosbornauthor.com

TWITTER

http://twitter.com/KEOsbornAuthor

INSTAGRAM

@keosbornauthor

EMAIL

keosborn.author@hotmail.com

FACEBOOK

http://facebook.com/KEOsborn

With a flair for all things creative, *USA Today* Bestselling **Author K E Osborn**, is drawn to the written word. Exciting worlds and characters flow through her veins, coming to life on the page as she laughs, cries, and becomes enveloped in the storyline right along with you. She's entirely at home when writing sassy heroines and alpha males that rise from the ashes of their pasts.

K E Osborn comforts herself with tea and Netflix, after all, who doesn't love a good binge?

Explosive. Addictive. Romance.
http://www.keosbornauthor.com/

Made in the USA
Coppell, TX
27 March 2023